Fiction and
The Facts of Life

By Edith Konecky

Fiction and
The Facts of Life

By Edith Konecky

Hamilton Stone Editions

Library of Congress Cataloging-in-Publication Data

Konecky, Edith.
Fiction and the facts of life / by Edith Konecky.
   p. cm.
ISBN 978-0-9801786-7-8 (alk. paper)
I. Title.
PS3561.O457F53 2011
813'.54--dc22

2011006931

Hamilton Stone Editions
P.O. Box 43
Maplewood, NJ 07040
Web Site: http://www.hamiltonstone.org
Email: Hstone@hamiltonstone.org

Cover design and art by Kat Llewellyn

Also by Edith Konecky

Allegra Maud Goldman

A Place at the Table

Past Sorrows and Coming Attractions

View to the North

Love and Money

Fiction and the Facts of Life

LIFE

The cat is dead. Minnie. Minnie is dead.

All day the snow has been falling from a sky as leaden and dreary as battleships. The snow is coming down harder now than at any time during the day. Upon all the living and the dead. She was seventeen years old, a good age for a cat, but still. I took her to the vet yesterday, a cold day with a thin sun bleakly illuminating an earlier snowfall, piss-yellowed, exhaust-blackened, on the streets. New York. I knew the minute she stopped grooming herself. There were great clumps in her beautiful coat. I brushed and brushed. You can't brush out those clumps, and it hurt her to have me try. "If you can't do it yourself," I told her, but I still have the fading line of a scratch on my thumb, her gentle rebuke. She smelled bad, too, and slobbered uncontrollably. She was always such a fastidious cat, and vain. And loving.

I'm spending the afternoon with Rebecca, hoping for solace. She has two cats and I can hardly bear to look at them.

"I always knew that was the way you saw me," Rebecca says, her voice choked with pain.

"It's fiction."

"Ha!"

"If I did you with the depth and complexity you deserve, there'd have been no room left for anything else, like me. I'm not writing your biography, you know."

"Still, if you use a character based on me, you have a responsibility to me. I would never say some of the dumb things you have me say! It's your stupidity, not mine."

I didn't let her read it until it was in bound galleys. She was my first reader for my first book, and her response was crushing;

she can attain withering heights. She simply handed the book back to me and, smiling faintly, almost contemptuously, said, "Well, you've written a book." When someone, especially your oldest and closest friend, says something like that in which everything is held back, you are free to choose among a smorgasbord of negative critical judgments. Why was it impossible for her to find even one good thing to say? The book was not yet published and I had no way of knowing if it would be. Then it was, finally, and republished, and republished again and again. Though far from a best seller, alas, it was in many libraries being read and loved by many people and many of its chapters have been anthologized. Rebecca presented me with a copy bound in red leather with gold lettering and lovely red and gold paisley end pages. It must have cost the earth. I was moved and I prize that copy of the book, but under the circumstances, I don't know what her thinking to do it, and doing it, could have meant.

I tried one other time to let Rebecca read what I was working on, but after a few chapters I snatched it away. This was in Maine. Lisa and I were there for a month and Rebecca came to spend the last ten days with us. Lisa and Rebecca had always liked each other and gotten on well, yet having Rebecca there with us was the beginning of the end for Lisa and me. I was naturally closer in many ways to Rebecca than to Lisa. Rebecca and I are the same age and we grew up and are growing old together. Although Lisa and I were lovers, and had been for almost five years, and Rebecca has been happily married for most of the years I've known her to a man who has become almost as close a friend to me as Rebecca, Lisa was jealous.

"She's taken this place over," Lisa complained. "She's not our guest. It's her place. Her place and yours. You let her do it."

"What are you talking about?"

"You know what I'm talking about. The way she bustles around in the kitchen, makes the decisions, everything."

"That's the way she is. Helpful and efficient."

"It's not her place. It's ours."

"I don't know what kind of distinction you're trying to make. There are three of us here."

"Yeah, you and Rebecca. And then there's me."
"You feel extra?"
"Yes I do. I am."
"Oh, please!"
"It's like you're the parents and I'm the child."
"Nonsense."

But it wasn't nonsense, though Lisa, thirty years our junior, was the child, and began to act it more and more, sulking, riding off on her bike leaving behind a spoor of fury. Although Lisa and I were intimate in a way Rebecca and I had never been, Rebecca and I were intimate in a way that Lisa and I could never be, an intimacy born of all the years and their happenings, shared, commented upon, discussed, laughed hysterically about, filed away, forgotten. Which is why her reaction to that first book was so devastating.

Lisa wanted it to be the way it was three years earlier when she and I were there alone. An idyllic time. Mornings, I worked and she played tennis. In the afternoons we explored, took walks, made love, basked on the rocks looking out to sea, picked berries, walked into what there was of a town to buy lobsters at the only store, a shack on the small wharf where the lobstermen came ashore. Or we sat on the deck talking and laughing at the cats, hers and mine, who didn't get along. Minnie wanted only to be outside hunting, or following us onto the rocks, acting nonchalant, as if she weren't really following us but just happened to be going in the same direction. Lisa's cat, Bibi, was terrified of "outside," never having been there before. If we carried her out onto the deck she trembled, and the moment she was put down she would dart back inside, not to hide but to look longingly out at us through the sliding glass doors, wanting so much to be braver, or perhaps for us to be less brave and to come back inside with her where we belonged, where we were all safe.

It was late summer and the nights grew cold. We would go to bed early and pile the blankets from all the beds in the house on top of us and read to each other. We read Coriolanus and Troilus and Cressida and then, if we weren't too sleepy, we made love again, closing the door against the cats. Minnie pretended not to mind, but she did. Later, when Lisa and I split up, Minnie immediately re-appropriated Lisa's side of the bed.

We were happy that summer. I think we were in love. I think we were happy.

The cat's frightened heartbeat is imprinted in the palm of my right hand. I was holding her still on the stainless steel examining table while the vet, brandishing the needle with her death in it, tried to find a vein in her right hind leg. "It's all right, Minnie," I sobbed, tears streaming. "It will be all right." She was warm and soft. She was still struggling to get to her feet. She was alive. I started to say, "Trust me, puss," then didn't.

When I was little, I thought I was never going to be able to do those hard things grownups had to do. Never. How did they do them? How did they get so tough? Did they have to kill off their feelings? How did you kill off your feelings? Feelings weren't voluntary, they were simply there, part of you the way your eyes and appetite were part of you.

One of the first really frighteningly hard things I had to do was attend my grandfather's funeral. Hard things had happened, of course, but this was the first hard adult kind of thing I actually had to make up my mind to do and then do. It wasn't hard because it was Grandpa, but because I was going to be in the presence of --- I was going to see --- my first dead person, and it was someone I knew. Entering the chapel, I trembled uncontrollably and thought about vomiting or fainting. I had done a lot of involuntary vomiting but I had never succeeded at fainting. I told myself I wouldn't look into the coffin, I would try to keep my eyes averted or on the ceiling, but I did look. Naturally I looked. There, recognizably, was my stocky little grandfather with his neat rusty little moustache, in a navy blue suit, pale and still and silent. But he had always been pale and still and silent. Maybe, I told myself, the idea of a thing was worse than the thing itself. What surprised me as much as anything was that there was no blanket covering him. He was just lying there, fully dressed: shirt, tie, shoes, and that double-breasted navy blue suit, the same one he'd worn to my brother David's Bar Mitzvah two years earlier. It didn't look right somehow. Shouldn't he have been wearing a shroud, or something more suitable to the occasion? Pajamas and a blanket would have been better. He didn't look like someone who was at the beginning of his eternal rest. He looked interrupted. He looked like a doll that has been packed away until the next time.

I had never really known my grandfather. I couldn't remember a single word he had ever spoken except "Valnuts?" as he held out a bowl of them, unshelled, an offering, love. He had been so dominated and diminished by my grandmother that he could as well have been a deaf mute. I sometimes tried to imagine how their union had been effected, what he could have said to my grandmother to win her over, not only to marriage but to the marriage bed itself. He was a nice looking man with a neatly shaped head and straight regular features, and a neat and compact body, but he had no presence at all. He had produced three sons and, by that time, seven grandchildren, and except for one instance of red hair, he had passed along nothing recognizable of himself.

My grandmother Anna, noisy as always, was carrying on vociferously and dramatically, screaming, moaning, tearing her hair, rending her garments and, later, being restrained from hurling herself into the open grave. Obviously, he had meant more to her than she had ever let on. Or was this part of the mysterious religion she practiced, a ritual? Could Grandma simply be doing what was expected of her? If so, her performance was impressive.

Earlier, when I tried to voice my fear of seeing Grandpa dead, my mother had said with distaste, "Your vivid imagination!" As if she were speaking of acne or dandruff, as if it were a curse. But what could I do about it? My vivid imagination, like my feelings and, twined with them, was there, part of my equipment, part of who I was.

"You obviously never listen to me," Rebecca says. "You make me sound insensitive." She is close to tears.

"That's funny. Everyone who has read it says Becky is done so lovingly."

"But inaccurately," she says sharply. Oh, accuracy! I don't know what to say, but I feel terrible. I've hurt her. Although she has sometimes been insensitive, in spite of her keen intelligence, I would never characterize her as an insensitive person.

"I'll try to get you right in the next book."

"If you do write another book," she says with God Forbid in her voice, "just leave me out of it. If you need a mother figure, use your real mother." Old as I am, I do have a mother, but since I've come here to be comforted because of Minnie, in spite of the two resident cats, how can I deny that I'm using Becky as a mother.

'Mother' is inaccurate. You're occasionally my superego." My mother didn't apply for the job, so I had to appoint someone else. I like to have Becky's approval, or at least, her opinion, when I'm buying clothing or furniture. And, while I want Rebecca to meet anyone I'm involved with, and to like them, if she doesn't, tant pis. She usually does like them, though. Or at least she's interested. She's certainly interested.

"I never asked to be your superego."

"Who ever does?"

"Well get someone else."

"I would if I could. God knows, I could be a lot kinder to myself."

One of her cats stalks by, nose pointed toward the door as if some danger out there requires immediate attention. She is a lean, gray tiger, not very appealing. I feel the plump soft bundle of Minnie between my hands. I think of her sitting and looking up at me, her clear green eyes, her gaze steady, unwavering, sometimes for ten minutes at a time. How pretty, I always thought, made somehow content and peaceful by looking at her, then I'd return to whatever I was doing. But she would go on looking at me until I was aware that she was trying to tell me something. She was not a speaking cat; she was a looking cat. When I understood that she was trying to tell me something, I would wonder what it could be and in what sort of interior language. Sometimes it was that something was hurting her, sometimes it was simply that she loved me. In the morning it was that it was time for me to get up. Most often I would look at my watch and realize that she was telling me it was five p.m., time for her dinner. She was very good with time.

"Anyhow you were insensitive. I was furious..."

"Well, you don't have to cry about it. It's over."

"I'm not crying about that."

When we were in the country, or anywhere there was an "outside" for her to go to, when she wanted to go to it she would sit in front of the door looking up at the door knob. She would sit there patiently telling the door knob. Waiting for it to turn. In the beginning I thought how stupid she was. But she wasn't stupid. Sooner or later the door knob did turn, the door did open.

"I'm sure I told him," Becky says. "I know I did. He probably forgot. It just didn't mean as much to him as it did to you. It probably didn't mean anything to him."

"Thanks so much."

"Well, it's true."

Truth. Accuracy. She still hasn't said a single word about the book itself. She has chosen to focus on this one small section, loosely based on a real event in which my central character, the aged protagonist, reluctantly spends an evening at Becky's house with someone she was briefly but importantly in love with many years earlier, a man she hasn't seen since the end of that never-consummated affair. The man, it turns out, doesn't recognize her, has no idea who she is. The protagonist, when she realizes this, finds it bitterly painful, because she herself has carried around the memory of this affair forever after, in some detail. It's a meaningful part of the increasingly heavy baggage of her life, not a part that she has ever chosen to jettison.

This small section of the book has nothing, really, to do with Becky. Becky is incidental. It has to do with memory and its betrayals. It's about the sadness of time, of growing old, of what we are left with, of attrition, of losses.

In Maine, when she was reading that earlier manuscript and I was in a chair across the room with a book in my lap, trying not to read her face, trying to pretend I wasn't there and that if I were I didn't really care, but nonetheless feeling the charged air, Rebecca made a small sound and I jumped and said, "What?"

"The Waldorf," she said, her first words in the hour since she began, "wouldn't have had self-service elevators in the forties. They would have had manned ones. They probably still do."

"Yes. Of course." So she had gotten that far. She was past the wedding scene when my young couple are on their way up to the bridal suite. There was a lot of pushing of buttons in the elevator, but I could easily replace all that with a bored, short, 4F elevator operator. In fact, he could make the scene funnier. He could comment on it. He could be part of it.

Ten minutes later, Becky spoke again. "You really should make up your mind whether to spell 'marvelous' with one 'l' or two."

"I can't."

"One is all you need."

A silent quarter of an hour elapsed during which my distress increased.

"Do you have any idea," Becky said, giving me a pained look, "how often you use the word 'though'?"

Oh shit, I thought, she's reading this book like a copy editor. I'd spent the last four years writing it. Out of my gut! I was her best friend. I crossed the room and snatched the manuscript away.

"I don't want you to read any more," I said. "I can't stand it."

I think she was relieved. I vowed, then, never again to let her read anything of mine until it was in print. A bound and printed book is a fait accompli. For better or worse, it has authority. Immutability. It bears the stamp of the publishing house that saw something in it, enough to make an investment in it, no matter how laughably miniscule. It is an object. It can be held easily in the hand. It can be lifted and put on a shelf between others of its kind. Alphabetically, if you like. It is not an amorphous pile of pages still groaning with indecisions waiting to be resolved. You can like it or not, but it is there, one of many, perhaps too many, subject to a range of responses. A published book, even if it dies an early death, has been delivered into the world.

I have been asked to read the work of many writers, established as well as aspiring, and to view the paintings of a number of artists, and even if I have sometimes been less than thrilled, and God knows I have, there has always been something positive I could find to comment upon. I almost never give negative, "helpful" criticism until I first mention what I like, what is commendable. It's hard to accept that Becky can find nothing. My writing is so much a part of me. I know that Becky loves me. We are in other ways so close, so in tune that we really hardly have to use words with one another. So how can it be?

Still, I didn't keep the vow I made then and now I'm sorry.

"When you're writing fiction," I tell Becky, "you're always going in and out of other people's minds."

"So it pleases you to imagine."

"Naturally. Of course in the writing it never is someone else's mind. It must always be some part of your own mind, since you invent the characters."

"We all try to do that. In real life. It's called empathy. And I wish you would invent them."

She's so angry!

"We invent them in life, too, or at least what they're thinking or feeling," I say. "How do we ever know?"

"Some of us listen! And we know when others find us sympathetic and understanding. We know who our friends are."

I ignore this. "I no longer ever, ever say to anyone, 'I know just how you feel.' Tully cured me of that; it infuriated her. 'No you don't!' she would scream. 'How could you? That's so arrogant and presumptuous.'" I was merely trying to express sympathy. But Tully was right; the words were wrong. The most I now allow myself to say is, "I can imagine how you must be feeling." Even Tully, who argued with everything I said, could hardly argue with what I imagined. "But there are some minds and feelings I can't even begin to imagine," I say.

"Mine, for one," Becky says.

"There was a man at the book party Tuesday night," I say, trying to change the subject. "An older man, good-looking, charming. A poet. And, as it turned out, he'd read my first book and was a fan. Percy. His name was Percy. I'd never heard of him."

"So?"

"He used his hands a lot when he talked, sort of like an Indian dancer. Very graceful. I thought he might be gay but he has a wife, grown children no longer at home, even some grand-children."

"So?"

"They live in Maine, he told me, he and his wife. In the woods. In a house without electricity or plumbing."

"No plumbing?"

"A pump from an underground well that comes through the kitchen sink."

"That's the plumbing? An outdoor privy?"

"He described it. Proudly. A double privy, he said twinkling, beautifully painted."

"Oh, yech. In the winter? In Maine? At night? If I had to choose, I'd rather have a toilet than a husband."

I laugh. It feels like the first time I've laughed in a week. I'd wondered at the time about people's minds. Was this man Percy terribly poor? He had a car. He bought books. Did he live this way because he thought it romantic? And what about that wife? Chamber pots? Chopping down trees, splitting wood, cooking, baths? What for? They may not have been out of their minds, but they were certainly out of mine.

When the vet showed me the X-ray, I wasn't surprised. The cancer was perfectly round, just under the jaw. And large. It looked at least an inch in diameter. An inch is a lot on a cat.

"Isn't there anything you can do?" I asked.

"Not really. We don't have much success with radiation or chemotherapy."

"What happens next?" I asked.

"The jaw will break and she'll be in terrible pain. She won't be able to eat. A cat's greatest pleasure is eating, especially at this age."

"What would you do?"

"I know it's hard, but the time comes when we have to bite the bullet."

He must have been through this hundreds of times, but still he managed to look at me with profound sympathy, handing me the carrying case with Minnie inside, crouched in a corner. Safe. She thought she was safe. I was supposed to take her and go. Go home. Go home and wait for the cancer to eat through her jaw. Wait for her agony. Wait for her to begin to starve to death. Then, when it was unbearable for her and for me, bring her back. And do it.

"Do it now," I said, and the vet looked surprised, then nodded.

"It's really the best thing," he said.

We had a hard time getting her back out of that wicker carrying case. She cringed in her corner and held on, damn it, for dear life. She knew, she knew. But what chance did she have against two people, four adult human hands, destiny? Oh! stop being so soppy; what chance do any of us have? Stop thinking about it; it's done.

"Why are you crying?" Becky asks. "Minnie?"

"Yes. Do you think the sun will ever come out again?"

"No."

This cheers me up. I blow my nose.

"Everyone's dead," I say.

"What do you mean?"

"There are so many people crossed out in my address book that I bought a new one last week. Dead. Or lost in other ways, and names I can no longer connect with faces or anything else."

The new book looks so barren that, lest my heirs, executors, posterity, consider it a reflection of the state of my life, which it is, I've still not thrown away the old one.

"I have a Roll-a-Dex," Becky says. "I just yank the dead cards out." She's so efficient. But until recently, her phones were still black rotary dial phones, not push button ones. She deplores gadgets. Not me. I'm instantly drawn to the New & Improved, not just buttons to push but programmed buttons, buttons with memories, happy to free up space in my already overstuffed brain for all those other numbers that identify me. I'm not one of those who ever had a problem moving from manual typewriters to electric ones, to electronic ones, to word processors, computers, both desk and lap. I can hardly wait for what comes next. Human beings can be awful and destructive and monstrous, but as far as I'm concerned, one of their better qualities is their restlessness and greed, which give rise to their inventiveness. Not long before she died, I heard Mary McCarthy speak about her resistance to The New, as though it were, ipso facto, shoddy, her devotion to her manual typewriter, her eschewal of food processors and word processors and electric can openers and plastic charge cards. She made herself and others of her persuasion sound like purists, the rest of us barbarians.

The more effort you put into a thing, she insisted, the better it will turn out. That sounds almost true, but it isn't. I had the utmost respect for Mary McCarthy but my Cuisinart-chopped liver is just as good as my hand-chopper chopped liver, and so much quicker and easier. As for my charge cards, they give me a very real sense of power; behind them lies the full faith of my financial responsibility, such as it is. I, too, was devoted to my original Underwood typewriter with its nickel-banded clickety-clack keys and two-tone ribbon, but I never felt wedded to it for life. My serious writing life started in first grade with a wooden pen that had a half-circle-grooved bottom into which you fitted metal (aluminum? Did we have aluminum then? Look it up.) pen points that required frequent changing. You bought the points in cardboard boxes and if you were passionate about what you were writing and pressed too hard, you would spoil the point and probably tear the paper. The pen was dipped in an inkwell that was fitted into the upper right hand corner of your school desk. Tiny blobs of paper and other soft debris would accumu-late at the bottom of the ink, and there was something satisfying about fishing it out with your pen. Except for ink smudges and blots, and the dependency on your own handwriting, which they therefore had to teach you in those days, the system worked well enough. You learned to write a certain Mr. Palmer's way, (I think it was a mister but it could have been a Ms.}, clear and round and legible. Not until your character firmed up did your handwriting change and show some of the true you. Today that all sounds so quaint. Why? Because we had no hesitation about moving on to the next thing, an Eversharp guaranteed-for-life fountain pen, and, later, ballpoint pens, felt-tipped pens, and for those most serious about getting things down on paper, the Underwood. That Mary McCarthy chose to stop there, all else aside, doesn't mean she was a better person than I.

Furthermore, what about being able to hear Jessye Norman sing Strauss's Four Last Songs on a compact disk? Was Mary McCarthy still listening to her scratchy old 78's on her original windup gramophone with the megaphone coming out of the fox terrier's ear? Did she never fly? If she drove, did she insist on a manual shift? Did she write checks, or did she go about paying the telephone company and the department stores with bags of cash? The more I think about it, the more annoyed I am at this inverted snobbery!

"What makes you think you're so superior for not getting a push-button phone?" I scream at Becky. "Why don't you have an answering machine?"

"Why would I want an answering machine? I'm not running a business here. Whoever wants to talk to me will call back."

***

I dreamed of Tully last night, I don't know why, and today she keeps popping into my mind. I haven't thought of her in months, except occasionally to wonder what in my book enraged her, or was it something in my last unanswered letter. She never wrote to me about the book, either, and that means she hated it. The book isn't officially out yet, but I put her on the list to receive bound galleys. Why wouldn't she hate it? She hardly appears whatsoever, and when she does, what I said wasn't particularly kind. At best, she would feel slighted. And she'd be right; I slighted her. Not personally, but deliberately, because I didn't want to deal with her in that book. Two important ex-lovers weren't necessary. I could and did make Dibbs stand for both. It was fiction, after all, as I keep insisting to everyone.

I don't remember what was in the dream, just the feeling. We were young. At least, we were more than twenty years younger than we are now. But I woke up remembering what it felt like, the excitement, the exhilaration, the ecstasy of it. It was so intense. God, to be able to feel anything like that now, even the pain of it when the pain comes.

Are there ever enough friends to fill the loneliness, or does it need a lover? Though I truly thought I could learn

21

to live without anyone, that I was mature, now, and self-sufficient, I find that often I do miss that one person. Does everyone? Two people revolving around each other, interested in almost everything about each other. And if not interested, bored, but at least with an object, not the absence of one.

I am listening to this celestial trio from Der Rosenkavalier, the Marschallin and Octavian and Sophie, the voices of three women, and it makes me weep, I can't help it, it's so glorious, so full of yearning and tenderness and *shmerz,* oh that Strauss, what notes, imagine having all that in your head, all those lines, to be able to hear that all the time possibly even in his sleep.

Before I ever met her, I had a premonition that Tully and I would be important to each other. I'm not sure I thought of it as "an affair," and if I fantasized anything, I doubt if it was sexual, although I'm not sure. Dr. Kantfogel had more than once said to me, when I brought up the possibility, "You're not a lesbian, Rachel. Forget it. There's nothing in your Rorschach, transference, dreams. Nothing. Go to bed with a woman already and get it out of your system." Ever since, I knew that some day I would take his advice, although I minded the wording, that business of getting it out of my system as if it were something disagreeable I'd eaten for which I needed an enema. Also, I had begun to suspect that there were limits to Dr. Kantfogel's expertise. He was such a macho little man that I think he couldn't imagine that any woman, at least any young, attractive one, could possibly love another woman while he was alive in the world, short and crippled though he was. It was probably my fault. I may have led him on. During the desperate upheaval of my transference, I fell passionately in love with him and pleaded with him to come get on the couch with me and 'make love` (Even if I'd wanted to, which I didn't, I still wasn't able to say the word 'fuck'; it hadn't yet become such easy currency). To his credit, although he did several times lie down beside me, all we did was neck. He taught me how to be a better kisser, so he may have felt it was part of the therapy. It was very sweet, and I never minded thinking about it later, when I knew that one's psychiatrist wasn't supposed to do that sort of thing, and when I even knew why.

Erato was my first artists' colony. I hadn't known such places existed. The goal of my analysis with Dr. Kantfogel, who was more or less Freudian, was to make me the happy mother/housewife instead of this discontented, neurotic one given to panic attacks. "I think I was meant to be a writer," I kept trying to tell him. "So," he would say, "who's stopping you? If you're a writer, write." He finally sent me for a battery of tests and, in their dry statistical language they seemed to agree that yes, I should be a writer. So as soon as Jed was in kindergarten, I went back to school to keep myself disciplined, and began to write like mad. Within a couple of years, I had published three stories and acquired a mentor who diagrammed my stories on the blackboard and explained exactly what I had done, much of which came as a surprise to me.

"Now you have to write a novel," he said. "And it might help if you went to Erato."

"What's Erato?"

He told me. And so, a few months later, I sat in my car in the driveway. I had managed to turn on the engine but I couldn't bring myself to shift into gear. I was too busy saying the world's longest goodbye.

"Better get going," Peter suggested. "You'll run out of gas before you get out of the driveway."

Slowly, I eased out of the driveway, out of Red Maple Lane, out of Scarsdale. A half dozen times I was tempted to turn the car around and go home, but I was on the Throughway, always miles from the next exit. As each exit neared, I had to urge myself to go beyond it to the next, there would still be time to change my mind.

I knew why I was terrified; I had discussed it with Dr. Kantfogel. He had given me tranquilizers to take if I needed them, security blankets, and assured me that of course I could do it, that I was ready. He pretended to be proud of me, like a good father, but he was proud of himself. Hadn't he made me?

"I'll disintegrate," I said. "Pieces of me will fly off. I'm going there just as ... me."

"Exactly," he said, beaming. But he was a liar. He had done everything he could to try to make me happy with "my role." He would have denied it, insisted that he was challenging me. As usual, he couldn't lose. Either way, if I had settled, if I had not, he was right.

"That's how I've always defined myself," I said. "Mrs. Peter Levin, Max Goldman's daughter, Jed and Henry's mother."

"You're not going to stop being any of those things. It's just that for the time you're there, you won't be responsible for anyone but yourself."

What could be more frightening?

By the time I reached the Northway, a little more than midway, the terror in my bowels had subsided. In fact, it seemed to have disappeared entirely. Not having to be responsible for, or to, anyone but myself suddenly began to seem like the most glorious and unprecedented freedom. What a solid, reliable, little blue car I was driving. How blue the sky was. How the sun made everything it touched sparkle. How sweet the early October air, wafting in through the open window. My head was stuffed with words and ideas that needed to be put in a certain still-to-be-decided order on clean white paper. On the radio, Ella Fitzgerald was singing "Got the World on a String," and, at the top of my lungs, I sat on her rainbow singing along with her in my off-key voice.

The fear began creeping back as I drove up the winding gravel road to Erato, past the twin ponds covered with green slime, and around a bend where a monstrous gray castle with spires and turrets loomed. Soon I would be meeting the people within, some of them famous, *real* writers. They would try to engage me in conversation, the kind they were accustomed to, assuming that I was one of them, and I'd blow it. I had no idea what such people talked about, and on what level; I had never met any of the people whose work I had read, except for Dorothy Parker. Her brother, who sold dresses for my father, had just died. I was sixteen. I went with my father to the wake and there she was, she and her handsome soldier husband who was off that night to the war. They were both very drunk, but this in no way diminished my awe. In the hour we were there, I never spoke a word, and my ears were so full of pounding, rushing blood that I never heard a word she said, though I heard every word spoken by my father, who, as though Dorothy Parker were just anyone at all, mortified me by talking about the dress business, his idea of conversation.

How long would it take these Erato folks to find me out? They would know at once that I wasn't one of them. After all, just what had I done to deserve admission to this fairy-tale place, this august company? Published three short stories, big deal! Who knew if I would ever manage to write another and get it into print?

I parked the car in the shade of a row of tall, stately pines, where a few other cars were parked, and emerged into a pool of wonderful air. It smelled like a cedar closet. I stood for a moment, breathing, trying to decide what to do next. I was to go to the office, and yes, there was a little white wooden sign directing me there. But just then a woman emerged from it and walked towards me, smiling.

"Rachel," she said in a soft, sweet, sad voice, holding out her hand. "Welcome to Erato. I'm so pleased to meet you. You're such a beautiful writer."

I clasped her hand as though it were a lifeline. Whoever she was, I wanted to fall at her feet and kiss the hem of her drab, muted garment. Instead, I stood there, grinning.

"I'm Martha, Eudora Caldor's assistant. Your room and studio are in Winter House at the end of the drive. Meals are in the dining room here." She handed me a chain with three keys. "You can drive right to the steps leading to the back door," she said, after explaining what the keys were meant to open, although they were clearly marked. "Shall I send one of the men to help you unload your car?"

"Oh, no," I said. "I can manage easily." We smiled at each other again and parted, and I drove to the back of Winter House, It was about two o'clock in the afternoon. I told myself that everyone would be in their studios working, and I'd have a few hours to settle in before having to face anyone. The thought calmed me while I began unloading the car. But when I got inside, through the back door, I saw two women in the kitchen. They were having an argument. They were both extremely voluble women, opinionated and impassioned, I would soon discover, and all their conversations were arguments. Because my arms were loaded, I kicked the door shut behind me. They stopped talking and turned to look at me.

"Hullo," one of them said, getting up and coming out to greet me. "You must be Rachel Levin."

"I am." I said, surprised. "How could you tell?"

"We were expecting you," she said, and smiled. Nice smile, white teeth. Southern accent. Around my age, maybe a little younger. Short, curly black hair. Tall, thin, vibrant with energy. Handsome. "I'm Tully Jackson. And this is Lizzie Hunter." The other woman had followed her out of the kitchen. Lizzie Hunter. Pretty, buxom, huge

black-rimmed spectacles, long hair, fresh-skinned, impos-
ing presence, wearing a gray wool jumper, the hem almost
to her ankles. She looked like a suffragette, a bloomer girl,
someone to lead a march holding a placard smeared with
slogans.

But T. L. Jackson! How odd that she should be the first
Erato-ite to speak to me. A week earlier, I'd had a letter
from Martha, the woman who'd come out of the office to
greet me and who, I would later see, was a sad, spiritual,
sighing woman who ran the colony office as if she were
doing penance for some unimaginable sin committed in a
dark and distant past. In her letter, she told me that it would
be a small group, since the main house was closed for the
winter, and she listed some names. I recognized the names
of a critic, a novelist, and Tully, a Southern Writer who
signed herself T. L. Jackson, just beginning to receive
recognition. I had read a few of her short stories, and,
though neither her name nor anything in the writing gave
away her gender, I was pretty sure she was a woman. I dug
out a recent quarterly with one of her stories and reread it.
It was very good. She wrote with a lot of energy and humor
and I, who was just beginning, felt that she was probably a
rising star in the tradition of Katherine Anne Porter or
Flannery O'Connor. I felt awed. It was then that I had my
premonition, or perhaps it was a fantasy, that our destinies
would not only cross but lock. Premonition? Fantasy? It
could as well have been a plan.

"We're having tea," Lizzie said. "Will you join us?"

"No, thanks. I just had lunch." I had stopped for it in
town, stalling the moment of my arrival, trying to gather
courage. "I want to unload and get unpacked." Before I
change my mind and race back home, I did not say.

"Here, let me help you with that," Tully Jackson said,
taking the heavier suitcase from me.

"That's okay," I protested, but she was already marching down the hallway with it, leading the way. "Which room, d'you know?"

"Number three," I said.

"That's this one, right here," she said, rounding a bend in the hallway and pushing open the heavy door. I followed her inside. It was a small, pleasant room, painted white. Small desk, narrow bed with the usual auxiliary furniture in dark wood, mahogany, leaded-glass bay window, an adjoining white-tiled bath, larger than the bedroom.

"Nice," I said, pleased.

"Hope you don't have to work at that tiny desk," Tully Jackson said. I was still too scared to really look at her. "That's a desk for poetry, or *billets doux*, not fiction."

"In a pinch, I could set myself up in the bathroom," I said. "But I've got the attic studio. Where are you?"

"Upstairs in the back. The servants' quarters. I love it."

We sounded like two girls at school. "Well," I said, "I'd better get the rest of my gear."

She followed me out to the car. Lizzie, who had been waiting in the kitchen for her return, came out, too, and they both loaded up and helped me inside.

"Great service," I muttered, embarrassed.

"You don't travel light, do you?" Lizzie said.

"I've never learned how," I apologized, struggling with my typewriter and the heavy bookbag containing my thesaurus and Webster's and the dozen books I'd brought along to read, as though I were going to a desert island. "With a car it seems pointless not to take everything."

"Not like us peons who have to backpack it in buses," Tully said cheerfully, holding the screen door with a booted toe. "So much quipment It's a good thing you're a writer, not what they call around here a visual. You'd have had to rent a truck." Her southern, backwoodsy talk, I decided, and it would later be confirmed, was a lowering of the barriers, her way of telling me that we were going to be friends.

Friends! Take away the "r" and you've got what we would soon be, in the sense of immoderacy, of addiction.

"What do you write?"

"Short stories," I said.

"Me, too."

"I know. I've read some of your stories. In the Georgia Review." She beamed. "You're awfully good," I said, then thought that maybe I'd sounded patronizing, which was the last thing I felt, but she beamed even brighter. "I wasn't sure if you were a man or a woman." T. L. Jackson. "In New York, single women use initials in phone books, hoping to ward off heavy breathers, but that ploy has become such a clichè that they're a dead giveaway."

"When I started writing, I wanted to pass as a man. It's one of the things Lizzie castigates me for. Lizzie's a writer, too," Tully said, as though Lizzie might be too shy to tell me herself.

"Non-fiction," Lizzie said. "I'm writing a book about women."

We were back in my room, with my luggage spread everywhere, waiting for me to sort it all out and tuck it away.   "Women!" I said, though I wanted the small talk to end and for them to go away. I needed to be alone, not only because I wanted to get settled, but because I wanted, after that, to collapse. It had required all my emotional energy to leave the kids, Scarsdale, Peter, Dr. Kantfogel. This was too new, this emerging, untried, unproved self. I was exhausted. People who know who they are don't have such a hard time of it. It took Tully to put it into words for me, to tell me, as she did many times, that I didn't know who I was. Also that I wasn't in touch with my feelings.

"Women," I said again. "What about them? It's a fairly large subject."

"Indeed it is," Lizzie said. It was only the beginning of

the modern women's movement. It was even before consciousness-raising groups. My feminist consciousness had not yet begun to rise much, though I think my instincts were all in place, waiting for the yeast of catchwords.

"We discuss it endlessly," Tully said. Her eyes, deep, deep brown, almost black, sparked and crackled. Gorgeous eyes! "And so, like it or not, will you." She looked at her watch, perhaps sensing my need. "Well, back to the mines! We generally meet in the living room around five for a pre-dinner drink, if you'd like to join us. Lizzie and I and the others."

"Thanks," I said.

When they were gone, I sank onto a corner of the bed, feeling not only exhausted but elated. And terrified. I knew. I trembled with it. My life was going to change, and Tully was going to be the instrument of that change. I knew almost nothing about Tully, yet I knew that. How did I know? I have fallen seriously in love three times in my life, and each time I knew almost instantly that it was going to happen. How do people know? Maybe there really is a chemistry, an electrical charge given off, but I doubt it. That kind of instant attraction must have to do with readiness and will, which are all you really need to make things happen. I was sure Tully felt it, too, though she later denied it. "I saw you as a typical suburban matron," she said. "In that navy blue suit with the pleated skirt, driving that cute little sky-blue Chevy Corvette."

"Suburban matrons almost always drive station wagons," I said. "Or Cadillacs so vast they can barely see over the steering wheel." But it was true. I had arrived in proper attire, looking very much the suburban matron which, no matter how uncomfortably, I was. It was a warmish day and under the suit I was wearing a girdle, bra, and stockings, garments I was soon to renounce forever.

Whatever Tully took me to be, however, didn't prevent

her during those first days from directing much of her attention and considerable charm my way, which is, of course, flirting.

She read the three stories I had published, the extent of my opus to have made it into print. "I started late," I explained. "I gave it all up to be your typical suburban housewife and mother and I only went back to it two years ago when Jed started kindergarten."

"Why did you do that?" she asked, aghast. "Give it up?"

"I didn't think I could manage both," I said, which was only the smallest part of the truth. It would have taken hours and hours to tell it all, and I didn't want to bore either of us.

Although my stories were in what writers call "prestigious" publications, Tully didn't seem terribly impressed. "They're good," she said, "but you haven't found your voice yet." I had no idea what she meant. What could she know about my voice? They were well-written, literate stories, and I had written them, so how could they not be in my voice? I had learned to love writing from, among the contemporary women, Virginia Woolf and Jean Stafford and Elizabeth Bowen and Iris Murdoch, though you'd never know it now since I have found my voice.

Tully asked me what I was working on and I told her a novel. I had, in fact, quite a lot of the novel, and she asked to see it. She promised to read it that night, and I gave it to her with trepidation. I lay awake and tossed half the night, imagining her reading it. What part was she up to? What if she hated it? Or worse, if it bored her and she couldn't really read it at all and had to skim and lie to me? I squirmed and thrashed in my narrow bed, feeling that half of me lay naked and exposed in her room, the more important half. And how honest would she be with me? Could I trust her?

In the morning, she was waiting outside for me to go to

breakfast on the path to the dining room. At the sight of her, my heart leaped into my throat and I had trouble breathing. I had been crazy to think that Tully and I were going to be anything to each other. All my premonitions were nonsense. I could never manage it, not with this woman. I was much too scared.

"Good morning," she said cheerfully, falling into step beside me. She peered at my face, which I kept resolutely turned from her. "What's the matter? Are you all right?"

"I'm fine."

She laughed. "You're afraid of what I'm going to say about your book, is that it?" Ha, ha, ha. For a split second I hated her. "The book is good. It's better than good. I was up half the night reading it. I was completely involved."

My breath came back and I was able to look at her. She was smiling at me, amused, fond and speculative, the look a mother turns on a beloved child who has been bright or silly in some unexpected way.

"You don't have much confidence in yourself, do you?"

"Not yet," I said. "I'll have it when I earn it. Or so I hope."

She touched my arm. "Well, believe me when I tell you that your book is better than..." and she rattled off the titles of several recent novels about young women by critically acclaimed male writers. I laughed. "It is," she insisted. "I know."

"What you know," I said, "is the way to my heart." She had withdrawn her hand from my arm but I still felt it there.

"It needs a little tightening. I hope you don't mind, but I read it with a pencil. You don't mind, do you? It's the teacher in me." She taught writing and contemporary literature at a mid-western college for young ladies from well-to-do families. "I teach debutantes," she'd told me during the drinking hour the previous night, "none of whom will ever again write anything more profound than thank-you notes, but at least they'll write those grammatically, and possibly even gracefully." Her students, she said, were still at an age where they believed they had souls and were eager to expose them, so occasionally the writing would be of some interest. But soon, of course, they would have more important things to think about.

Tully was on sabbatical. She had been at Erato for four months. In those days, if they judged you both worthy and needy, you could stay forever. She had another two months to go.

"Nothing serious," she said. "Just a little line editing. We can go over it later today. Why don't you come to my studio around four?"

At four I found her in what had once been the servants' sitting room, stretched out on a wicker and leather chaise. Because the room faced east and got no afternoon sun, she wore a green cable-knit sweater with a shawl collar. She was shod in ankle-high buckskin boots, which I found quaint. Her feet, I noted, were smaller than mine. My manuscript was in her lap, and she had obviously just been leafing through it.

"Pull up a chair," she said. The room was cluttered with furniture, much of it wicker, which had not yet returned to favor, the sort of practical, not too comfortable furniture the turn-of-the-century wealthy would consider serviceable for the servants. I dragged a straight-backed oak chair alongside her chaise, and sat awkwardly on it, at right angles to her.

"Whatever I've bracketed," she said, pointing with her pencil, "should go. Here. Let me show you how much better this sentence is without these extra words."

Oh, she was right! I could see it at once. I marveled. How masterful she was! What an ear she had! As she spoke, I watched her face, her beautiful, expressive hands, listened to the words she spoke in her soft, sure voice. She doubted nothing about herself.

I loved her.

Also, I saw that she had already established a hierarchy in which I was somewhat subordinate. I never questioned it. Her stories had been collected and would be published in a few months by one of the more literary houses. She had an agent, one of the good ones, and I did not. She had a respected editor who respected her. She taught. She spoke with authority. Furthermore, she was exotic and I was ordinary. Hers was a world that hitherto I had only read about, one with a literary tradition. She was southern, a lapsed Catholic, a lesbian, her father had been a judge in a small town, she had two handsome, overbearing older brothers, one of whom, in classical southern literary tradition, had sexually diddled with her during part of her childhood. Though I didn't yet know all this about her, I knew this: she was a real writer.

It never occurred to me, then, that she might have found my background exotic if only because it was as different from hers as hers from mine. I was like practically everyone I knew.

She went on turning the pages of my manuscript, showing me sentences, words, that she had marked for expulsion. Over and over, she was right. "You must never feel that what you've done is graven in stone," she said. "Rewriting is the heart of good writing. And after a while, you'll see, it's fun."

Would I ever be able to see my own mistakes? I was so ashamed that I hadn't; they were now so obvious.

"I've marked it through to the end," she said, "but you get the idea. No need going over all of it with you."

She put the manuscript back in its box and handed it to me. I started to get up. "Wait," she said, and laughed. "You're not dismissed yet. We haven't really talked about the book. Would you like a drink? I've got some Scotch."

"Yes. I'll go down for ice."

"No, don't. If Lizzie's there, she'll wonder why she's not invited. I'd rather she didn't know."

Oh, that's it, I thought, my heart sinking. She and Lizzie are having an affair.

"Let's drink this one neat," she said, pouring a careful minimum into two bathroom glasses. The bottle was nearly empty. She looked at it ruefully. "This is the last bottle of Scotch I'll be able to afford for a while," she said. "Unless *Mademoiselle* buys my Kit Lansbury."

"Your what?"

"Kit Lansbury. That's a *nom de plume* for my junk writing." She said *'nom de plume'* as she had earlier said *'billets-doux,'* in a way that made it clear that she was not one for fancy phrases, especially French ones, that her use of them was half in jest. *'Nom de plume'* seemed perfectly acceptable to me, not at all an affectation, hardly even French.

"Whenever I bad need money, I write a story for the slicks. They pay pretty well, and I seem to be able to do it without much trouble."

"Do you have any here? I'd love to see them."

"I could dig out one or two. They're not worth reading."

Later, when I read the two she had with her, I was impressed. They were skillful and funny and moving, and driven by her special energy. I wouldn't have been ashamed to have written either of them, and I would have published them under my own name.

"It's just a craft," she said, but it was more than that. Her inventiveness and imagination were there in the plot, in the details, in the way her characters, though without the depth they would have had in her "real" stories, were nonetheless alive. I was full of admiration, but by then there was nothing about Tully, although I scarcely knew her, that I didn't find wonderful. That's what falling in love is; I couldn't imagine why everyone wasn't madly in love with Tully. She seemed remarkable in every way, and unflawed. I was bewitched. *In love.* The real loving comes later, more slowly, when the scales fall and familiarity brings a truer seeing, a more accurate one. Then, unless you are too disenchanted and disappointed, and there is always some of that, the love grows more profound, less hectic. I could never make Tully believe that, however, because of who I was, a New Yorker with a big, critical mouth, daughter of my parents. Anyhow, that wasn't what she wanted. She wanted the *in* love.

But that lay some years in the future. This was only our third day. I sipped her Scotch, trying to make it last, planning to buy her a new bottle. I would call it a token of appreciation for the help she'd so generously offered with my novel, though I would have given it to her without reasons.

"Who is Thomasina?" she asked.

Thomasina was the name I had given my novel's protagonist, God knows why, a young undoubting woman, mysteriously (I hoped) innocent and fresh and unspoiled, open to life, but not yet marked by it, a *tabula rasa.*

"Is she you?"

"Oh, no!" I said. "Well, maybe one tiny aspect of me, of a much younger me."

"How old were you when you married?"

"Twenty-one."

"Why so young?"

"I didn't know it was young then. My father had been calling me an old maid for three or four years by that time."

"Weren't you in school?"

"Yes, but that didn't matter. As far as he was concerned, school was just marking time for a girl. A waste. Marriage was what counted."

"What a bastard! But you knew better."

"I did and I didn't."

"Where was your mother in all this? Did you marry just to get them off your back?"

"I married to get away from home, yes. And because it was what everyone I knew was doing. It was what came next."

"Oh, Lord! I can't imagine it. Were you happy?"

"Happy?"

"Yes, happy."

"No. Were you?"

"We-ell," she laughed. "No. But I did what I knew I had to do, not what anyone else thought I should do."

"You were lucky to know."

"How could you not know?"

"It was easy."

"Because you didn't know who you were."

"That's just another way of saying the same thing. Why didn't I know?"

"Because they kept seeing you as they wanted you to be, not as you were, and you kept trying to be their version of you because you wanted to please them, or because you weren't aware of anything to put in its place."

"I was too young to know who I was. Look, Tully, I started seeing a psychoanalyst when I was twenty-five and I just quit. At least I think I just quit. Weren't we going to talk about my book?"

"We are talking about the book," she said, not at all nonplussed. "How old are you?"

"I turned forty in August. It was traumatic." I wasn't just saying that. It *was* traumatic. It marked the time when I realized that nothing in my life would change unless I changed it.

"Wow! Fifteen years of analysis! How come?"

"I had a breakdown. That's what they called it then.

And there were problems with the marriage."

"What kind of problems?"

"Really, Tully, this is an inquisition. I thought southerners were supposed to be so polite and well-mannered."

"I'm not being rude, just practical," she said. "Sooner or later I'm going to know everything about you. Might as well be sooner."

How cocky she was! How sure of herself. Anyone that sure of herself must have it right. But I was already sold.

Still, it took another three days. We were in my room, speaking softly, because it was late. In the room above mine, Lizzie marched to and fro, as she had been doing every night. She was an insomniac, but not the kind who thrashes about in bed, or reads. It was her thinking that kept her awake, and she was a pacer/thinker. A marcher, really, with a firm, definite step. From the sound of it, her bedroom slippers were wooden clogs.

"I don't want Lizzie to hear us," Tully said. "I'd rather she didn't know I was here in your room."

"Why not?"

"I just think it would be better if she didn't know."

"You're having an affair with her," I said.

Tully laughed. "No, of course not," she said. She had been telling me about herself, her life since she had taken her Master's degree at Iowa, where she had met and fallen in love with Margaret, the woman she had been living with ever since. She was trying, now, to leave Margaret.

"It's the real reason I've stayed at Erato so long," she said. "I love Margaret. I'll always love her, but she's not good for me. I've got to wean myself away as painlessly as possible, because I don't think I can ever go back." From what Tully had told me about her, Margaret sounded, despite my jealousy and immediate prejudice against her, wonderful, a paragon. I was half in love with her myself. She was beautiful and brilliant, what Tully called "a real

lady." After going on to get her doctorate, she had bought
the farm they shared and was already assistant dean at the
college, the real money-maker of the pair, though Tully had
endless money-making projects: raising earthworms and
breeding Labradors and figuring out how to get their toma-
to crop to market ahead of everyone else so that they could
still get a good price. She talked like a real farmer, but,
then, Tully was a talker; she could talk like a real anything.
And, of course, and above all, Tully had her writing, which
Margaret respected, encouraged, and supported.

"I can't imagine why you would leave someone like
that," I said.

"Do you want to go to bed?" Tully asked.

"No, I'm not tired."

"I mean do you want to go to bed with me? Do you
want to make love?"

I began to tremble and hoped it didn't show. "Yes," I
said. "No. I don't know."

"I'll settle for the 'yes' since it was your first choice. But
why don't you know?"

Because I'm scared, I did not say. But why this inordinate fear?

"I won't know what to do," I said. Tully was sitting on
my bed and I was in the armchair. I got up and went to the
window, my back to her. There was a big Norway spruce
outside the window, partially lit by a path light. I was here,
in this place, among these people, people in the art world,
because I had published three good stories and there were
those who believed I would publish more. It was late, but it
was my first tottering step toward independence. And
wasn't independence freedom? Wasn't I free?

"You don't have to worry about knowing what to do,"
Tully said, softly. She had gotten off the bed and was
standing behind me. "If that's all. Is it?"

"What if I don't like it? It could destroy our friendship."

It was the sort of thing one thinks but doesn't say. If anyone had said it to me, I would have been put off instantly. Not Tully.

"You've never made love with a woman? I can't believe it. How did you ever grow up?"

"I sometimes wanted to," I said. "Sometimes acutely."

"Then why didn't you?"

"I didn't think that just because I wanted to do something, I should."

"You were frightened."

"Yes. There was no place in my life, in my world, for anything like that."

"You were living a lie."

"It wasn't that simple. I fell in love with men, too. Once I was madly in love with a man and a woman at the same time."

She put her hands on my shoulders and turned me towards her. I forced myself to look at her. Her expression was sweet, bemused, her dark eyes gentle, loving. She put her arms around me and kissed me. I must have swooned into that kiss; it was such a relief after days of what I hadn't recognized as sexual tension. After a while, she took my hand and led me to the narrow bed and we somehow managed to lie on it, facing each other. She held me for what seemed like a long time, just looking at me. Overhead, Lizzie was pacing like a pony, clop, clop, clop.

"Thank God," Tully whispered, sounding relieved. "I like your close-up face just as much. Possibly more."

"What do you mean?" I said, touching her hair.

"I once started to make love with a woman I thought I was attracted to, but when I saw her close-up face, close up like this, she looked entirely different. I couldn't do it. It was embarrassing."

"Your close-up face looks all right to me," I said, running a finger along the rim of her ear, then down the line of her jaw. "Why didn't you close your eyes?"

"I never close my eyes during love. Afraid I might miss something. I need to see the person." She was running a hand slowly along my side. I was beginning to feel urgent. I wished she would stop talking. I drew her close-up face closer and kissed her and we began, slowly, to make love, I don't know for how long, since love-making time isn't real time. Lizzie's pacing overhead had ceased. She was either lying with her ear to the floor or had finally worn herself out and gone to sleep.

"No, don't get up," Tully said. And slowly, slowly, we went on making love. I think Tully talked almost the whole time, but I shut my ears, totally absorbed in our bodies, in my skin, my nerve endings.

It was so different with a woman, softer, gentler, more varied and inventive, less programmed, somehow. Maybe not in every way better, really, but different. I loved it.

"See," Tully said. I think she was smiling, but it was too dark to be sure. "You didn't have any trouble figuring out what to do, did you?"

"I didn't do anything," I said.

She laughed. "Of course you did." She began to put her socks on. Was she going to leave?

"Why don't you stay?" I asked. But she wouldn't. Was she afraid we'd be discovered, found out? I couldn't have cared less. I wanted everyone to know. I felt elated and, somehow, triumphant. I got up and walked, naked, to the window, and looked out again. The trees were so tall and thick I couldn't see the sky, couldn't see if there were stars. I heard Tully laugh.

What are you laughing at?" I asked.

"Your walk. You swaggered."

"I did?"

"Like a man," she said. She rolled off the bed. "Sleeping with a woman doesn't turn you into a man." This confused me, because I hadn't for a moment felt during lovemaking like a man. There would be times, years later, when I sometimes would, but never during the years with Tully.

"You mustn't get confused about gender," Tully said. "It's not the sex, you know, it's the person."

When she was gone, I fell blissfully asleep, eager to get the night over with so that it would be another day with more Tully. I could hardly wait.

But Tully missed breakfast the next morning. I didn't see her until dinnertime. I had been in a fever all day. I don't know what I expected from her at dinner, but whatever it was, I didn't get it. She was her usual vibrant, talkative self. She smiled at me from time to time, but there was nothing particularly reassuring in those smiles. When we left the dining room and were walking back to Winter House, she and Lizzie were in the middle of an argument about a book they had recently read.

"Of course she's a feminist," Lizzie said. "There's not a better book about the boredom and loneliness of marriage and motherhood. Here's this still young wife with four small kids and a husband who won't or can't really open up to her about anything substantive, and every minute of her day occupied with the demands and needs of all of them..."

"Yes, I know, and it's wonderful, but..."

"The loneliness, loneliness, loneliness.... there isn't anything for her, and she's dying. And this is a woman who loves her husband and children."

"That's all true, I know what you're saying. My point is that when she finally gets someone who listens to her, who's interested in who she really is, who talks to her, it's a man, and the first thing she wants from him is sex."

"Well, that kind of rapport for a starving woman can be a powerful aphrodisiac."

"Doesn't she have friends?" I asked. I hadn't read the

book.

"The only two women she knows," Tully says, "are nitwits."

"I know a lot of women," I say, "and most of them don't get that from their husbands. When they really talk, it's with a close woman friend."

In my days of compromise, I finally accepted, or thought I did, the fact that I would rarely be able to have a really meaningful conversation with Peter. It wasn't so terrible, I told myself. That kind of connection was something I knew I could get from my friends.

By this time, we were in the living room, talking about Erato.

"I guess there's something to be said for institutional living," I said.

"You call this institutional living?" Lizzie asked. "It's heaven."

I thought about heaven, people's idea of it. "Heaven is a kind of institution, too."

I wanted desperately to be alone with Tully, but I could see that it might be hours before that happened, if it happened at all. What if Tully didn't want to be alone with me, and obviously she didn't. What if last night was it, as far as Tully was concerned, one night of love. She had told me of earlier lovers, and there had been a multitude of them. She had spoken of them with pleasure, the pleasure of a collector, I suspected, trying not to think that she was bragging, though perhaps she was. Probably I was nothing more than the latest of those conquests. A little therapy, she would tell herself, to unburden this suburban matron of her suffocating heterosexuality. Do her good. Oh God, if that's all it was I'd be devastated, completely undone. How would I proceed with my life?

Lizzie went to her room for her Irish and I went to mine for my Scotch. Tully went to the kitchen for the ice and glasses. I had run into town that afternoon for a few things, and I came back to the living room with my purchases.

"I've brought both of you presents," I said, handing them each their package. Tully's was a liter of Scotch. Beaming, she read the note I had tied to the neck of the bottle, thanking her for the help she'd given me with my manuscript.

"You didn't have to do this," she said, smiling, "but I'm glad you did. Have a drink on me."

Lizzie held aloft the fuzzy purple scuffs I'd bought her, her expression more puzzled than pleased.

"Bedroom slippers?" she said. "What a peculiar...I mean, what on earth?"

"They're soundless bedroom slippers," I said, catching a glance of amused complicity from Tully. "It's really a self-defense gift, something for both of us. It was either slippers for you or a rug for your room."

"You can hear me? Oh, that's right, your room must be right below mine."

"You're not much of a sleeper," I said.

"A very light sleeper," Lizzie said, "and, apparently, a heavy non-sleeper. Sorry if I've kept you awake. I've had a lot on my mind. Problems with my marriage. Problems with a lover."

"What a rich, full life you lead," I said.

"Full. Not rich." She began to talk about it. Three hours later she was still talking and, unable to keep my eyes open another minute, I excused myself and went to bed. I don't know what time it was when Tully came into my room and slipped into bed with me.

"D'you still love me?" I mumbled, waking up.

She kissed me. "You mean after twenty-four hours? I have a feeling this may go on a while longer. This feels serious to me."

It was a strange time, the rest of that stay at Erato. I wrote like a madwoman, mostly poems. The novel would have to wait. I hadn't written much poetry before, but these poems overwhelmed me and I had to write them. They were mostly about Tully, about my feelings, which were as acute and intense as an adolescent's. As was my lust, and my glorious sense of freedom. I felt like Sleeping Beauty, brought to life after a long sleep, though I hadn't thought before Tully that I was less than fully awake. I walked around in a constant state of lust. But it wasn't just sex. It was the place, it was living in this other unsuburban world among creative people to whom the mind mattered, was crucial, because of the nature of the work we were all engaged in. Because our senses brought the world to our minds, they seemed sharper and our perceptions heightened. We respected and enjoyed each other. There were, among us, a leading literary critic, a pipe-smoker with a thick mane of silver hair, quite deaf; an older man, a wonderful writer whose stories I had been reading in *The New Yorker* from the time I was sixteen; a British woman poet of considerable renown in her own country, reclusive; a witty composer who knew the names of all the trees and birds, and who believed that two benevolent ghosts entered his room each night and led him gently into sleep; a young Indian woman who made mysterious, beautiful paintings; Lizzie, Tully, and me. For me, it was a whole new world, and I was dazzled by it, though it took me a while to feel that I might really have a place in it. But gradually, when I saw that that they were interested in what I had to say, that I could make them laugh, that my poems kept coming, I began to feel less and less of a fraud, until I was almost as much in love with myself as I was with them. Self-love, the sine qua non of libido.

But even in that company, it was mostly Tully's words I hung on. She was opinionated about everything and she had such energy. She spoke with animation, with enthusiasm, not only in her voice, but in her eyes, her expressions, her gestures. I couldn't take my eyes or ears off her.

She brought me new writers, new books, new attitudes, new ways of seeing. She taught me why some things I didn't much care about were good, or why some things I thought were good were not. She made me see in a way I hadn't seen before.

I don't know what I gave her in return. Security, maybe. A seven-year resting place where she could safely fall apart and begin to mend again. Some years later, long after we had ended and gone on to other lovers and other lives, she told me, "You were so beautiful. When you walked into a room, I was so proud."

I was stunned. I had never thought myself beautiful. I had never thought anyone else thought so either. I knew I wasn't as ugly and ungainly as my parents had often made me feel, but it would have helped if someone had told me what Tully had just said at a time when it mattered. And I was stunned, too, because it was such a macho, possessive thing for Tully to have felt. Proud. I was beautiful and I was hers.

"Why didn't you tell me that then?" I asked, trying to digest this news.

"I'm sure I did," she said. "I must have."

"I'd have remembered."

"Didn't you know you were beautiful?"

"Of course not!"

"You probably wouldn't have believed me, or even heard what I was saying. There are things people don't hear until they're ready for them."

I'd have been ready.

If I make it to extreme old age, are these the things I'll

sit in the wheelchair remembering? Will that withered old woman with the afghan on her lap doze off thinking about how Tully and I grabbed at an hour here, an hour there for making love? We would meet for lunch, usually in my studio, the only room at the top of the house, a silent and private aerie. We could step out of one of the long, narrow windows onto a walled rooftop, the midday sun filtering through the treetops draped about. We would sprawl on the roof, eating our sandwiches in the good warmth of that October sun, and then we would go back inside and make love on the cot, though more often it was necessary to make love first and then eat lunch. Lizzie was away during the day, in her log cabin studio, so we felt freer.

"I want Lizzie to know," I told Tully. "I mean, I don't care who knows."

"I'd rather Lizzie didn't know."

"Were you having an affair with her? Tell me the truth."

"No. I always tell you the truth. I always will. She was flirty with me and I'm pretty sure she wanted to have something. It might hurt her to know I'd passed her over for you. I put her off by talking a lot about Margaret."

"Lizzie's married," I said. "She has a child. She has a lover."

Tully laughed. When I heard what I'd said, I laughed, too.

"That's how removed I feel from the real me," I said.

"This is the real you," she said indignantly. "The other is a lie. How could you have lived that way?"

***

The wind must have changed; the snow has turned to rain. Becky's house doesn't have many windows. It's a brownstone, or what in a lesser neighborhood and without the bows and bays, would be called a row house. Both sides of its length are uninterrupted wall. The windows are on the narrower front and rear, and these are mostly blocked by an orgy of trees and shrubs in the small patches of gardens outside, drapes or intricately carved shutters on the inside. You are snug and private in this house, but if you want to know the weather you can't simply glance up from whatever you're doing, as I can in my apartment. You must make an effort. I have made the effort of getting up and going to a window and peering out of it through the branches.

"It's stopped snowing," I say. "It's raining."

"Yes, I know."

"You can't know."

She looks at me, perplexed and annoyed. "You're very cranky," she says. "What's the matter with you?"

The answer that comes to mind is: nobody has ever loved me enough. Of course, I can't say this. Self-pity, she would say with loathing and scorn, and she'd be right. Missing Minnie, I'm feeling profoundly sorry for myself. Yet, people have loved me as much as people usually love anyone. For what it meant, Peter did. He'd probably have gone on loving me until one of us died. Tully loved me for seven years until, as she said, I drove her away. Others, too, and so, in her way, even Lisa. It wasn't their fault that they stopped loving me and went on to love other people. It was probably mine. I never, with all the psychoanalysis, got free of my parents' legacy to me, the inability to love myself enough to trust anyone's love for me.

"What's wrong with me is that my cat is dead," I say. "Her love was unconditional."

"What we should do," Becky says briskly, as though we are going to spring to our feet at once and do it, "is go right to the animal shelter and get you a kitten. It's the only thing to do. You'll be so enchanted with her you won't have time to brood about Minnie."

"I can't. Not yet."

I feel drained, dull, dead. I'm supposed to be happy. I have this new book about to come out. Oh, big deal, I tell myself. Of course I'm apprehensive and excited but publishing a book is so iffy. It's like laying an egg. You lay it but it's the publisher who sits on it for about a year. You both wait to see what will come of it. Will anyone like it? Will it be reviewed? Will it sell? Will it be in the libraries? Will it have a short life, a long one, a good one? The suspense! More often than not, a little chick struggles out, says tweet once or twice, then falls on its side dead.

Poor chick. Poor old hen.

"Tully used to tell me that I was the angriest person she'd ever known," I say to Rebecca. "Whatever happened to my rage? I miss it."

"Where is Tully now?"

"Last I heard she was in Mexico."

Although it was at Tully's insistence that we more or less stay in touch, periodically she stops writing to me. This is in response to something I've written in my latest letter, something she finds offensive. She was so sure of herself when I first met her, so cocky, that it shocked me later, when we'd left the cushioning of Erato, to learn how touchy, how raw and unprotected she really was. Emotionally, she is a perennial neonate, and I'm never sure what will offend her. There is her terrible, insatiable need to be seen, to be heard, respected, adored, revered, even idolized. This is different from my own need, which is simply to be loved by my lover, in spite of me. When I write to Tully, I am not to say anything at all personal, not even what I am thinking or feeling, and I don't know how to write letters like that. Her own accounts of her comings and goings are like polite letters to an aunt. They irritate me, and so I occasionally do try to push our correspondence to a different level, not of intimacy, but at least of two old friends who still care about each other. Once, in response to God knows what, she wrote me the most scathing letter I've ever received, so full of loathing and excoriation that if I had believed her, I would have had to kill myself, wipe myself off the face of the earth. She left me nothing. The letter made me cry, then it made me feel poisoned, and then, after a few days, I destroyed it. There was no point answering it. I certainly didn't need anyone in my life who thought these things of me, who made me feel so rotten. But after a year or two of silence, she called to say that she was coming to New York to see an agent, and asked if she could stay with me. Warm, friendly. When I brought up the letter, she seemed never to have heard of it. "I said that? I wrote that? I did?" and laughed, not even embarrassed. "You must have gotten me at a really bad time." She had been having depressions, she told me, bad ones, and had turned not to psychologists, but to psychics and homeopaths.

"I liked Tully," Becky says. "I always did."

Becky was the first person I told about Tully and me, because I didn't think she'd be shocked. Surprised and curious, I think she was, more than anything else. I was feeling ecstatic, triumphant, and glorious. Also, selfish and irresponsible. It was what I had felt, pulling out of the driveway that first day, leaving that first time for Erato, terrified. This is for me, I kept telling myself, trying to gather the strength to leave. This is just for me. This is something you've never had before, Rachel, something that's just for you, because of your work, your own accomplishment and efforts. Of course it's selfish. When I'd been at Erato a second time, I got to know two men, well-known poets, and saw how ruthless they were in pursuit of their art and of the experience that fed it. How the other players in their lives must have suffered, I thought. As sensitive and feeling as they were in their poems, there was never any nonsense in their lives about `selfishness.' They knew what they had to do, and they knew who they were. There was never a moment's self-doubt. Men had a God-given right. Women, at least the ones I knew back then, rarely felt that. Everything else came first: children, husbands, laundry, dinner. I'd had twenty years of that and it was a hard habit to break, even for a short time. What was I doing? How could I leave Jed and Henry? How could I bear to be away from them for so long? I reminded myself that Peter was there for them. I could never have done it without him. He was there every night and weekends. And the live-in housekeeper we had then, Annie, whom they adored. I hardened my heart.

"Were you there when Tully and I came home from Erato?" I ask Becky. "I can't remember."

"You mean at that welcome-home party Peter gave?" Becky says. "Of course. I was shocked that you brought her home with you, and even more shocked that she came."

"Yes, it was awful. Tully didn't want to come. I almost forced her. Anyhow, nobody knew but you. Two women? Nobody thought anything of it. Not back then."

"But you and Tully knew," Becky says, sternly.

"I was so nervous walking up from the car to the house, and I'm sure she was, too. Peter opened the door. I was introducing him to Tully when the lights went on and everyone screamed 'surprise!' It was like one of those I'd-just-sat down-at-the-piano jokes."

"Do you think Peter knew?"

"No. Not then." I don't know exactly when he knew because he never asked, never mentioned it. Ever. The first time I knew that he knew was about two years after we'd finally separated. He brought Jed home at the end of a weekend, left him playing outside, and came up to tell me that what he couldn't understand was how come our sex life had always been so good. He wasn't really telling me, he was asking."

"He read somewhere that when a marriage is bad the sex is bad. It doesn't necessarily mean he knew."

"He knew. Someone among our more percipient friends probably sat him down one day and broke it to him." I wondered who. "You know, he never paid the caterers for that party."

"How did you find that out?"

"They called and told me. I was appalled."

"You could have paid them."

"I wanted to, and I would have, but by then Peter was in bankruptcy, something he hadn't bothered to mention. You know, that scheme that couldn't miss? He always had one somewhere on the back burner. Anyhow, the lawyer told me I couldn't pay the caterers."

"Why?"

"Because there was a long list of creditors and if anyone was going to be paid, they'd all have to be paid the same. That's the law." I felt awful about it. Still do. Especially since I was the excuse for the party.

"What did you tell him when he asked?"

"You mean about the sex? Well, the truth is that in those last years it wasn't all that great. It was merely satisfactory. But I didn't tell him that. I mumbled something dumb about our both being sexually healthy animals. He liked that. He liked thinking that about himself, and it wasn't a lie."

"He always lands on his feet, doesn't he? Things come so easily to attractive people. They don't have to work nearly as hard."

"He must have operated over the years with thousands of dollars of other people's money, never repaid."

"Do you think Peter's wife knows?"

"I doubt it. Whatever she thinks, and she probably doesn't dwell on it, she loves him anyway. He's landed on his feet there, too. He found the perfect wife for him, and it didn't take very long, either."

"Giving you that party, whether he paid for it or not, was sweet of Peter, just the sort of thing he would do," Becky says. "Paul has never, never given me a party and we've been married almost thirty-five years. It would never occur to him, and if it did, he wouldn't have the least idea how to go about it."

She sounds bitter. Their marriage has lasted. She and Paul love and respect each other. They're happy.

"So he doesn't give you parties."

"Or presents that I don't have to return," she says with exasperation. "How can he not know after all these years?"

"He gives you other things. Yours is one of the very few good marriages I can think of that isn't good because of blindness or stupidity."

"You don't take anything in my life seriously," Becky says, moodily. "You're so self-involved you think nobody feels anything but you."

"What are you talking about?"

"Even in the old days, when I talked about my sister or my mother, all you ever did was laugh."

"I did?"

I probably did. Her sister's life was a wild soap opera. She'd had a series of lovers, all of them awful, and she'd borne a child by each of them. She married most of them, too, usually without bothering to shed the earlier ones. Accident-prone and a hard worker, she was always recovering from some ghastly injury sustained in her current star-crossed endeavor. She was so predictably outrageous that it was hard to take the stories of her exploits seriously. Because she didn't live by any of the rules, she didn't seem quite like a real person. I don't know how she survived, but she did. As for Becky's mother, I was too fond of her to imagine that Becky could have been seriously upset by anything she said. You forget how it is with other people's mothers, unless they are venomous or abusive, as Becky's mother certainly was not.

"I can't remember that," I say. "But if it's true, I'm sorry. Does it really bother you that Paul is incapable of buying you the right present for your birthday?"

"And our anniversary," she screams. "Of course it does! Why, after all these years, shouldn't he know me?"

"He knows you. You're not easy. Your taste in things is unique and he isn't you."

"I know what he likes!"

"You've told him what he likes. You even buy his clothes for him."

An important part of what Becky does instead of being an architect, or a drama or dance critic, instead of writing scholarly books or even editing them, instead, that is, of doing any of the work of the world at which she would excel, is to design the externals (as well as those internals under her control) of her life according to certain strict, careful standards acquired and, when necessary, modified along the way and applied to her home and everything in it, including her own image and Paul's. Things must look right in order to be right. She has style. I once made the mistake of saying she was fashionable. "I am NOT fashionable," she said. "I'm stylish."

"When Peter was about to be discharged from the army," I recall, "I went to a tailor and picked out what seemed to me a lovely tweedy blue wool fabric, and had a suit made for him." I bought him a pale blue shirt and a bright red bowtie with polka dots to go with the suit. After all the years of khaki, I couldn't wait to see him in this bright plumage. I felt like a little girl dressing a doll. Not that I ever dressed dolls when I was a little girl."

How happy we were, how his face glowed when he shed his uniform and put on the clothes I'd bought, and pinned his ruptured duck, the emblem of his discharge from the army, onto the suit's lapel. How handsome he was! It had been such a long war.

"But it wasn't really his self-image. He wore it, but I don't think he liked it much." Except for an occasional tie, I never bought him another thing to wear. But he took very good care of himself. "He spent much more money on his clothes than I would have, or than I did on mine."

"He had to go out into the business world. He had to look successful. And you never really cared how you looked."

"Yes I did. Do."

"Well, it doesn't show," she says kindly. "Here you are, still chewing this ancient cud, and I'm sure he never gives a thought to you at all."

"Of course he doesn't, why should he? I'm a writer. Writers never let go of anything."

But which comes first? Am I a writer because I can never let go of anything? Isn't that neurosis? And isn't creativity a way of dealing with neurosis?

"Life is just a bed of neuroses," I can't help saying. "Writers are constantly ruminating on their lives because that's what feeds their work. That's probably what you mean by my self-involvement."

"Partly. What I mean by your self-involvement is the extent to which it makes you unaware of others. You think you're the only one who feels pain."

"That's untrue," I say, stung. "People are constantly unburdening themselves to me, or coming to me to be saved."

"Well, you must be different with other people than you are with me. I'll make tea," she says, getting up and going into the kitchen area. In spite of the sciatica that has plagued her for the past few years, her walk is brisk and purposeful.

I think about whether I'm different with Becky than I

am with others, and of course I am. I'm a little different with everyone than I am with anyone else, but I suppose I'm more different with her. She is the one person on whom I sometimes allow myself to lean. She is always so definite about everything and I am so ambivalent. She has firm opinions and mine are so soft. She is always telling me. I am often asking her, but not always. She disapproves of me more than anyone else I know, rarely allows me to feel good about myself, makes me question everything. I don't know why I respect this in her. Masochism? Maybe I need someone to re-enforce my frequent bouts of self-loathing. There is, however, an on-the-other-hand. I totally respect and love her and we often laugh together harder and better than I ever laugh with anyone else.

"Getting old is a pain in the ass. Literally," Becky says, coming back with the tea tray.

"It's the hardest thing I've ever had to do. I'm tired of it. I wish it would stop."

"Some people seem to take it in stride," Becky says, pouring. "I'd just as soon be dead. I've joined the Hemlock Society and I've written a living will."

"You're so practical," I say. "What I hate is being invisible. I have to make such an effort now to convince people that I'm there, younger people that is, and it really isn't worth it. All that energetic small talk and being witty and making your eyes sparkle."

"It would be a pleasure to feel invisible," Becky says. "I hate the way I look. I hate what's happening to my body."

"I keep thinking it will go away, being old. Every morning I take it for granted that when I'm brushing my teeth and I look in the mirror it will be gone and I'll be my real self again."

"It was so hard to grow up," Becky says. "Who would have thought it would be even harder to grow old?"

"Yet so different."

"All those lessons. All that seeing everything for the first time, fresh. All that raw, tender feeling. Ugh! I wouldn't be seventeen again for anything."

"Or even twenty-five. Forty is about the right age, don't you think?"

"To be frozen at forty? Yes, that would be a good plan. To reach forty and die at that age forty years later."

"I didn't mind fifty either. What about staying at fifty for another fifty years?"

"Don't be greedy," Becky says. "Of course, I can't stand anything any more. You're supposed to mellow with age, but my indignation seems to be boundless, and while I never suffered fools gladly, I can't suffer them at all now."

"I've noticed that," I say. I know a group of women our age, ardent feminists they are, too, who go regularly to have their spots erased and their faces lifted. They have estrogen replacement therapy and they go on having periods, or something like. They look terrific. I mention this to Becky.

"What's the point?" she says. "Inside, it's all happening anyway." Becky will do anything to avoid taking even an aspirin.

"Inside isn't what you were talking about. You were talking about your body. Anyhow, it may not be happening, at least not at the same rate. That's the point. And they have all this energy, and they don't join the Hemlock Society and think about suicide."

"They're too busy taking pills and having operations."

"They're too busy marching and signing petitions and having love affairs."

"Do they have love affairs?"

"Yes, some of them. The ones whose husbands are dead or fled or infirm."

"Paul is losing his mind."

"What I hate most in my life now," I say, "is the loneliness."

"Nonsense! You have loads of friends."

"It's not the same."

"The same as what?"

"Having a husband who's losing his mind. Anyhow, Paul isn't losing his mind. Why do you say that?"

"You don't regret having divorced Peter?"

"Not for a minute."

It's true. When I think of the twenty years of my marriage, wifing and mothering, although there are vivid memories, they are like bursts of color against a predominantly gray background. I can hardly remember myself in that time. I feel strangely dissociated, unconnected to that earlier me, as if she were someone else. I suppose she was, if what Tully always said was true, that I didn't know who I was, that I was living a lie, being the person others expected me to be. But it seems peculiar to be a character in a life without natural progression and continuity. Life, I always thought, is a river that trickles down from a mountain, widening as it flows, emptying at last into the vast dark sea. Such a neat and satisfying image. But not for me. I changed my life in those months at Erato with Tully. I did it deliberately, consciously, although I often felt and behaved like a passive player.

Tully and I were scheduled to leave Erato at the same time. She was planning to come to New York for a while, because earlier that year, in Ohio, she had seen her first real, professional play. The Lunts were touring with Duerenmatt's "The Visit," and she was knocked out by it. She was coming to New York to see as many plays as she could, and to write her own.

As the day of our departure neared, we both grew increasingly nervous and upset at the prospect of being cast out of this easy paradise. Everything would, inevitably, change.   I knew that ahead of us lay turmoil and pain, no matter how we finally managed to arrange the future.

We left the day before I was expected to arrive home. We wanted to spend one whole night together. I looked in the yellow pages and telephoned a motel in a resort town an hour south of Erato. The reservation clerk asked if I wanted a room with one bed or two, and I said one would be fine.

The motel turned out to be an ancient, depressing Kozy Kabins kind of place, with a swinging neon sign out front saying, " ACA CY."

"What you reckon that means?" Tully asked, slipping into her backwoods persona for the occasion, wanting to cheer me up. "Some kind of sickness they have up here?"

"It's a flowering shrub," I said.

It was a sad night. A gas heater in the cabin whooshed on and off at frequent intervals throughout the night, casting an unhappy blue light over the room. "Puts me in mind of Cousin Murf's place up in the hills," Tully said. "Course he keeps chickens in there with him for the company since Cousin Willa's passing. It's none of my bidness, but chickens seem a sorry substitute for a good wife who cooked up your grits every morning for forty-seven years, and the good Lord knows what else. Come here, woman." And then, reverting to Tully, she held me and said, "It will be all right."

We were up most of the night making love, then not able to sleep, making love again. In the morning we stayed in bed as late as we could, legs and arms twined around each other, then checked out and wandered through the few streets of the town, poking into shops. I bought presents for the kids. Tully's watch had stopped working, and I bought her a waterproof, shockproof, foolproof Timex she admired. Mid-afternoon, we went to a restaurant for "our last meal." I had told Peter I'd be home in time for dinner. I didn't mean to get there any sooner.

I was to drop Tully at the train station, where she would

go on to the city. Lizzie, who had left for New York a week earlier, had offered to put Tully up until she found a place of her own.

"Come home with me," I said to Tully, when we were nearly there. "Just for tonight. Tomorrow I'll drive you into the city."

I couldn't imagine how she was going to manage; she had exactly nineteen dollars and a pocket full of change. She was perfectly calm about it. How I admired and envied her insouciance, I who never left the house to go to the corner without first making sure I had at least fifty dollars in my wallet, plus my American Express card.

"Something will turn up," she said, cheerfully. "It usually does. I have a hunch they'll buy my Kit Lansbury." A few days later they did. They paid her enough to live on, if she was careful, for three months.

"I can't come home with you," she said.

"Why not? We have a guest room."

"It wouldn't be right."

"It's an offer I'd make to almost any friend I was driving home from Erato. It wouldn't seem at all unusual."

"I couldn't."

"Please. I can't stand it. I need some ...," What did I need? "... transition. Connection. Anyhow, you have all that stuff to haul with you on the train."

She came. And all the lights went on and it was a surprise party. Horrified, Tully excused herself almost immediately and I took her up to the guest room, which was also, and primarily, my writing room.

"I'm sorry," I said, choking on tears. "I'll bring you food and drink."

"I'm not hungry. I don't feel well. I'll just call Lizzie and tell her I'll be there tomorrow, and then I'm going straight to bed."

I kissed her and left and went to my party. I even

managed to have a good time. I was glad to see my friends and family after being away so long. Being in love made me high to begin with but I got even higher. When the caterers had cleaned up and followed the last of the guests out, Peter and I were alone. The boys had long since gone to bed. We went upstairs and closed the bedroom door. Peter put his arms around me.

"God, it's so good to have you back."

"I'm sorry, Peter," I said. "It was so sweet of you, that party. I want a divorce." I began to cry. He let go of me and, looking stricken, went into the bathroom without saying another word. I sat on the bed and wept, overcome by grief and remorse, and above all, guilt, aware every minute of Tully in the room across the hall. Peter came out of the bathroom and got into bed and pulled the covers up to his ears.

"Don't you want to talk about it?" I asked, dismayed, since I had girded myself.

"There's nothing to talk about."

Nothing to talk about! I couldn't believe it. A couple of years later, waiting together in an airport for Henry's plane to land, bringing him home from college, I asked Peter what he had told his family about the reason for the divorce. I wanted to know. I had never heard from any of them again.

"I told them it just hadn't worked out," he said, shrugging.

Nothing to talk about. It just hadn't worked out.

We had been married for twenty years! At least, I thought we had been married. I was stunned. As far as they went, both statements were true, but was this why our species had gone to all that trouble to invent language? The worst of it was that those words must have been adequate for Peter. I'll never know, but they could well have covered the range of his feelings and his thoughts. If that was true, was there any reason for me to feel guilty? The whole thing, half my life, was a mirage.

So, then, where had I been all those years? Hadn't I been a total, willing collaborator, as much a party to my own delusion? More, really, since I was the one who was supposed to be so smart, who was always looking for meaning, for truth, and for the words with which to express them. I was supposed to be the digger, the planter, the gatherer; Peter was merely the hunter, the one with the spear, the one who dragged the carcasses home to the cave. His not to reason why. What was the reality? What was it that I felt it so important to graft onto that reality?

Reality is so simple. Delusion, illusion (they are, of course, the same), and fantasy, are so much more complex. The need for them comes out of such a different, poetic, romantic place. Once that place would have been called the heart; now it's probably the left brain.

The reality is that we were husband and wife in the eyes of the law of the society in which we lived, and in the eyes of everyone who knew us. We had lived under the same roofs during the twenty years of that marriage, having satisfactory, and sometimes very good sex with some regularity. Under those roofs were paintings and furniture that we had chosen and accumulated together, and books and records. We had tossed our genes into the pot and created those two new lives and watched and helped them grow. There were albums full of photographs he had taken, mostly of the children and me. The children and I broke things, he fixed them. I cooked the dinners, we all ate them. We shared friends, laughed at many of the same jokes, occasionally even wept together, went to the same parties, movies, plays, concerts, weddings, funerals.

That was a lot. Why wasn't it enough, that reality? Why was I so ready to throw all of it over, and for what? Why should I so often have felt lonely? Why had there always been a part of me that felt empty and unused? Why did that part loom so large, when I could hardly even name it? It wasn't merely the work, my work, because by then I was working. It was something else.

The reality is that he told me almost daily that he loved me and that I believed him. The reality is that I don't remember ever telling him that I loved him. Why didn't I? Why didn't I love him? I knew him so well, his skin, his teeth, his genitals, his chest, his elbows, his ears, his smile, his humor, his lies, his dignity. I was so comfortable with him most of the time, so angry at him the rest of the time, and, when the anger stopped because I had finally learned that it was useless, so bored.

All that was the reality, yet almost all the time I yearned to feel something real. What did I mean by that? To love someone? To be in love? Yes, but to be that, it had to be with someone I respected for qualities Peter didn't have, someone who could surprise me, someone who could, as Tully did, talk to me during lovemaking, reminding me that we were in this together. Someone who could go with me to levels of passion and awareness I knew were there. Someone who would love qualities in me I wasn't even sure I possessed, but who, by loving them, would at least lend them to me. All these years too late, because I had found my work, I was ready for what had earlier terrified me because I felt unworthy: a lover who was worthy of me.

Dr Kantfogel would have told me, as he often did, that if my ego was strong, intact, I wouldn't need anyone to validate me. It wasn't validation I needed, it was intimacy. I knew that I'd no longer go to pieces without it, that I was no longer that frail, breakable reed, but with my strengthening ego, it was what I more and more wanted.

I thought of Tully sleeping across the hall from us, so near, so alien.

* * * *

The book is finally out. Readers either love it or, if they are among my friends or acquaintances, I may never hear from them again. I don't know why this is. I can't imagine that there is anything in it to shock or offend anyone of my generation, or of later ones. My mother's, yes.

"I told you not to tell your friends about it," I whine.

"I couldn't help it. I was so proud. How could I not have shepped a little nockis?"

"You can't say I didn't warn you."

"Now I know how Philip Roth's mother felt."

Maybe I shouldn't have told her about the book. She might never have found out. But of course I told her. I told her for the same reason she told her friends.

"Why couldn't you have written a book like other people write, with a story, made-up people in it? In another century, another country? Or even about animals, bears in caves. You tell everyone you write fiction, why don't you? Instead, an open letter to the world, look at me, I'm a... one of those. I don't know what to say to my friends. They keep asking where's Rachel's book."

"Tell them the publishers decided not to do it."

"I considered that, but sooner or later somebody will hear about it and then what. They'll know I was ashamed. Better to brazen it out."

"Good for you. Try to act as though you're still proud."

"My daughter the freak."

I have always been her daughter the freak, even years before I so much as thought about acting on any of my unheterosexual inclinations. This has been the dominant element in our relationship: she, trying to force me into the mold, her notion of what a normal child/girl/young woman/woman/middle-aged woman/practically old woman should be in her behavior, life-style and, especially,

64

dress; I, resisting, passing through a chronology of helpless indignation and despair, shame, resentment, anger, indifference, deafness, indigestion, and, finally, amusement. Bemusement, too, since I'm really too old to have a mother.

But we were talking about the kind of book I should have written for the sake of my mother's friends.

I spent a lot of time, not long ago, writing what I thought was an entertaining book with a lot of plot and a large cast of characters based more or less on movie types, who may be the same types one finds in all those mass-market paperback books with embossed covers, lots of gold and silver and neon blue, but I wouldn't know because I've never been able to bring myself to read one. Still, I think part of me was trying to write one of those, only in a sort of literary way. which may have been where I went wrong. It was such a relief not to have to probe deep inside those people, and into myself, not to have to be tearing off my skin. I believed I could let them just say what they had to say and light cigarettes and pour drinks and have some small, recognizable emotions while they worked their way through the plot. To tell the truth, I enjoyed writing that book. With the least encouragement, I might have gone on writing books like that.

But I did not receive much encouragement and I only let it see a handful of publishers. What's a writer to do? It's not that I don't have any imagination, it's that my serious stuff and my true voice spin out of my experience of life. It's autobiography up to a point, but only up to a point. I take something out of the closet and dust it off and look at the back of it, the front of it, and hold it upside down, and maybe I use it in one form or another, and maybe I don't. And of course I invent new scenes, even new chapters, to strengthen and re-enforce the reality as I prefer to see it, giving it the meaning I want it to have, and convince myself that it does have. This is true of my characters, too. Most are done in shorthand, compressed, or they are amalgams of several people. How much, after all, can we really know about anyone, even those we're most intimate with? Still, I do what I can to disguise everyone but myself, invent much of what they say, change their height, the color of their hair and eyes, and move them to Roslyn Heights. One of my characters, Deirdre, in real life had fiery red hair. It seemed as integral to the book as it was to the entity that was Deirdre, that her hair be flaming red. It nearly broke my heart, and it took a lot of strength, but I dyed her hair raven black for the book.

Still, don't think I didn't worry about it. Once the book was scheduled for publication, I began to have qualms, and, frequently, nightmares. I've already described Becky's feelings, but everyone I ever knew would recognize her/himself in it and feel cheated. My mother, now over ninety, would die of shame. I would be sued, lose my closest friends, alienate my children. I would be shunned, hated, dismissed, and probably murdered by Deirdre, in her paranoia. She would accost me, screaming that I had stolen her words and her soul, and would draw a small silver pistol from her ruined purse with the frayed, hanging straps, and shoot me through the heart.

And for what? The book won't be reviewed. Out of politeness or curiosity, people who know me will read it. After a month or two, it will drop from sight, but never from the memories of the few readers it managed to offend.

But then, though too late for my publishers who gave up on it after the first week and turned their full attention elsewhere, it does begin to be reviewed, and most of the reviews are passionately favorable. Strangers are reading it and buying copies to give as gifts to other strangers, friends of theirs. Publishing a book is not, after all, a laid egg, it's a rock dropped into a sea. For a moment or two, it causes widening rings to ripple the surface. I get invitations to speak, to read. I am not displeased; more grist for my grinding-down mill. I get fan letters, and even love letters. The latter come as a surprise. I am a Leo, and flattery is the arrow that unfailingly goes straight to my heart.

"Dear Rachel:

"It may be that I am writing to Ann. [Ann is the protagonist of my book]. I know Ann. She is as much me as she is whoever she is, even if she is you. Though my writing is not like yours, I feel as though I could have written your book, by which I may mean that I feel that we may be the same person."

The letter goes on, charmingly, to tell me about herself. Woven through the letter are adroit references to events in my book, proving that she has read it well, perhaps even memorized it. Her name is Alison Block. She is in the drama department at Berkeley, "merely an adjunct." She is an ACA, the adult child of alcoholic parents. In self-defense, she became an actress, or, depending on your point of view, an hysteric. She no longer acts. She too writes, mostly criticism, reflections, essays. The packet that brought her letter is stuffed with Xeroxed tear sheets of her printed essays, culled from a dozen little magazines and other tiny, esoteric publications. There are also two of her published books. I will read all this later, but I can't help wondering why she wants to make herself so known to me.

She lives, she tells me, in a large, drafty Victorian mansion owned by a former actress and erstwhile friend, now an antagonist, strung out and brain-damaged by drugs. The younger of Alison's two daughters, grown-up and several years out of school, is temporarily living there, too, trying to save up enough money to get herself and her current boyfriend to some warm island where they can paint without having to wear clothes. Also living in the house is a former, intermittent lover who goes back a number of years. He moved in a year ago, after the earthquake. It has taken only this one year of living under the same roof to convince her that it is an ignominious relationship based almost entirely on her masochism, which he can be counted on to feed. He argues with everything she says, gives her nothing but his rage and disdain. It is an impossible situation, and to escape it in order to work, she has rented a tiny room in a friend's damp, unheated basement. She is writing this letter from that room. She hasn't yet figured out whether she's feeling cozy or claustrophobic, but her joints have begun, occasionally, to ache.

She's learned that I'm scheduled to be in the bay area in a few weeks to read at a feminist bookstore/coffee house, one of her hangouts, where she first heard of my book. She would like to arrange a paid reading in the women's studies department of her school, if she can get my schedule from me.

"Are we our words?" she then asks, cryptically. "Sometimes I think that's all we are."

Delighted, I write back at once. I give her my dates, and thank her for sending me such a cornucopia of her work. I tell her that I will write again when I've read it. I put the books aside, and that night, in bed, I begin reluctantly to read, at random, the loose pages. Reluctantly, because I'm in the middle of a good book which I would prefer to be reading. But very soon, I am captivated. Alison Block has a voice, sophisticated, witty, ironic, strong. She is a raging feminist, by which I suppose I mean that there is what seems to me an excess of anger, but she has range. She has been well-educated and she seems to have remembered everything she ever read (how I envy that!), and she is honest and funny. Among the pages, and on the back covers of the books, are reproductions of photos of her. I study them. On the Xeroxed pages, she looks a little like the not-yet-old- and-bedridden Colette, with wild hair and sharp cheekbones. Attractive, interesting. On the book jacket, she is older, her face a bit rounder, the cheekbones less prominent. I read on, well into the night. She is someone I would love to know. By the time I am falling asleep, I have begun to think that she may be someone I would love to love. When I fall asleep, I dream of her. In the dream, she is Colette. In the dream, she is someone I already love.

When I recognize the strong, distinctive handwriting on the envelope of her next letter, I feel a rush of pleasure and anticipation, a lifting of the heart, while another part of me, standing off in the wings, takes note of what I am feeling and comments on it, not uncritically. In the letter, Alison proposes a date for the reading, and a fee she is ashamed to mention but does, alas all she could wheedle out of the department. This information takes up only a fraction of a long letter filled with delightful anecdotes that tell me more about her. She is an eccentric. She goes to parties. She has been to a reunion of her college graduating class and has discovered that the young women who were her friends then have all died and been replaced by mostly stuffy, suburban types with good-looking husbands running to fat, and that she is the only one who seems to feel that the world is coming to an end. But she, too, has died and come back not only as Chicken Little but as a somewhat flamboyant eccentric in thrift-shop clothing, who hangs out in coffee houses, trailing feathers. Her college, small and expensive, was attended by daughters of wealthy men although she was one of the scholarship students because: When she was twelve, her mother died, and a few years later her father quite dramatically disowned her because of a poem she'd written about him in her diary. Who would dream that a busy, successful, alcoholic brain surgeon, now on his third wife, would stoop to read his seventeen-year-old daughter's diary?   A poem is enclosed that is probably the one in question:

> **Drink, Daddy**
> *In the middle of that inferno, your life,*
> *Your mouth goes slack, you curve your spine,*
> *Recoil against your evolving,*
> *Your brain's precision,*
> *The dexterity of your hands,.*
> *Your erect and elegant stance*
> *All the civilizing brush-strokes:*
> *Discretion, politeness, the use of words*
> *Like "right," "wrong," "good," "evil."*
> *"No," you roar, "I never meant to come this far,*
> *Neanderthal is good enough for me".*
> *Slope forward, dangle your arms,*
> *Glaze your eyes, spew vomit on your shoes,*
> *Then, grunting, crawl into your cave*
> *And pull the rocks up over your head.*

As in the first letter, there are frequent, artful references to my book to demonstrate that attention is still being paid. She asks again if I think we are our words, and concludes the letter by confessing that after reading my book, she was in love with Ann for a whole week.

I write back, accepting the date, the fee, (it will pay my plane fare) and go on to tell her that her writing did, indeed, ring my bell, and, typical New York provincial that I am, opine that she is wasted in the boondocks, that she deserves to be more in the world. Though she undoubtedly already knows it, in the belief that one can always stand to hear that kind of news again, I tell her why she is so good. I tell her about the grace and ease of her writing, its natural rhythm, her intelligence, wit, style, and above all, her extremely likeable voice. I suggest magazines she should be writing for, national ones, and I urge her to write a novel. Then I take a deep breath and tell her that a week isn't long enough for me, that I think I may have been in love with her longer than that, and that she'll have to do better. I tell her that of course we are our words. Ultimately. Why else would we keep groping for them, since speech is our most direct and immediate way of being, ignoring how often we use words to mask ourselves. I sign the letter with love, remarking that this is something I've never done before with someone I haven't met, but what choice have I?

There is one more letter before my departure. In it she writes, almost by the way, that people are sometimes disappointed when they meet her. At a party, a woman tells her that she writes like a thin person. She tells the woman that she hasn't had sex in a year and has been pigging out in an inexpensive Italian restaurant that serves twenty-seven flavors of pasta. The woman advises her to see a psychiatrist. I am forewarned. I now know these things about Alison Block: she is overweight, unhappy, a talker. I can hardly wait to meet her.

On the plane, at about the midpoint when everyone is watching the movie that I've already seen, and my mind has strayed from the book I'm trying to read in the half-dark, I imagine Alison Block. I review the range of fatness possible, from pleasingly plump to heavy to obese, from solid fat to lumpy, rippling, bouncing fat, rolls and rolls of it. I soon lose interest in this, too, telling myself it doesn't matter, she has probably exaggerated in the way that fashionable, vain women who are accustomed to wearing a size eight do when they have moved up to a size twelve. My Alison Block is poised, sophisticated, charming, witty, brilliant, and wise. She is her own woman, well at ease. She will know how to love me.

I haven't had sex, either, and it's been well over a year. But my fantasies of Alison, buoyed by her letters, and even more by her books and bits and scraps, have reawakened my libido. I feel years younger and ready for lust. But Alison, I remind myself somewhere over North Dakota, in all her writing is undeviatingly heterosexual. There is no hint, really, that she expects anything more than the friendship of someone who is, perhaps, a kindred spirit, something not so easily met at my age. I like the fantasies I have been having, but I must remember that they are fantasies. I must stop being such a baby. This is real life, not a novel that I am writing, where I am in control and can shape things the way I want them to be. Not that I can always do that even in my novels, where the unexpected is always happening, and characters I thought were all wound up and pointed to go in one direction defy me and go in another, already knowing more about themselves than I do.

I am staying with good friends in Berkeley. Phoebe is a fiction writer, whose work I admire and respect, and her husband Daniel is a physicist. I love them both. When they come to New York they stay with me, though not in such style. Their guest room is really a guest room, attractive and comfortable, just redone before my arrival, whereas I give them my tiny, cluttered study with its fold-out sofa-bed, a form of medieval torture, and they must settle into it amidst all the machinery and paraphernalia of my trade.

When I've unpacked, I tell Phoebe that I must call someone named Alison Block, who has set up a reading for me.

"Alison Block? Oh, I know her," Phoebe says. "I went to school with her."

"Small world," I say.

"Berkeley is a small world."

"What's she like?" I ask.

"I haven't seen her in years, but I read her stuff. I always agree with everything she writes, and occasionally I send her a letter praising her for her courage."

"She sounds intelligent."

"She's brilliant. Eccentric, though."

"How?"

"Oh, it was so long ago. She was a few years ahead of me. She was stagy and talky and flamboyant. When she was there, you always knew she was there."

Presence, I think. Alison has presence.

"What did she look like?"

"Tall. Attractive. I don't really remember. She's probably changed, anyway. It's been … oh my God, is it possible? … over thirty years."

I call Alison Block and get an answering machine on which, for the first time, I hear her voice: strong, clear, musical, flashy and dramatic. "You have reached the Voice of Pure Reason," she says. "Sorry. I'm out to lunch." Too cute, I think, leaving my message. I'm against answering machines as a form of entertainment; their purpose is to carry the word. My son, Jed, when he got his answering machine, (he was among the first, as he is with all gadgets), taped a production number for it. Eerie, menacing background music, and Jed with a perfect Transylvanian accent, or so it was easy to believe, telling callers that he's just stepped out for a leetle bite and will be flying back at dawn, so if you would kindly leave your name, number, and blood type... Funny once, less so the second time, unbearable thereafter.

Alison calls back that evening. I am shy with her. Maybe she is with me, too. For a minute we talk about the Phoebe connection, and then we don't say much beyond arranging where and when to meet. She lives a few blocks from where I'm staying. We arrange to have late breakfast the following day at a restaurant we can both walk to. I walk to it. I've already begun to lose my fantasy of Alison. Words on a page are one thing, a voice on the telephone, no matter how intriguing, is a little closer to reality. There is more of a body around a voice, a body that contains the mechanism, a body with eyes in it, too, and hands. I have been reading much more into our brief correspondence than could possibly have been there. In a moment I will see Alison, the completely unimagined, unelaborated one, and her words and gestures will be entirely hers, not those I've grafted onto the person behind the words in the books and letters. And she, too, will see me and hear me and what will she think?

But then I remember that the fantasy has been mine, not hers. I only fantasized that she might, perhaps, also be fantasizing. I've even had the temerity to invent her fantasy for her, all of it harmonious with mine.

It's a bright sunlit morning, and when I go through the door into Pamela's Kitchen, I am nearly blinded by the darker interior. It's a small place with several long, rustic tables, each seating a dozen people, family style. Someone at the center of one of these tables waves and calls my name. She is sitting with her back to a window so that I see only her broad bulk, motioning me to the free place across from her.

"Hello," I say, sitting down. "How did you know it was me?"

Stupid question, but they are almost the last words I will say until the waitress comes to take my order. Alison, to my surprise, for I'm not late, in fact I'm a few minutes early, has not only already gotten her meal but has begun to eat it. Her plate is huge, piled high with two pork chops, pancakes, scrambled eggs, apple sauce, a basket of muffins and buns and butter beside it.

"You came in alone,'" she says, answering my question, "and stood there obviously looking for someone, and, besides, you look more or less as I expected you to look. This is a yuppy place, a yuppy neighborhood, most people come at least in pairs, here, especially on Sundays when

they've rolled out of bed together, though there are families, too, as you can see and hear, it's not like the cafes on
Telegraph Avenue, where almost everyone comes in alone
carrying a book or a newspaper but, no matter, it's convenient and the food is good, I think, at least they give you
enough of it, though Goddess knows food is my enemy, but
I won't have time to eat again until fairly late tonight, if
then."

Gradually, as my eyes grow accustomed to this lesser
light, Alison begins to appear. Her head is swathed in
something, large, amber-tinted wraparound sunglasses
with thick lenses conceal her eyes, a large purple shawl
covers her neck and shoulders, and she wears long silver
earrings, and purple lipstick so dark that it is almost black.
What I can see of her face is round, the cheekbones gone. I
can see only the part of her that rises above her breakfast,
but she is broad, not yet obese but possibly close, especially
if she continues to eat breakfasts like this one. It is impossible to make out what she really looks like, not only
because of all the covering, but because I am so distracted
by the stream of consciousness that continues to roll forth.
Her mouth slightly pursed to shape the words, she speaks
in a strong, carrying, stagy voice, a voice with range, a
voice that she would have no trouble sending to the back
row of the upper balcony. An elderly couple sits beside us,
also across from each other, and now a party of four women
are shown to seats on the other side, filling the table.
Alison's monologue seems to embrace us all. It's hard to
know what she's really talking about because she is trying
to talk about everything. There are familiar strains, familiar, I realize, because she is quoting herself and I have
already read those bits. She leaps from de Beauvoir to
Emily Bronte to Gertrude Stein to Woody Allen to the
Persian Gulf to her father to phallocentrism to Bella Abzug
to "this serious question of lipstick" to Godfather III and

the Zeitgeist to her friends who are witches to cats she has known to existential angst and deconstruction and Derrida and Lacan to seventeenth century poets to abortion to ageism to Fellini to Andromache to "Jimmy" Baldwin to Freud and incest and Virginia Woolf. There are no transitions or, if there are, few of them show. Seamless. She leaps about with the aimlessness of one of those crazy water beetles that zigzag in random geometric patterns on the surface of ponds. I try to follow and grow dizzy, but I somehow manage to order and eat a decent breakfast and even to get my coffee mug refilled twice.

"Take off your glasses," I say at some point. I don't say please, I don't say why I want her to take them off, I don't feel I have the time for more than those four words. I want the glasses off, if only for a second, because I have begun to feel that I'm being talked to by a wall, and I can't really know what this woman looks like until I've seen her eyes, and all of her face. Startled, she takes the glasses off instantly, and her face at once becomes more human, more plausible, though the light isn't good enough for me to see the color of her eyes. I nod, and the glasses go back on, and so does Alison.

What is clear to me is that I have never met anyone quite like this. She is brilliant and amusing, I think, and tremendously well-informed, well-educated. But there is something hysterical about this barrage of words. Perhaps she is nervous. Obviously, she believes that we are indeed our words and that if she stops talking for a minute, she will disappear, or give me time to think. And what, then, will I think? And say? She hasn't really asked me anything about myself. Having carefully read both of my published books by now, she may feel she already knows everything there is to know about me. Whatever the reason, after two hours I feel we haven't made any contact and I'm both exhausted and perplexed.

When we get up to leave, I am surprised to see that she is as tall as I am. Almost, she can carry her weight. We walk out into the sunshine and, still talking, talking all the way, she walks me back to Phoebe's. We part outside, having arranged that she'll pick me up and take me to my first reading at the bookstore/cafe. She'll try to get her friend Callie to tape the reading, would I like that? I no longer know what I would like because in some new way I have ceased to exist.

"Well?" Phoebe asks when I get inside. "how did it go?"

"I don't know," I say, and I don't. "She's brilliant. She's interesting. She's probably crazy. She talks too much. I think I have to take a nap."

It's not a nap I need so much as to be alone, to be quiet. Maybe to listen to music.

*****

A seismologist who predicted the earthquake, which I watched last year on television, has predicted a new and even worse one, due to strike today, my last day. During the week that I've been here, some of the residual destruction has been pointed out to me. I can't say I'm not a little nervous. New York is a city where you don't think about earthquakes or tornadoes or tidal waves. Winds may some-times reach gale force, but you'd hardly know it. What you worry about in New York is your fellow man, bad enough, but you have the perhaps false sense that you're not entirely out of control, that if you're cautious you're not completely at the mercy of the whimsical forces of destruction. It's the difference between being on a plane with a stalled engine and a car you're driving that's lost its brakes. In the latter case, there are still things you can do, the end is not certain, the ground is solidly there beneath you, but from the mo-

77

ment you step aboard a plane, you surrender all control over your own life to some man (usually), or two, whom you've never met and know nothing about. What an act of faith! Although for infidels like me, something even more is required, a degree of resignation not unlike that forced on you when you're a patient in a hospital. In fact, there are many similarities between airplane passengers and hospital patients. You are expected to stay quietly in your seat/bed except when you need the lavatory, meals appear on trays, stewardesses play nurse, you must somehow suffer through what is really empty time, trying not to worry too much, the destination is arrival or cure, you will either survive or you won't.

"No," Alison tells me, that '"no" referring to something she's thought, not to anything I've said. We are in the nice, clean Bart train with its comfortable upholstered seats and carpeted floors. I'm particularly nervous when traveling on the long Bay Bridge or underground, where we are now. The Bay Bridge will come later, when Phoebe drives me to the airport. I debate the choice but I can't decide which is worse, to be buried alive or to crash from a height into the sea, there to drown if one isn't already crushed to death or, more mercifully, dead of a heart attack.

"If there's an earthquake it will come on my birthday," Alison says, "four days from now." She will be fifty-seven, she tells me. She was born the day Prohibition was repealed and she always felt that gave her permission. I don't see what this has to do with earthquakes, but she is already talking about something else. We're on our way to my final reading, the one arranged by Alison. The first two, in the bookstores, went so well that I'm no longer nervous. In fact, I've begun to enjoy these readings, even to feel like a ham. "Why can't New York subways be like this?" I ask, interrupting her. "Is it because New Yorkers are so much less civilized? Or is it the condition of our subways that decivilizes us? Which comes first?"

"Society or the ape? Society, of course. It makes the ape."

"But the ape is society. Society is the ape."

"Oh, this is too useless. No, I'm afraid it's too late for this kind of speculation. The ox is in the ditch. Alas. It's doomsday time."

"What does that mean?" I ask.

"Doomsday...?"

"The ox is in the ditch. You've said that half a dozen times. What does it mean?"

"Why, I ... don't ... know," she says, a little taken aback, or do I imagine it? I haven't yet learned how to interrupt her. This is a first. "I suppose it means that the wheel is no longer turning. The mills have stopped grinding. Things aren't working. The center will not hold."

"I see. Then the ox has tumbled into the ditch, probably dead. Alison, do you have trouble falling asleep at night?"

"No, I pop right off. Why do you ask?"

"I would think your mind isn't able to stop long enough for you to fall asleep."

"My mind doesn't stop when I'm asleep. It goes right on. I'm a rattle. I'm sorry. If you just hold up your hand, you know, like with the dentist when it begins to hurt, I'll stop until you're ready for me to go on." She pauses for the smallest moment, then says, thoughtfully, "I guess the reason I talk so much is that I'm afraid I may say something."

I laugh. This is about as personal as she has yet gotten with me. I'm no more to her than an empty, and probably unnecessary, ear. After that first breakfast, I stopped considering the possibility of Alison as a lover; she's too much a force of nature, like the earthquake we've been anticipating, though more overwhelming than destructive. I'm a little sorry about it, because I'd so much enjoyed my fantasies; I hated to let them go. But I've been too busy to give it real thought. I need quiet time to get into my mind, and there hasn't been much of it. In addition to Alison, and the readings, I've been seeing other friends, catching up with their lives, meeting their babies, looking at their paintings, commiserating with them about their dwindling love lives.

Between times, home base is Phoebe and Daniel with whom I try to discuss all of it. They're funny and so am I, so we laugh a lot and enjoy each other. Having friends at the other end of a continent is ideal. You only get to see them once or twice a year, so when you do, you see them in depth. It amazes me how at home we feel with each other, when I'm here, when they're with me in New York. They even feel free to quarrel when I'm around. Their quarrels are always the same. Phoebe takes a stand, in no uncertain terms. Daniel, who doesn't agree, will be gentle, patient and reasonable. For Phoebe, though, his kind of logic is beside the point, and it drives her up the wall. She gets angrier and angrier. Daniel begins to sound annoyed, but Phoebe is intractable. Daniel will say, "All right, Phoebe, that's enough," but it's not enough for Phoebe, who goes right on. In the end, Daniel will seem to agree, to submit, but he never does submit. He goes right ahead and does whatever it is in his own way. Although I used to be terrified of my parents' arguments, the quarrels of long-married people have come to amuse me; even when there is genuine anger, you know nothing is really at stake, there is really nothing ugly in them, it's just another way of touching. I was never sure of that with my parents. It was always my father's explosive loss of temper, my mother's almost immediate submission and silent tears, in spite of which my father went on and on. There was so much anger in him that the tiniest dent became a blowhole through which he could unleash it all, making room for more to gather until the next time. I was always certain my father's wrath was so great that, like lava pouring from a volcano, it would engulf and destroy whoever was in its path. Yet he never struck any of us; though powerful, he wasn't a physical man.

I follow Alison off the train at our station, and up the escalator. The small auditorium is only half full when we arrive, but women are still straggling in. It's all women, I see. It was all women at the bookstores, too, but they were women's bookstores, a recent phenomenon, shops that sell only women's books, whatever *they* are. I think of myself as a feminist, but certainly not as one who reads only women, and not one who writes only for women. Men who have accidentally stumbled on my books have often liked them, and I'm glad. I mention this to Alison.

"Hardening of the categories," she says with a little wave of her hand. "You're also known as a Jewish writer, but who would think of calling Muriel Spark a Catholic writer, though Goddess knows Catholicism comes up in her writing more than Jewishness comes up in yours. Eat half, Muriel Spark says, order everything, but eat only half. That's her diet prescription, advice I should take, but if I did, I would only order twice as much to eat half of. She gives other stern advice in this last book: if you're a writer keep a cat, how I miss having a cat but nomads can't keep cats. It's a sign of reaching a certain age to give stern advice, but who knows, never mind, I'm going to introduce you now."

Instead of reading, I deliver a talk I prepared about writing and its perils. I have never given a talk before, never having been an academic nor an authority on anything. I pretend I am Virginia Woolf and this improves my posture. There is a microphone, so I needn't push my voice. I watch my timing. I look up at my audience at strategic moments. I speak slowly or, at least, not at a conversational clip. Sometimes I smile. Nobody fidgets. Occasionally, when they're meant to, they laugh. Here and there a face beams at me, the faces, I later learn, of women who have already read my books, looking up with shining, excited eyes, as I imagine I did seated before my idols. I feel... what do I feel? It's a new feeling. I feel, yes, that's it, I feel almost powerful.

I like the feeling.

Alison has taken a seat in the front row and, wonder of wonders, she sits quietly listening to me. This, I realize, is the only way, in this long week, that I have been able to get a word in edgewise. I don't really want to stop, but the talk is only eight double-spaced pages long and it comes to its inevitable end. After the applause, no one gets up to leave. One of the women asks me if I would please read from my book and I am easily persuaded. I read a short, funny chapter, and when that is over, they ask questions or make comments, and I respond, and so the time passes.

When we get outside, Phoebe and my previously stowed luggage are waiting for me in the station wagon. She is driving me to the airport. I notice that I am still standing straight, unslouched, and I feel exhilarated. I say goodbye to Alison.

"Write to me," I say. "I may miss you."

"Of course," she says, in her deep dramatic voice. "Of course I'll write. But you'll be coming back soon, won't you? Why don't you move here?"

I thank her for everything and get into the car. Not much later, I am airborne, thirty-thousand feet up, though no higher than I already am. And I haven't been attacked by an earthquake.

*****

Three days later I'm home, having detoured en route to Albuquerque for a weekend with Henry and the kids. Henry's wife, Patti, is still too angry at me to have joined us, except when it was absolutely necessary. Who can blame her? I wanted a mother-in-law chapter and I needed her to behave like a daughter-in-law, resentful of my presence, which, on one memorable and ghastly occasion, she did. I could have made it up but I was lazy. There were too many perfect little things that really took place; my imagination could never have equaled them. More than that, when I wrote it I was still hurt and angry. Of course Patti recognized herself. Neither of them will ever forgive me but with Henry I have the advantage of mutual love and a past the length of his life and considerably more than half of mine. Also, Henry read the whole book and, some weeks after having finished venting his husbandly spleen, told me that he thought it was wonderful. I cried when he told me that. Patti never read anything but that one chapter, (why would she?) and then she destroyed their copy of the book.

My mother flew out from Florida to Albuquerque for the weekend, too, and whatever bolstering my ego had gotten from my week as a minor celebrity soon slipped away. My mother treated me as she always does, with a loving despair because I'm still not the daughter she had in mind, but maybe it's not too late. Yes, even at my age. She's over ninety and can't break the habits of a lifetime any more than I can or ever would have by becoming that daughter. She tries, but she can't help it. "You need lipstick, Rachel," flies out of her mouth when we have barely greeted each other. Why do I need lipstick at midnight in an airport, a small one? I am constantly under the scrutiny of this self-appointed fashion-maven's eye. "That jacket is too short, Rachel! Can't you see that? My God, those shoes!"

But I'm happy to see her, plowing on as always, indestructible. If she ever despairs, I haven't seen it. She came close once, that weekend.

"I let my membership at the club lapse," she told me., gloomily "I've had to give up golf."

"Why?" I asked. Golf, she always said, was what kept her alive. Golf and cigarettes and her daily pre-dinner Scotch.

"I have no one to play with," she said with disgust. "All my friends are falling apart. Flora with her arthritis and her neck in a brace. And Ethel can't walk at all, she's in a wheelchair. Millie has emphysema and never goes any-where, except downstairs to the cigarette machine."

"You'll have to get a new batch, younger ones," I said. "If you plan to go on living this long."

She laughed. "These are my younger friends. The others are dead."

But I really came to see my grandchildren. My mother is constantly flying up to New York, on any pretext, but Henry and Patti can't get away so easily. Alexondra is seven and a non-stop talker, not unlike Alison. I love the way she takes up our relationship, after all the months between visits, exactly where it left off. She holds my hand and looks into my eyes and very seriously tells me all the important things. And Sherry is in her first year at the University, although she has only just turned seventeen. Her whole life has changed, lots of new friends, basketball games, chorus, all sorts of campus activities. Every minute that she was required to spend with us was obviously a torture of boredom for her. I know exactly how she felt.

When I get home, I am as deflated as a punctured football. There is a letter from Alison. I look at the postmark. She would have had to write it immediately after I left, that same day. I tear it open.

"Yes," she wrote, "I do love you." What can she mean by that 'yes'? What can she mean by that 'do?' Have I ever asked her? "Come back to Berkeley and live with me. We'll find a suitable apartment, and protect each other against unnecessary incursions and intrusions. My Goddess, do you think people can do that for each other?" Later: "I don't know anything about love. I just muddle through from one day to the next. I want to have a cat again." The letter, as it progresses, builds upon itself, increasing in enthusiasm, as though she is whipping herself up into a froth. She goes on to outline her financial situation (hopeless), with some optimism concerning future prospects, as men used to do in proper marriage proposals. She assures me that she really is capable of companionable silences, once again saying that she babbles on only out of fear of saying something, and a little later, restraining herself, "But if we were to marry, we would cease to correspond. (Emily Bronte)." As usual, a charming letter.

I read it over three times, smiling all the while. All that week, during the times we were together, there was never a hint that there was anything more in her mind than what came spilling from her mouth. Yet she must have been appraising me and fashioning revised fantasies, since what could she have seen of the real me, or heard, effectively blocked off as I was by her strategy for keeping not only me at a distance from her, but herself from herself.

But apparently Alison's volubility can be put on automatic pilot, freeing her mind for other things. What a talent! And what do I feel? Obviously, since I'm still smiling, I am pleased. The more I read her letter, the more she loses weight and gains tenderness and the capacity for what her letter promises, charmingly sophisticated intimacy. She has made the decision to love me, I who haven't been loved in this way for what seems an eternity, and who have resigned myself, however reluctantly, and with considerable ill-grace, to the deathly celibacy and absence of adventure appropriate to one my age. I feel myself fluttering awake. Who knows? Maybe I am still alive!

My first impulse is to telephone Alison, and then,

because the time in California is wrong, to answer her letter, but I restrain myself. I know I have some thinking to do. I love being loved, but is this love, and do I love? I'm crazy about the woman on the page, but what of the woman herself? Is that woman her words, as she apparently keeps asking herself and others? If not, then whose voice is that? And what about the deluge of spoken words that tumbles and sprays out of her like water from a broken pipe, threatening to drown us all. I'll wait until tomorrow to answer her letter.

There is also, in my accumulated mail, a letter of acceptance from Erato, to which I applied six months earlier when I felt that by the time it came through, if it did, the excitement of publication would be over and I would be ready to get seriously back to work. I've been offered a two-month stay, commencing in less than a month. Ordinarily, this would be welcome news, but now, because of Alison, I hesitate. But then I write to accept my acceptance. There is always an eager waiting list at Erato, desperate for my place if I should cancel. I give myself time to change my mind.

That night, waiting for sleep, but not too anxiously, since half-sleep is once again comfortable and interesting now that expectation and fantasy have come creeping back, I realize that I can't know anything, and that neither can Alison, until we have spent more time together. I'll ask her to come to New York. But what if she does, what then? I try to imagine lying beside her in bed, and I can't. I try to imagine her asleep and not talking and I can't. I try to imagine sex with her, and I can't. I don't feel even the tiniest modicum of lust though, perversely, I feel lust for the Alison on the page, in the letters, in the essays, and even the Xeroxed photos on those pages, photos from an earlier time. I figure I'm about ten years too late for the Alison I'd have lusted after and I wonder if it's my ten years or hers.

If it's hers, then I am shallow and superficial. After all, the real, the true Alison is not the body she has chosen to walk around in but the Alison who is carried around by that body. I do love the Alison inside the body, and it isn't an asexual love. Nonetheless, physical love is about bodies.

Maybe, given time?

I write telling her about Erato but there are a few weeks before I'm scheduled to leave. Why doesn't she come to New York for those weeks and then, if she'd like a New York winter, she could stay on and water my plants.

If we really should fall in love in those few weeks, I'll cancel Erato. I don't mention this. I'm cautious. I've left myself every possible out.

Meanwhile, I'd better start the new book.

If I can start a new book, maybe I'll be able to start a new cat.

****

I sit down at the desk feeling the usual terror. With a computer, at least, it's no longer the bright, expectant blank white page, waiting. The screen in this word-processing program is black, like a night sky, like a hole, like my empty mind. It's a comfort to know that whatever I write on it is as easily deleted as saved. I can fiddle around, waiting to see what will happen. The big question is what will happen. What if nothing happens? What if there's nothing there?   I think Alison. I think Tully. I think bodies. Bodies and Souls. Collisions. Never mind the title, you can think of one later. Since you haven't the vaguest notion of what the book is going to be about, how can you give it a title?

Call it NOVEL #5. So the computer will know. So that I will know where to find it.

CHAPTER ONE

From the moment he came through the door, Julian knew that the house was empty. Still, "Jilian," he called, and heard her name echo through the hall. He glanced into the living room and then the kitchen, where the late afternoon sun was setting in the sink among last night's soiled dishes, still waiting for them to finish making love. "Jilian," he called again, hopelessly this time, then bounded up the stairs. She was gone of course. She had not felt, as he had believed, what he was feeling. A bitter pearl of disappointment began to form in his chest. Loosening his tie, he went into the bedroom.

She was there, lying on the bed as, hours earlier, he had left her. "Jilian," he said again, going to her, though perhaps she was dead. But how could she be dead?

They had met and fallen immediately in love only two days ago. Carefully, he sat beside her on the bed. How beautiful she was, how cruelly beautiful. Her pale, flawless skin, taut over the good bones, gave her in death the look of an ivory carving. Only the thin, nacreous eyelids, almost translucent but shielding forever those marvelously expressive eyes, seemed vulnerable. Yes, and her soft, perfect mouth. Moved as he always was by perfection, he began, silently, to cry, then took her hand and lifted it to his breast. It was still warm.

"Oh, Jilian," he cried.

"Oh, what?" she said, stirring, her eyes fluttering open. His heart leaped. "What's wrong?"

"Oh, Jilian," he said. "Oh, thank God. I thought perhaps you were dead."

"Why on earth would I be dead?" she asked.

He felt his face flush with relief and embarrassment.

"Because I'm madly in love and I don't trust my luck," he said."

She snorted. "So you're one of those?"

"One of which?"

"Fate, or whatever, has nothing better to do than to take away your lollypop? How arrogant, how self-involved that is. How masochistic! Well, I suppose masochists are self-involved."

"Oh, my lovely, delicious, funny, all-flavor lollypop. Why is that masochism and not an understandable reaction to the fear of losing this sudden, unexpected, God-given precious gift?"

She giggled. "We're certainly talking in clumps of adjectives, aren't we?" Then she snorted. "Precious gift! You don't even know me."

It was true; he didn't know her. "Except in the biblical sense," he amended, sitting on his lust. "But oh, how instantaneously, immediately, completely I've come to adore you. Why are we quarreling?"

"We're not quarreling. We're having a little talk. We haven't had any of those, really." "There hasn't been time." As he leaned to kiss her, she raised herself to meet him. It was hard to know which of them needed the kiss more. Furiously, they melted into each other.

"I missed you," she said, coming up for air. "While I was awake. Never leave me again for six whole hours."

"If there had been any way not to, I'd have found it."

"You look so different in a jacket and tie," she said, trying to separate him from them. "Oh God, I don't even know your clothes. I don't know anything!"

They had met Friday evening at the Miller's annual lawn picnic, an informal affair with volleyball and much jumping in and out of the swimming pool. Instantly magnetized, across a crowded lawn, they moved toward each other and introduced themselves, enjoying the alliterative and rhythmic coincidence of their names, ("Julian and Jilian/ Went to the pavilion/ where they joined in the etcetera"), they had chatted for about twenty minutes, chiefly to listen to the sound of each others' voices, and then she had taken his hand and said, "Let's go."

They had gone to his house because he lived alone in it, whereas she was a houseguest of the Millers. Her home, a large studio, she told him, with a small attached apartment, was in Wellfleet. She painted.

They had come here, then, and gone straight to bed, and stayed there for most of the two days since, coming up for air only to satisfy the lesser urgings of other orifices. The only other intrusions were the half dozen times the telephone had rung. And then this morning had arrived and there was no way for him to avoid going to work. He had never before thought of it as work.

＊＊＊＊

Well, it's a beginning, I tell myself. That's a beginning? I reply, are we writing one of those glistening neon-covered paperbacks? I don't know yet, I don't think so, we'll have to wait and see.

I awoke this morning and, instead of springing from bed, which I no longer ever do, I lay in a limbo state, neither asleep nor fully awake, my mind ranging about as it would have done in full sleep; I was awake and dreaming. Thoughts came and went of their own volition, with no control from me, no directing or ordering. For some reason, this morning I was my father reviewing my (his) life. I rarely think about my father any more. I didn't mourn his death; it was incredibly freeing for me. But here he was, so vivid that I was both inside, being him and outside, seeing him. We went from scene to scene; we were in the dress business, almost always in a panic about

90

the coming "season," we were fussing around raising chickens, we were lord of the manor, we were knocking down beautiful estates and building ugly garden apartments. We were busy every minute because we didn't trust anyone else to do anything right and hence had to do it all ourselves. We strode through offices and across interrupted landscapes, supervising, we danced on ships, happily. We were angry, we were charming, we perspired and our face turned red, we were proud of my mother (when there were new people about) because she was so young for her age and so good-looking. We were in a fury at my mother because she never wanted anything in her life that might entail responsibility. We didn't really love anyone, never had. For a few years, we had one friend we respected and liked, a manufacturer of refrigerators, (wealthier, even more forceful than we), but he died.

I shook my father off, finally, because it was time to force myself to get up (for no special reason), and I thought what a nice memorial service I had just given him, and I wondered why. Perhaps because we are approaching the thirteenth anniversary of his death, and because it recently occurred to me that if I'm genetically programmed by him, I may have about thirteen years left. Thirteen. Soon we'll be down to one-digit numbers.

But then there's my mother by whom I'm pretty definitely not programmed since, except for her sense of humor, in no way do I resemble her. For several months, she's been struggling with a crisis of indecision. The ocean-front building in which she, and most of her surviving friends live, has been sold.

"To an Orthodox Jew," she told me at the time. "Nothing's open on Saturday, not even the coffee shop, even though the people who run it aren't Jewish. There are a lot of rumors flying around about more changes to come."

A few weeks later: "He's co-oping the building. We

either have to buy or get out."

"They can't put you out at your age," I say.

"That's what you think. They can do whatever they want in this state, at any age. If they had special laws protecting seniors, nobody could ever do anything."

"How much are they asking for your apartment?" Hers is a prime apartment, two bedrooms, two baths, nice terrace, facing the ocean, dazzlingly bright, just high enough.

"What's the difference? It would be crazy to buy at my age. But I hate the thought of moving."

"Don't worry about that. Marcia and I will come down and do it all." Marcia is my brother's wife. We supervised her last move, though my mother was a dozen years younger then. When my father died, she didn't want to stay in the vast penthouse apartment where they'd been living.

"It's too big," she complained. "When I'm in the back, in the bedroom, I'm a million miles from the front. I don't feel safe. Anyhow, what do I need it for?"

So we helped her move to a smaller apartment in the building next door. Her cadre of friends followed. Half a dozen of them have since died, far from prematurely, but there are enough left for the regular fiercely competitive Wednesday, Friday, and Saturday bridge games. "I'm looking into some of those villages," she told me a few weeks back.

"What villages?"

"Those places for old people. You get your own apartment with a kitchen and everything, but they have a dining room and included in the rent are breakfast and dinner. They thorough-clean the apartments every week and change the linens, and there's always a registered nurse on the premises."

"Are the apartments nice?"

"I don't know. Flora and I are going to look at a couple of places on Friday." Flora is her best friend. It would be unthinkable for my mother to settle in one of these places without Flora being there, too.

"Oh," she says, "and they have activities."

"You mean like basket weaving?"

"Who knows. Movies once a week, exercises, indoor and outdoor swimming, whatever. Something every minute."

"It sounds ideal."

"And they drive you places. To the bank, the market, the doctor, even concerts and movies."

My mother has a driver who comes three mornings a week. She also has a once-a-week cleaning woman. She has her life very much in order where she is.

"Flora is dying to move there. She only wants to get away from her kitchen." Though five years younger, Flora is not holding up as well as my mother. Heart, arthritis. She is in constant pain. I honestly believe that if it weren't for her love of my mother, she would have died years ago. In more than one way, she took my father's place. An ex-business woman, good with figures, she does my mother's bookkeeping, pays her bills. My mother, who has cannibalized my father's temperament, isn't always very nice to her, however. She's critical and impatient with her. She yells at her. Flora's jealousy of other close friends of my mother drives my mother crazy. There are constant dramas.

Still, they are as bound to each other as any married couple.

I call my mother Friday night. "How was it?" I ask, hoping one of the places she went to see was perfect. I have begun to feel that this would be the ideal solution, and to understand how lucky she is to be able to afford it. Independence with full support. There are emergency call buttons in all the apartment's rooms, and gadgets on the front door that indicate if it has been opened that day. If it hasn't, they come in to see if you're still alive. There is no way you can lie helpless on the floor for more than a few hours. Not like me. I could be dead and decomposing for a week, still apologizing on the answering machine. Sorry I can't come to the phone. I'm dead.

"I don't know how it was," she says, her voice dismal. "I never got inside. From the outside, it looked beautiful."

"So why didn't you get inside?"

"I tripped in the doorway and broke my shoulder."

"Oh God."

"It could have been worse. It could have been a hip."

"Why didn't you call me?"

"They took me to the hospital for X-rays. And then I had to hire someone. She's here with me now. A very fine woman from Trinidad. I could never dress or undress myself. You'd be surprised how many things you can't do with only one shoulder."

"Does it hurt?"

"I'm taking pills. The arm is in a sling."

"I'll come down."

"I don't need you. I have Majesta. She drives a car, she cooks, everything."

"I've never felt such sustained lust," he had told her, waiting for her to agree that neither had she, but she only smiled and made a small purring sound deep in her throat.

"Aren't bodies marvelous?" she said. "They bring us all this exciting news."

He thought of the people they were studying at Gerutopia. How he hated the name.

"You won't think so when you're old," he said.

"Shhhh," she said, stroking his hair. But it was hard for him, fresh from his day with them, to put aside the men and women, octogenarians and up, in the study he was doing.

"Emily Barnes fell and broke her hip this morning. Or her hip broke and she fell. If she'd broken a wrist one would know that the fall caused the wrist rather than the other way around. In either case, the news from her body wasn't exciting."

"Shhhh," she said again. "Later. We'll talk about it later. Carpe diem."

For the first time, the love they made was slow and careful. "I love your forearms," she said. "I love your shoulders," he said, "your breasts, your stomach." "*What* stomach?" "This place, here," he said, "where so much of the processing is done." "I love your prick," she said. "It's strong, yet elegant." "My God, an elegant prick," he said.

They went on naming and caressing the parts they loved until there were no more parts to name and then they came to the place where speech was no longer relevant. They came out of that place very slowly and lay entwined, breathing.

"Where did you learn to make love so well?" he asked, feeling an unexpected surge of rage.

"I'm thirty-seven years old," she explained. "I've got to

make a phone call."

Sooner or later, he thought, this was bound to happen "Use the one in the study if you want privacy," he said.

She picked up the bedside phone and dialed. "Mark," she said, "I'm glad I caught you, darling. ... It's Jilian.... Yes of course you know my voice ... How are the pets doing? ... No, that's why I'm calling. I won't be home today. Can you manage a few more days without me? ... I'll tell you when I see you... Yes, well, they'll just have to go on missing me... Thanks, darling, bye."

Naturally she had a life that was going on somewhere else, he thought, tying the belt of his robe. She hadn't sprung full-blown from anyone's brow or miraculously risen up on the half-shell. She was, as she had pointed out, thirty-seven years old. What had he expected? Still, he couldn't help what he was feeling.

On the other hand, she obviously meant to stay, at least for a "few more days."

"What about you?" she asked, reading his mind or his face. "What were all those phone calls?"

"I don't know." he mumbled, "I haven't played back my machine."

"Mark is my neighbor and cat-sitter," she said, gently, and a very good friend. When you live in a place like Wellfleet all year round, everyone else who lives there becomes more than an acquaintance. As for the pets, they're cats."

"How many have you got?"

"Six," she said.

"Oh," he said, dismayed, "you're a woman with cats."

"Summer people. They abandon them."

"And they become your responsibility."

"Not only mine. Do you object to cats?"

"Not individually. Only in packs."

"They're not a pack. They're all individuals."

"Well, maybe when I get to know them."

"You may never. We may find that we're incompatible."

"It won't matter."

She laughed. "It's odd," she said, "beginning a love affair with no courtship. The orgasm before the foreplay."

"None of the suspense of romantic love."

"This is romantic enough for me, "she said. "Let's get married. We can sort out all the rest later."

"I can't," he said, thrilled by her proposal. "I'm already married."

"You're what?" There was no sign anywhere, in bathrooms, closets, kitchen, bedroom, that a woman had ever lived here. She said as much.

"No woman ever did live here. I lived there. With her and the children. We haven't gotten around to the divorce."

"Children?"

"Two girls. Twins. Eight years old. Gwen and Polly. You'll like them, maybe even more than the cats."

"Don't quantify my love," she said, angrily. "I have separate categories. I don't ask a cat to be anything more than a cat. I require more of children, especially other people's."

"I'm going to take a shower," he said. "And then I think we'll go somewhere for dinner. I'm famished."

****

Alison considered my offer, then wrote a long letter declining my invitation. She had been up all night, she said, examining what she had done, what she was doing. Out of the desperation of her unhappy circumstances, she had constructed an elaborate fantasy that it would be unfair and impossible to expect me to live up to. My book was charming, had struck a chord of recognition, and my apparent stability, both emotionally (hah!) and financially, were attractive and tempting, though they were at the same time repellent. She was, after all, a gypsy, a beachcomber, a Celtic nut. She could not see me living her life, and she was sure that she could not live mine, three meals a day and all that.

Who was she, that enormous eater, to disdain three meals a day? I am angry, disappointed, relieved. I feel rejected, as I am, and hurt.

But how wise, how prudent she is. I write back and tell her this, more than half meaning it. I tell her that the fantasy has been mutual. But if we had proceeded, I say, we would soon have floundered in sexual failure and, if I were ever to get a word in, it would undoubtedly be one that bored her.

I think about fantasy. I have had letters from other strangers, an unhappy 22-year-old lesbian who dreams of showing up on my doorstep. I take her in and care for her. I buy her clothes and cook for her and am nothing like her mother. Then, there is the woman from Tennessee who sends two dozen roses to show her gratitude for my book, and writes to tell me about her husband's suicide twenty years earlier, and how she reads his horoscope in the daily paper to see what kind of day he might have been having, piecing out his unlived life. An actress telephones (my number is not unlisted) from Los Angeles at what must be seven o'clock in the morning there to say she has just finished my book, and how much she loves it, and she can't talk now because she is due on the set, a new television sit-com, in half an hour, but she'll call when she's in New York next week and perhaps we can meet. I tell her I have Lyme disease, since that is what, at the moment, I think I have, and she shudders at the other end, and doesn't call again.

From time to time, there are others.

People feel that they know me after they've read my books, I suppose because the voice sounds so real, so personal. But the persona I have chosen for my narrator is only a small part of me. I have left out so much.

I wonder if all love affairs don't begin with fantasy, with inventing the other and responding to the excitement of their invention of you. I have rarely waited to get to know the person before I fell in love. If I had, I might never have been in love. No, that's not true. Getting to know Tully, Dibbs, Lisa, made me love them more even while the intensity of the in-loveness waned.

CHAPTER TWO

The hip was a dreary nuisance, of course, but she was used to dreary nuisances. In time, if she had it, it would mend or not mend. The pin would hold or not hold. A hip replacement was a possibility if there was anything solid enough there to anchor it to. Eventually she would be able to walk with a walker. She might then advance to a cane. Slowly, the pain would recede. Pain was a familiar. She would cope.

She was yet more grist for Julian Keller's voracious mill. He would pepper her with questions. He would want to know with exquisite precision how she felt, not so much physically as emotionally, spiritually, psychologically. They would have long conversations and he would give her tests and questionnaires to elicit what he thought she might not be able to articulate, or had not the insight or imagination to perceive. Little did he know!

He had already begun, even as she lay on the floor moaning. After the fall, she had done what she was supposed to do: pressed the emergency call button they all wore around their necks, like key children. She had been a key child. Her mother had been a bookkeeper in a coat factory. When Emily came home from school, she had to let herself in to the gray, empty house, but there were always fresh cookies waiting for her and a note reminding her to drink a glass of milk.

A nurse came running, the gerontologist right behind her. And only a moment later, Julian Keller, who knelt beside her while the gerontologist, Dr. Felix, was taking her pulse.

"What happened?" Dr. Keller asked.

"I fell," she managed to say. "That is, I crumpled. I am now lying on the floor." She always made an effort to be thorough with him.

"Yes, I see."

"It's her left hip," Dr. Felix said.

"It's my left hip."

"I'm injecting a sedative," Dr. Felix said.

"What do you feel?" Julian asked.

"I feel that I am unable to get up off this floor."

"And how does that make you feel, Emily?"

"Oh really! How should it make me feel!"

"Of course," he said, blushing, taking her hand and gently pressing it. "Helpless and frightened. Not in control."

"Betrayed," she mumbled, succumbing to the sedative.

She had agreed to be part of this study. Why not? A change of scenery, a diversion, a little special attention, the opportunity to be a participant in something, something that might even be meaningful. My God, a participant! Or so she had thought then. Now, as her fear subsided, her anger rose.

"Listen carefully, Dr. Keller, I am going to tell you something important." She thought she was shouting, but her voice was barely audible.

"Julian. Call me Julian."

"Dr. Keller..." she was falling asleep, "this ...such as it is ... is ...my... _life_."

As she swam off, she thought she heard him say from a great distance, "I love you, Emily." The last word. They always had to have the last word.

***

Just over the flu, I go down to Florida for a week. There is absolutely nothing for me to do, thanks to Majesta and orders from the internist not to go swimming and from the dermatologist to stay out of the sun. For months I've been having what I myself, finally, after numerous doctors and their tests, have diagnosed not as Lyme disease but as chronic fatigue syndrome. I don't mind not having anything at all to do. I sleep a lot and read and do a little writing in what, since the advent of my computer, remains of my longhand. The important thing is, no matter what condition I'm in, I am there for my mother because of her accident.

"Why don't we go see a couple of those villages?" I suggest one morning, feeling a miniscule burst of energy.

"Not yet. I don't want to think about that yet."` But she gets up from the chair where she is smoking after having quit for a few months. I was so proud of her for being able to quit smoking at her age, now 93. She'd been a smoker since she was eighteen. She claimed that quitting wasn't even hard for her.

"Then why start again?" I wanted to know. "Don't you feel better not smoking?."

"I like to smoke. Sooner or later ... oh, I can't say sooner or later, it's already so much later ... something has to kill me and it might as well be something I enjoy."

She forages in the closet where she keeps her records, bills, checkbook, and emerges with a collection of bro-chures sent to her by half a dozen retirement facilities. They are quite elaborate. They include apartment layouts, menus, schedules of activities, details of services provided. I study them, amused by some of the activities offered: chair exercises, lip reading, pottery. I try to imagine my mother at a wheel making pots. I fail.

She was sleeping when Harold entered and said, "I heard you fell and broke your hip, Emily."

She opened her eyes. They were supposed to have as much privacy here as they wished, but of course they didn't. They were at the mercy not only of the doctors but of each other. There were twenty-eight of them at the moment, none of them younger than eighty. New ones came as others died or, in one case, resigned. Gerutopia was a small, exceptionally attractive nursing home, with every amenity, including a gym, sauna, and swimming pool on the glassed-in roof. Meals, shaped to the currently recommended pyramid of food groups, and also to their individual needs, were nonetheless prepared tastefully and presented artfully. All of it was free. This was a richly endowed experiment that seemed to be about going to heaven before you died. The members, as they were called, to emphasize their feelings of belonging, were treated by the staff with affection and respect. They had a certain degree of autonomy and had formed a governing body charged with making recommendations to the staff and settling occasional differences among themselves. Harold, who except for a small bridge in his lower left jaw, seemed exceptionally intact, and had been a lawyer before his retirement, had been named President. This, then, could be construed as a duty call, except that Harold had been hanging around a lot lately, even before her fall.

"Good morning, Harold," Emily said, wearily. There were fresh flowers, she saw, on her bedside table. Nobody had sent them; there were always fresh flowers.

"How are you feeling, Emily?"

"You can ask Dr. Keller," she said. "He collects the answers to those kinds of questions."

Harold laughed, slowly folding himself into her arm-chair.

"It's a small price to pay." He coughed, a short barking cough. "We can't really complain, can we?"

She hated being told that she couldn't complain. "And why not?" she asked.

"Because they've deprived us of anything to complain about."

It interested her that he had used negative words to say such a positive thing: they've deprived us. She wondered if he was subtle enough to have done it purposefully as a gift to her, knowing her penchant for finding the dark side. She looked at him with new interest.

"It is a deprivation, isn't it?" she said. Not having anything to rail against, what did it mean? Maybe she would discuss it with Dr. Keller. "That movie," she said, "Long ago, *Lost Horizons*, did you ever see it?"

"Ronald Colman," he said. "And an actress with, I think, only one name."

"Yes. They were in this mountain place, the Himalayas, perhaps, having as I recall, which could easily be inaccurate, a utopian life. But they weren't satisfied. They grew bored with stasis. They left it for the real world."

"They didn't age," Harold said. "But as they came down off the mountain you saw them suddenly become very old."

"Well, which would you choose?" she wondered. "To be eternally young in a false world, or take your chances with age in the real world."

"We don't have that choice, do we?" Harold said, cheerfully. "Here we are in this almost perfect false world with all our years on us, you with your broken hip, Marcus awash in his incontinence, Betty in her wheelchair losing her mind..."

"We're all losing our minds. We're all so useless."

"Most of us are as useless as we've always been," he

said, "but without the illusions. Gloria swims her forty laps a day, the Four Jades have their ferocious bridge game almost daily, which they've probably been doing all their lives, you're writing your memoirs, Vernon is still building his ships, Walter prowls around looking for ways to make trouble, and I'm doing what I've always wanted to do, never really had the time for."

He painted. Big, splashy paintings. She had no idea if they were any good. He painted fast, perhaps to make up for lost years. His paintings hung in the hallways and the public rooms. Soon there would be no wall space and, she supposed, they would have to begin taking his paintings into their rooms.

"Hobbies," she muttered, unfairly. "Is that why you quit practicing? I always thought one of the advantages of a profession like yours was that you could do it till you slumped over onto your desk."

"Do you mind if I smoke?" He smoked brown cigarettes, or were they cigarette-sized cigars? They smelled vile.

"Yes," she said.

"I always hated the law," he said, unfazed, taking his empty hand out of his pocket. "Almost everything you do in general practice is boring, the same things over and over. Wills, trusts, estates, closings, contracts. And I was dying to paint."

She wondered what he really looked like. She herself was always shocked to see her face in the mirror, that mask that had grown over her true face.

"You could have done criminal law. Trials."

"No, I couldn't. I agree that everyone's entitled to a fair trial and the best possible defense, but I don't have the stomach to defend someone I know is guilty of a brutal crime. Seems like the worst cynicism to me, to get some wanton, depraved monster off because I'm clever at what I do, at finding the soft spots, loopholes." He fidgeted in his chair. Again his hand went to the pocket that held his cigarillos, and came away empty. He glanced at his watch.

"I've got to go," he said. "It's almost time for lip-reading."

"You're doing lip-reading?" she asked. "Is your hearing going?"

"Like everything else, it's not what it used to be. Anyhow, might as well be prepared. And I like to watch television with the sound off."

So did she, but it was usually baseball games she watched with the sound off. She had always been a Yankees fan. And she didn't need to go to lip-reading classes to understand the players' oaths. She sometimes wondered why, in the age of television, players hadn't been trained to control themselves for the sake of the children watching. Or why Parental Guidance was not advised before games. All that cursing, so clear on television. And spitting. They all spat, almost constantly. What was it about baseball? In no other sport did they spit!

Harold got slowly to his feet. "I'm sure you'll be all right, Emily," he said. "The physical therapist will have you dancing in no time. And I'll want the first dance."

"You shall have it."

"I'll come back later, if I may. I like talking to you." She smiled. She liked talking to him, too.

CHAPTER THREE

"I don't know anything about you," she said, soaping his back. "That is, I now know you were ... are... married and a father. But what about, well, your politics for instance? For all I know you could be a Republican, or worse."

"Leftish," he said. "Pretty far."

"Oh, good."

"Actually, I'm probably politically naïve."

"Me too. I keep thinking how much better everything would be if they would only listen to me. It seems so simple."

"Do you tell them?"

"I write letters to The Times occasionally. Sometimes they print them. Well, once."

"Tell me about your love life," he said, taking the soap from her and doing her back.

"No. Tell me about your marriage. Why did it fail?"

"The marriage," he said, as though it were the title of an essay he was about to read. "Cora is an extraordinary woman. She's a political activist, militant, always organizing and marching and heading up committees. When she was at home she was glued to the telephone. The rest of the time she was marching or at meetings. She's out to save the world, and she'll do it, too. "

"Did you mind that?"

"No, I was proud of her. Even the twins, though they sometimes feel neglected, are proud of her. What a lovely, graceful back you have." He ran his finger down her spine.

"Was it she who told you that you were politically naive?"

"Often. But I knew she was right. We grew apart in such opposite ways. Hers is the larger, grander view. Mine is almost microscopic. It's individuals that concern me, even though I'm trying to learn general truths from them."

"And did she mind that in you?"

"I think she respected what I was doing, but she grew distant with me. She didn't have the kind of vision that could quite get someone like me into focus."

"What about your incredible sexiness?" Jilian asked, leaning back into him and wagging her tail, causing him to drop the soap. Grinning, he kissed her neck.

"Sex for Cora was something she liked but was usually impatient with, the way she was impatient with buying clothes for herself. If she had to spend more than ten minutes in a shop, you could feel the tension mounting. It was almost impossible for her to be a private person."

"She sounds like someone I'd like."

"Yes, I'm sure you'd like her. I do."

"There was no way for you to accommodate each other?"

"It began to seem pointless even to try. We had a circle of friends with whom we'd meet for dinner, social evenings. The women did all the talking, passionate talk, and the men sat back and mumbled, or talked to each other. I couldn't stand it."

"You wanted to be the dominant one?"

"I wanted to be equal."

"I think we're sufficiently cleansed," she said. "Let's get out of here and into something dryer, like a martini. Not that I've got anything to wear. I've only got the clothes I came in, and they've been on the floor for three days. Even my car is still at the Miller's."

"Details," he said.

She called the Millers.

"Jilian! Where the hell have you been?" Betty Miller roared. "Someone said you went off with Julian. We tried calling, but wherever he was, he wasn't answering his phone. We decided he'd murdered you and was in the basement walling you up."

"Not yet," she said. "I'm really sorry, Betty. It was thoughtless of me. It was one of those peculiar instantaneous physical passions, lust at first sight, but now I need my clothes."

"It's over?"

"No. But it will keep. Do you want to have dinner with us?"

"Dinner! We had ours two hours ago. It's almost eleven o'clock."

"A bedtime snack, then?"

"Thanks, no."

***

I'm sleepy, and it's still morning. Writing is a soporific. Or else this part is too boring.   No, it's not knowing what will come next. Should I have Betty Miller decline Jilian's invitation because it makes her uncomfortable to be with people who've just spent three days fucking? Will we have to know that much about Betty Miller? She's not likely to show up again. What is this book going to be about, anyway? Shouldn't I know a little more than that it's about bodies, young ones, old ones? Youth and age? Sex and dying? Lust and love? Creativity?

What else is there?

They picked up her clothes and her car, and she followed his Mitsubishi to the local Brasserie, the only place in town that stayed open late. They both ordered onion soup and steaks, rare, with baked potatoes and a huge salad. It was as if they had spent three days bleeding and were badly in need of transfusions.

"Now that we have carped our diem, tell me about the woman who broke her hip," Jilian said.

"Emily. Emily Barnes."

"Yes."

He realized that he'd have been thinking about Emily constantly if it hadn't been for Jilian.

"I know that if we were contemporaries, she'd have been the kind of woman I'd have loved."

"You mean sexually?"

"I think so, yes, also. Because of the kind of woman she is."

"What kind of woman is she?"

"Intelligent, gracious, witty, introspective, dissatisfied..."

"You know more about her than you know about me."

"Yes, but I will learn you."

"When you're so strongly physically attracted to someone, you begin to look for qualities to love," she said. "You need to. It's different from learning to love someone and then having the lust develop from that. That way is so much safer."

"Yes." Because if you don't find those qualities, and alas, they aren't always there, he thought, then in time the lust goes. He stared at her, wondering who she was.

"I haven't yet begun to do that," she said, "Look beyond the lust. Oh, this steak is soooo good. It's a shame red meat has gone out of style."

He loved the way she ate, her appetite, the honesty of it. His mind strayed back again to Emily.

"It's strange to think that it's only the accident of time..."

"You mean Emily? I'm beginning to feel jealous."

He grinned and reached across to squeeze her hand. "But I'm also madly in love with you," he said. "Madly, passionately, contemporaneously and, I suspect I'll discover, for life."

"So, then," she asked, "what is it you're trying to prove in this study?"

"I don't think we're trying to prove anything. It's merely a study in which we're attempting to probe and chart the stages and ramifications of aging in the most optimal environment, a place where the aged can be reasonably happy."

"Happy?"

"Not depressed. At peace. Able to enjoy. Perhaps even hopeful."

"Don't you need some sense of a future in order to be hopeful?"

"Tomorrow can be a future. Tonight can be a future."

"Are you a sociologist?"

"No. Actually I'm a psycho-biologist and an anthropologist. I have advanced degrees in both. I can't wait for this meal to be over so that we can stop talking and go back to bed."

"Do you not like talking to me?"

"I'm sure I do, but at the moment it's not paramount."

"Then I'll try to be more amusing. I'll tell you about my life."

"Oh, please."

"I'm a D.A.P.," she said, swallowing. "Daughter of alcoholic parents. My father was a neurosurgeon."

"Oh, God, an alcoholic with a scalpel!"

"He claimed he never killed a patient. He claimed he

never botched one, either. When his hands began to shake too badly, he was responsible enough to quit. When he did, he divorced my mother and spent his remaining years marrying and divorcing other women."

"And your mother?"

"My mother read books and drank gin all day. She was a cross between Jane Bowles and Zelda Fitzgerald, though she didn't write. Instead, she did the Charleston. She kept a pet three-toed sloth that used to hang upside down from the dining room chandelier. Once, in the middle of dinner, both sloth and chandelier crashed down into the ragout of lamb and while my mother was comforting her sloth, whose name was Brady, Daddy, laughing all the way, took me to McDonald's for hamburgers, or whatever those things are." She chewed for a while. "Daddy had trouble leaving my mother. He really loved her. She made him laugh."

"Then why did he?"

"Drinking had a peculiar effect on her. It made Daddy invisible to her."

"What do you mean?"

"It was as though he wasn't there. She didn't see him or hear him. If he touched her, she brushed him away as if he were an insect."

"Did she see you?"

"Alas, yes, though less and less in the right way."

"You were an only child?"

"Yes. I began to feel like an orphan. I went around the neighborhood offering myself for adoption. So they sent me off to boarding school, a good one thank God, where I began to paint darkly. It took me about four years to lighten up."

"Are your parents dead?"

"He is. She's alive. When Brady died, she went on the wagon. She lives in Santa Fe with a woman lover."

"How old is she?"

"She must be about seventy, not old enough for your club, but you could put her on your list."

He reached for her free hand again. "My poor Jilian," he said. "What a sad and disturbing childhood. How did you turn out so well?"

"I haven't turned out so well and it wasn't, really, so sad and disturbing. Only at moments. It was often glamorous. They had interesting friends, most of them artists or people in the theater. I listened to a lot of good music and I discovered that I had what Madame Calame called 'a painter's eye.' School saved me. Madame Olivet's Lycee, which included high school and two years of college. All girls. It was in a town about twenty kilometers outside of Paris, but we made frequent trips to opera, theater, museums, galleries. I had a very good education, and I saw a lot of great art. We made a few trips to Italy, too, those of us who painted, to Florence and Rome. I could hardly call myself deprived."

He was still holding her hand. It was enough to send little tremors down to his groin. He felt stupid, like an adolescent; it was remarkable. But still engaged with her steak, she withdrew her hand to pick up her knife. From this, he concluded with a small sinking of the heart, that she loved him less than he loved her, or at least less than she loved the steak. He watched her eat, and the thought of what the interior of her mouth was doing aroused him even more. Please let her not want coffee and dessert.

"I love watching you eat," he said.

"What shall we have for dessert?"

***

The bird feeder needs refilling. The cat sits vigilantly beside the window to which the feeder is attached, waiting to pounce. The window is closed, of course, and she knows this, but short of springing against the window glass, her body does what it must. Yes, I have a new cat, and months have gone by since that afternoon at Rebecca's. The cat's name is Allegra. She looks as much like Minnie as I could manage, also a calico, but her personality is entirely differ- ent.   On my first trip to the ASPCA, there was no one I wanted, but I went back and they had just picked her up on Laurel Avenue in the Bronx and brought her in. She was a starved four-month old and, unlike the other cats, who all pleaded with me to save them, this one crouched in the cage, facing the back of it, wanting only to be left alone. A cockroach zipped across the floor of the cage but the cat, cowering in fear, ignored it.   "I need to see her face," I told the attendant. She opened the cage and took the cat out, turning her reluctant face toward me. What a face! "Okay," I said, grinning, "wrap her up."

She cried pitifully in the cardboard carry-box on the back seat of the car. Unlike Minnie, this one was a talker. When we got home, I took her out of her container, showed her where her litter box was, and put her down. She ran under my bed and stayed there for two weeks. I had to lie on my stomach and shove her food under the bed for her, while she backed off. For those two weeks, I couldn't coax her out, but while I slept, she would come out, use her litter box neatly and efficiently and dance around in the living room, knocking papers off the table-tops. She is very neurotic, but slowly, slowly, she's beginning to come around. She now sometimes sleeps on top of the bed, with me, curled in my armpit. She isn't trusting and cuddly and dignified, like Minnie, and she won't sit on my lap, but she makes me laugh.

She loves being in this place, or so I imagine, where there are birds, though they drive her crazy, chickadees and nuthatches, mostly, some noisy blue jays, an occasional

cardinal. She crouches near the window, her tail waving
madly. The feeder attaches to the windowpane with two
suction cups and the birds come within inches of her nose.

It's October. The leaves are waving their annual gorgeous farewell, gold and scarlet and beautiful shades between, fluttering to the ground where they weave a bright
carpet. It's as if they put on this show as a plea to us not to
forget them in the long winter months ahead, as a promise
that they'll be back in fresh bright greens come spring. And
oh, the fragrances! I can't breathe the air deeply enough.

I reread what I've just written and see that I have used
bits of Alison for Jilian's childhood. Is that what friends are
for?

CHAPTER FOUR

With the help of a walker and Peggy, the physical therapist, Emily took her first small, careful steps. She couldn't imagine that she would ever be able to walk normally again, but she was exultant nonetheless. She had often heard that broken hips were one of the preludes to dying, but she had made the decision to live. A cracked hip was no reason to die.

Now, sitting in what Peggy promised was a temporary wheelchair, she picked up the Helen Nearing book she was reading, *Loving and Leaving the Good Life*. Scott Nearing, who had passed his 100th birthday, had decided that it was time to die and was arranging to begin starving to death. There was nothing morbid about this. Scott had lived a long, strong, fearless life and wanted to die in control of it as he had been from the time in early manhood when he was buffeted about by others because of his radicalism and his uncompromising purity. But unlike Emily, the Nearings believed in an afterlife, believed that death was merely a passage between one sphere of life and another, higher one. Emily had never been able to believe in anything that might be a comfort to her, including and especially God. The solace alone was reason to discredit it, to confirm that it was a convenient, sometimes necessary, human invention. Her intellectual stringency permitted her no more than an occasional happy fantasy, an indulgence she never mistook for possibility. She was very hard on herself. Any afterlife she might have would consist of what her ashes or her decaying body happened to nurture, and she did not really care about this. If she fed a pregnant rat and therefore had some responsibility for the lives of that rat's litter, so be it.

What she did have to hold onto was her life which, in

writing her memoirs, she now held in her hands, feeling the shape of it. She had had a generous allotment of years, and while her life hadn't been particularly happy, it had, for the most part, been interesting. Writing it down, she was learning, put memory in her control instead of her being at its mercy. Memory had a randomly recurrent circularity, a disorganized messiness. It floated in and out at its own will. But once she had recorded it, she found that she had tethered it, removed it from the ether within and set it outside, on the page. Thereafter, she was done with it, unless she chose to summon it. And if she did recall it, it was usually in the words she had used to concretize it. It had become, more than memory, her own creation, tamed and manageable.

So the notebooks accumulated on the table beside her bed, the latest one never far from reach, the box of pens beside them. She used notebooks with black and white marbleized stiff cardboard covers, lined white paper within, the notebooks given grade-school children in her day, the kind in which they first learned to write. She chose them because they were a nice, manageable size and also out of nostalgia. It seemed so fitting that they be used for her purpose, especially for the early childhood memories. She had thought two or three notebooks would serve for her childhood, but she was on her tenth notebook and still only twelve years old. Memory begat memory, and she saw now that childhood might well be the predominant period of one's life because, new and without precedent or history, no impression, no experience, no word, deed, shadow, or dream, was trivial. Her earliest memories had a Proustian clarity and intricacy that few of the later ones would match. The Life-Learning years, she called them, since every event was a lesson.

Because her handwriting wanted to run more quickly than her slowed hands, she was forced to slow her mind as well. This was tiring. She stopped frequently, waiting for renewed strength. She was in one of these pauses when Dr. Keller knocked and, at her bidding, strode in. She closed the notebook and laid it aside.

"Good morning, Emily," he said, smiling. "How are you today?"

He was an attractive man, and in the past week he seemed to have acquired something extra, a glow, not unlike the exhausted radiance women often have following childbirth. Falling in love had that same quality of renewal, of something born: one's self in relation to the newly beloved, one's new self as returned by the beloved.

He sat down in her armchair."Oh, Dr. Keller, I think I know what it is."

"Are you never going to call me Julian? How can I go on calling you Emily if you insist on being so formal? What *what* is?"

"You're in love. That's it, isn't it?"

He did three things simultaneously: blushed, looked surprised, grinned.

"Does it show? Isn't that odd."

"Happiness always shows," she said.

"You're an unusual woman, Emily. Tell me how you are."

"As you see me. Oh, we had what Peggy called 'our first little walk' this morning. Walk is hardly the word for it. I moved like a slug from one point to another about three feet from my starting point."

"It's a beginning," he said.

"It's a beginning," she agreed, thinking: what a time for beginnings. Was there ever an end to them? Then, knowing that he wanted more, she said, "Actually, I was elated. The discovery that one's moving parts are still capable of moving, no matter how reluctantly, is a great relief."

She kept a separate notebook for current events, entries

that she would later incorporate into the larger work. Earlier, she had recorded: "When it isn't working properly, the body demands almost all of our attention, as pain does. It is absolutely paramount. We become like infants, focused on this one commanding point of light, our hunger, our wetness, the bubble of gas, the cramp in our bowels. For the old it's bones, joints, muscles, it's all the drying up and dying parts, the dwindling, deserting hormones, the imperious triumph of gravity. For Dr. Keller, his body was his vehicle, a swift and graceful one, to carry him in and out of rooms, in and out of pleasure, and now, apparently, in and, perhaps not out, of love.

"Peggy wants to strengthen the muscles in your legs and arms," he said.

She nodded, trying to imagine it.

"With weights, I think. It will be hard work."

She hated exercise. Not only for the discomfort, but because it was so boring. She, who in childhood and early adolescence had never been still for a moment, whose physicality had been one of her great joys, who never walked if she could run, never ran if she could fly, who took such pride in her agility, her growing strength, the quickness of her reflexes.

"We're getting some new exercise machines," Julian said. "We expect them this week."

"Is it your feeling, Dr. Keller ... Julian ... that given optimum conditions we could live forever?"

"Why not?" He grinned.

"Oh, God forbid!"

"Given optimum conditions, you might want to live forever. Well, perhaps not forever."

"Infancy," Emily said, "the body multiplying and honing its physical skills and functions. Old age: the reverse, the body losing its elasticity, its juices, its faculties, its functions, deteriorating into death. One is as natural as the other. Why should we not be permitted our natural and inevitable decline?"

"No one can deprive you of that, Emily," Julian said. "We only want to see how much of it is attributable to avoidable societal circumstances, if the will and the ability to live flourish in proportion to the pleasure and comfort of life."

"Pleasure and comfort?" she said. "How trivial that sounds. What about usefulness? Work?"

He had given a lot of thought to that. "When your livelihood depends on your own efforts, you have a sense of purpose and meaningfulness," he said. "If you grew your own vegetables and brought them into the house and cooked and ate them, you would feel virtuous, as if your time had been well-spent."

"Yes. Why not?"

"Well, it isn't necessary to grow your own vegetables. In most cases, it's actually a waste of time and effort. It isn't even always necessary to cook them yourself any more than it's necessary to be a potter and make your own dishes, or a weaver of your own clothing. It might give you satisfaction, it might be fun, but it isn't necessary."

"Most work, then, is a form of gardening or weaving?" she said, "At some small remove. Its purpose being to bring in the dollars to buy the vegetables one hasn't had to grow."

"Yes."

"So then most work is meaningless. We do have to live, of course, but if the work itself means only the dollars for survival..."

"Yes, but survival is meaningful and, in many cases, for the lucky ones, the work itself is meaningful."

"Yes, of course," she said, impatiently. "But not in most cases. Except in the larger scheme of things. The coal miner and sardine canner may be doing something useful for others, but they're doing the work itself only because it's available and will put bread under their butter. I doubt that they feel the work is meaningful, or anything but arduous and boring, nothing they can take pride in. I'm sure they're delighted when the whistle blows and they can go home."

"Nonetheless, whatever the work, men often die soon after they retire. It doesn't seem to matter what they've been doing. If they can put on a suit and tie and go off to it, they feel connected to life. Not so for women, at least traditionally. They live on long after the children are gone and they've become widows, even when their *raison d'etre* has always been in the home. They may be lonely and bored and unhappy, but they live on. They are differently centered."

"They are trained to passivity. Men are not."

"All that has changed," Julian said, "and a good thing, too."

"Yes,"" Emily said, smiling, "now women are more and more in the world, they will begin to die younger."

She moved her wheelchair a few inches to the right to dodge a ray of sunlight that shone in her face. Her eyes were still luminous and Julian noted the good bones of her face, the cheekbones, the straight patrician nose. What a beauty she must have been; she was still a beauty, a beautiful old woman. Age had altered and shriveled her skin, thinned and whitened her hair, hollowed and maimed her throat, made prominent the veins that had once done their work in private. Beauty like hers often shaped character; things came too easily and too soon, what others had to wait and hope and strive for. Beauty could make its wearer arrogant or lazy, imperious or passive. Julian and she had never really talked about her life, though he had its bare outlines in her folder. Two husbands, a son who had died in Vietnam, and a late career writing sensuously and reverently about food for the newspapers. She had given this up, she said, when her sense of smell and taste had begun to diminish.

The people who came here all carried the heavy baggage of their lives, long and sometimes full lives, yet they seemed to arrive unlike their counterparts in the Home for the Aged, who lived much more in their memories; who scolded and wept, or sank into silence and went mad. Memory was supposed to be a comfort, he had always believed, moments, faces, feelings, pulled out of the pockets of one's mind to be, for a while, relived, to give substance to what would otherwise be emptiness. Memory was better than television because you were not sitting apart, silently observing, but were at the very center, as in dreams: the actor, the creator, the scene designer. Memory had become who you were, the shape and stuff of your life, the proof that you had been and were in and of the world. The past loomed, filling the vacant present, replacing the fled future, where once lay anticipation and hope. But for most of the people at the Home, warehoused until death, memory was a counting of losses, a desperate mourning.

The people here in Gerutopia, on the other hand, were still living in a now, a new and limited now, but nonetheless a now, and Julian was sure that that was the important, life-sustaining difference.

He glanced at the pile of notebooks on the table at Emily's elbow. He knew she was writing her life, and he wondered in what way what she was doing differed from ordinary remembering. Remembering in order to record it was a doing, an act, not passive.

"How is it going?" he asked, nodding at the notebooks.

"Slowly," she said.

"I suppose you have too many interruptions."

"I can shut them out," she said, "as you know, by merely shutting my door."

Harold now entered through that door.

"May I join you?" he asked, sitting down. "Don't let me interrupt. Go on as you were." He covered his ears with his hands.

"What are you doing?" Emily asked, frowning at his silliness. "You may listen to what we have to say. It's not private."

He was staring intently at her mouth.

"I think I got that," Harold said, grinning.

"Oh, the lip reading," Emily said.

"Private is an easy word. See what the mouth does?"

"Harold is learning lip-reading," Emily explained to Julian, "just in case."

"'Be prepared' has been my motto since boyhood. I was an Eagle Scout."

"Harold, I have a friend who paints," Julian said, rising. "Would you mind if I brought her here to see your work?"

"I'd be delighted," Harold said.

"This brown spot," Julian, said, touching Harold's brow. "Would you like the dermatologist to remove it?"

"No," Harold said. "It's paint. It will wash off."

***

How not to write a novel.

I am sitting here thinking about what I'm writing about. Writing is one of the ways I worry and almost the only way I think. Age is much on my mind here in my accumulating years. It comes in such a sudden rush. There are all those years when you are neither young nor old, then boom! you're old. It's a shock because for a long time you haven't been paying attention.

The truth is I'm not as old as I am; probably none of us is. It's a jolt to see a photograph of myself, or a reflection in a harsh mirror (bathroom mirrors are almost always kinder; how do they do it?) because my inner vision of myself, although in no way clear or precise, is still completely at odds with the reality. I am much thinner and younger, still athletic, and there is no heaviness under my chin. There may be a stomach but not this one. And when I get up out of this chair, where I've been sitting for two hours, I get up easily, effortlessly, gruntlessly, and without the sound of bones.

Someone, I forget who, wrote that we learn that we're old through others. When I ask for a senior citizen ticket to a movie, or drop half the adult fare in the bus's hopper and nobody gives me the slightest questioning look or, indeed, any look at all, I'm insulted. Gradually, I'm forced to accept their view of me. So that when a younger woman falls in love with me, as occasionally, but more and more rarely, happens, I am so grateful, if she is at all appealing, that I am almost instantly seduced. I become that younger self others are so heedlessly intent on denying me. I become arrogant and cocky, in a restrained way, instead of wondering what's wrong with this woman, why does she want someone quarter of a century her senior, someone who takes a tiny blood pressure pill every morning and Metamucil every night. What in her damaged childhood is this young woman hoping to repair by way of me? Oh, no. Instead, I think: here is a woman of discrimination and taste, let's see if she's worthy of me.

This happened to me so recently that the woman, whose name is Kate, is still part of my present, not yet memory. I am tempted to write about her, but this temptation conflicts with my need to get back to Tully. Although I know I'll never begin to get Tully right, she deserves more attention than she got in my last book. She only occupied seven years of my life, but they were a crucial seven years. She helped me change my life. She helped me to live as I was, an androgyne, and to believe in myself as a writer. I might have stayed with her for the rest of my life, but she was smarter and knew when it was time to move on.

In some ways, Tully lived my life. In others, I lived hers. Because she was in my territory, the balance was in my favor. So when the question of vacations arose and Tully began to talk about camping, I knew that in all fairness this was something I was going to have to do. Still, "Camping?" I said. "I'm Jewish." I had never known anyone before who had "gone camping."

"That's what us poor folks do," Tully said. "It costs a couple of dollars a day for the camp site and the rest is gasoline and kerosene."

"Kerosene? What's that?""

We drove to a huge emporium in New Jersey devoted entirely to necessities and niceties for the world of campers.

The first thing, of course, was the tent. She wanted a pop tent. I said I thought we needed at least a mom and pop tent. Since I was buying and was so reluctant to begin with, all the compromises were hers. We got something called a cabin tent, about ten feet by seven, with a pitched roof, zip-open screened windows on three sides and a zippered screened Dutch door on the fourth. It looked barely ade-quate to me, but it was the best they had. Tully felt that with this tent we could as well be living in Scarsdale, if only it were split-level. It came with a lot of poles and instructions and a promise that you could put the whole thing up in eight minutes.

From there we went on to the double bed: two air mattresses and two sleeping bags that could be zipped into one. (Zippers are crucial to camping).

Next the smaller stuff: the Coleman stove (two burners or four?) and the Coleman lantern. Tully talked me into the two-burner stove, and out of a second lantern, which I thought we might need for reading in, er, bed. Then the food chest, flashlights, pots and pans suitable for Coleman-stove cookery, plastic cutlery, etc.

"What about a toilet?" I said.

"Toilet? There's a bathhouse. It's never very far away."

"The middle of the night?" I said.

"You can go in the bushes."

"That doesn't sound like responsible camping," I said, and bought a plastic toilet seat on a crisscross folding aluminum support. It came with a package of blue plastic bags that were supposed to fit between the toilet seat and its aluminum support. It didn't look very sturdy and, in fact, wasn't, but I hoped it would do in an emergency.

"Keep in mind," Tully said, "that all this gear has to fit in the car along with us, our clothes, etcetera, and the food supplies."

"Never fear," I said, heady with the depth and sweep of my extravagance. If I was going to be cast forth into the desert again, a nomad, this time I would do it in the style of a sheik, not some poor Jew.

By this time, even I was eager to gather up all this stuff and transport it to a wooded place where we could assemble and arrange it and try to dwell in it. It was the way a child must feel with a dollhouse and all the little bits and pieces, arranging them in their places, in their rooms, imagining the life that goes on there. But I wouldn't know; I was never one for dolls.

We took a three-day weekend and went up the Taconic Parkway to a state campground a two-hour trip from home. Driving to our assigned site, I studied the other campers who would be our neighbors. They all seemed to be families with lots of kids and dogs and large fathers with beer bellies and duck-billed caps bearing messages.

Dogs barked. Babies cried. Children screamed. The rain fell steadily, but it was a gentle rain.

It took Tully an hour and a half to erect the tent, even with my help, or maybe because of my help. I held things and handed her other things. I read the directions to her step by step. Finally, it stood there with the rain falling on it and we both felt a lovely strong sense of triumph and went inside it to dry off.

Most of one's time spent camping, I soon realized, is devoted to simulating living conditions one ordinarily scarcely gives a thought to: creating shelter, lighting the dark, securing one's food against raccoons and decay, fetching water, trenching, a maneuver to prevent the rain from swamping the tent. Having established ourselves, with everything in place, we unfurled a canopy from the front of the tent to provide a roof over what could have been considered our terrace, opened beach chairs, and sat down in them. Tully was very happy; her eyes sparkled. She got out her guitar and sang "Moon River." We talked. We talked about the glories of nature. Somewhere nearby there was a lake and, given suitable weather, we would swim in it. We talked about how much better this was than going to a motel somewhere, at least she did. I said I preferred bathrooms in motels, hotels, resorts, rented cottages, to the public bathroom here with its lack of privacy and richness of odor. All my life I've had public bathroom nightmares. In them, the toilet cubicle doors never close and the floors are flooded with urine and other excreta, and I am, for some reason, usually barefoot. I am so filled with revulsion, shame, and self-loathing that I am inhibited from executing my urgent mission. When I tell her this, Tully looks at me with patient indulgence as one who loved her might have regarded the princess with her pea.

I suppose I have whoever was in charge of my toilet training to thank for the hurry she was in to get it over with, or to demonstrate my amazing precocity. I think it was my grandmother. She had prevented the fetus-me from being aborted by promising my mother that she would be my primary caretaker as, for a few years, she was. My mother had her hands full with my brother who was six months old when I was conceived, and who had exited the womb protesting loudly and, except for brief exhausted catnaps, had never stopped. A colic baby, they called him, but I think for those first years the world was too much for him --- too big, too bright, too noisy, too dangerous.

I loved my grandmother dearly and revere her memory, but I can still see her disapproving eyes and mouth, and hear her "shame, shame," as she shaved the index finger of one hand over the index finger of the other in the shame-shame gesture. How could she have guessed that she was poisoning camping for me?

So there we sat, Tully and I, under the dripping canopy, watching the water course down the trenches, during those moments not devoted to survival chores. I usually had a book in my lap but I rarely opened it because Tully talked and talked. She talked about other campgrounds she had known and other lovers with whom she had frequented them. Her adult life was an odyssey of women and cleared spaces in nature.

In my arrogance, because it was not in my plan to be one in a chain, I believed Tully had finally come to rest with me. I was her safe haven, her good Jewish mother. Hadn't I made it possible for her to have a long-deferred breakdown within weeks of our arrival in New York from Erato? But what a surprise to me, this strong, self-assured, gifted, cocky woman with $19 in her pocket dissolving in tears and tantrums that went on for weeks, then months, even after I had helped her find and furnish a terraced apartment overlooking the most gorgeous part of the Hudson river (we didn't think it wise or prudent to live together just yet) and across the street from one Jed and I'd moved into a year after Peter and I separated and I sold the house. I had also helped her buy a car and find a psychotherapist. But nothing was ever right, nothing was good enough. She had written a play that was being given an expensive, careful production in an experimental off-Broadway theater, but it wasn't Broadway, and she had disagreements with the director. She hated New York. She hated my friends and what she called their "judgmentality," which meant that she hated New York Jews. Of course, what she must have hated was me.

And she hated what she called my son Jed's rudeness, his lack of manners. In the south children never interrupted when adults were talking. What I tried to point out was that she would spend the rest of her life compensating for her well-mannered childhood. What I did not point out was that if Jed were forced to wait for a pause in her volubility, the house could have burned to the ground before he could have mentioned it.

Henry, thank God, was in his first year of college, at the other end of the continent, but I was trapped between these siblings, Jed and Tully, who, for different reasons, were so in need of my attention, and of course I tended to favor Jed who was a child and for whom the divorce was such a trauma.

People come to you with the terrible weight of their lives. What did I know about Tully when I first met and fell in love with her? What did I know about her mother, her aunt, her older brothers, her father, all of them crucial to the forming of her frustrations, prejudices, anger, fears, and most important, her needs. We are so innocent with each other in the beginning, dealing with surfaces, but all those buttons are there waiting to be pushed and, in our innocence, we push them and watch with horror the bombs we have set off. Our seven years passed with small successes, large failures. Tully's play received mixed reviews and did not, as she hoped, move to Broadway for a longer run. She would never write another play. In fact, it would be a few years before she would write anything again except for an occasional "true confession" for one of the magazines, confessions that I sometimes helped her plot, both of us laughing hysterically. I wrote and published, slowly, but with more and more confidence. Jed and Tully learned to like each other and Tully taught Jed how to play the guitar and to discover that music was his first love. Tully and I frequently went camping, sometimes to very nice places. We made new friends and in some ways our life together opened up. Still, I never knew what I could safely say that would not set off some ghastly scene, and I reached a point where I rarely said anything without thinking hard about it first.

Then Tully went off to Taos to write a novel, a serious one that she had been brooding on for several months. I was delighted; the real Tully was coming back. When Tully actually did come back, she had in tow a young, not very clean hippie woman with stringy dirty blonde hair. Tully was breathless with excitement, so I knew they were having an affair. I was devastated. Tully announced that she was leaving New York and going to live in the southwest, she gave her furniture to the superintendent of her building and asked if I'd give her my sleeping bag for her hippie; they would be camping their way across country and her new friend was unequipped. I came close to punching her, but didn't. I merely told her to fuck off, appalled by her insensitivity, and when they were gone I wrote one angry, heart-broken poem after another, and sent them to Tully. Tully liked them so much she forwarded them to an editor friend who thought they were wonderful and published them in her obscure quarterly.

And so, for a while, in my agony I returned to poetry. This is what writers do. They throw words at their pain in an effort to stone it to death. They obsess with carefully honed phrases. This provides some relief, but not much. I suffered for six months, until I fell in love again with someone who would eventually cause me even greater pain.

As for Tully, she managed to buy and restore an old Indian adobe ruin in Taos and make it into a comfortable home. She moved from one love affair to another, always, I think, with good intentions, but leaving in her wake a string of temporarily embittered women. Once it was her turn; she fell in love with someone who broke her heart and she became seriously depressed. After that first novel, which was well-received critically but brought her little money or fame, she again stopped writing for a long time. She was living in what I think of, perhaps unfairly, as dramatically beautiful marginal country among people with horoscopes and homeopaths and juice extractors and crystals and mystical experiences. I don't know how she makes her living except for teaching writing when she can. I don't know if she writes any more.

CHAPTER FIVE

Jilian's bag was packed when he got home that night. "I'll be leaving in the morning," she said. "I've got to get back."

"Why?" he said, stunned. The look on his face made her laugh.

"I have a life that precedes you," she said, trying to sound kind. "I have my work. My house. My cats. I have a show in three months."

"Sell the house," he said. "Move your work and cats here. I'll try to love the cats..."

"You don't have to love the cats."

"We'll build a studio out back. Lots of glass, skylights, high white walls, anything you want."

"We'll see," she said. "I have to resolve some other problems, too. There are loose threads, old relationships ..."

"Ah."

"Well what did you think?"

"How serious?"

"Obviously no longer, if ever, serious."

"How long will it take?"

"I don't know. I've made dinner. Do you want it now or later?"

"Later. Why must you be so secretive, so mysterious?" he asked, unknotting his tie, as they moved toward the bedroom.

"I'm not either of those things," she said. "What would you like to know?"

"Who are they, the 'old relationships?'"

Unbuttoning her blouse, she sighed. "There's only one. It's been fourteen years. He's a psychoanalyst and he's married. His name is Perry."

"Perry!" he said with disgust, helping her with her

brassiere.

"He has three children. He tried to leave his wife, but she slit her wrists. At least, she scratched them. He bandaged her up and promised he would never leave. I never asked him to, never wanted him to. I never wanted to marry him. I never wanted to marry anyone."

They were on the bed, in each other's arms.

"But you want to marry me, don't you?" His voice was hoarse. "I mean, we're probably forever, aren't we?" He felt like an adolescent, and blushed. She twined her legs around his, stroked his back.

"Possibly," she said. "It's so hard to see beyond lust."

"There's a chap at the home," he murmured, later. "Harold. He paints. I wanted you to see his work."

"When I get back," she whispered, her voice sinking into sleep.

***

Blanche (whom you've not yet met) is seated in a deep upholstered arm chair placed cata-cornered at the far end of the room, a warm, pleasing room, filled with good things: books, records, paintings, photographs, sculpture, rugs, a brick fireplace, dried heather and sea grass in a lovely blue porcelain vase. Blue is the prevailing color of this nest, and Blanche resembles some strange soft prehistoric bird, an odd mix of vulturine and avuncular. Age and illness may have given her the flaccid look. Her throat and arms and ankles have thickened. Like a bird, she has few facial expressions, her sharp brown eyes behind the tortoise-rimmed glasses don't change, her voice is low and insistent but uninflected. It's our third meeting and I'm still waiting for her to tell me what she really wants from me and how much she's willing to pay me for it. And I'm still wondering what I'm doing here and whether, at any price, writing her life is something I'd really want to do. What about Jilian and Julian and Emily?

"I feel a need to tell it," she says. "Why? You ask me why? It think it's commercial, that's why. I think it will sell. I don't need ego gratification. I'm in enough Who's Who's. That's not what I want."

"That's not what I mean," I tell her. "Is it because you want to give it form, a shape?"

"I don't know what you mean by that. Why should it have a shape?"

"Well, that's an artistic need, I suppose, an artist's impulse. Symmetry. Do you think by telling it you'll be able to make more sense of it? Of your life?"

"Ditto to that; why should life make sense?"

I don't believe her. Doesn't everyone want his life to make some sort of sense? "Then to get it out of your head where it gives you no rest," I say desperately, dramatically, "and onto the pages of a book where it will have its own life and leave you alone?" It's hopeless. I am talking about myself. I'm projecting. What do I know about her?

"You mean therapy? But I rarely think about it, I'm too busy. Well, that's not entirely true. I could be busier. They renewed my contract, but it's only for a couple of days a week."

"Maybe it's because you haven't been well and you're feeling your mortality? Is it that you feel a little powerless?" I am relentless. "Is it that you feel there's not much more future, and there's less and less in the present, an emptiness that you need to fill with the past?" I am also shameless, pitiless.

"No. I don't feel that old, that it's all over. Though I am feeling my mortality. The tests I've been going for! Tests, tests, more tests. It's not the cancer. The double mastectomy took care of that. Did I tell you what Alan said when I went to his office last week about renewing the contract?" I shake my head. Who is Alan? "`Well, Blanche,' he said, `are you clean?' 'What do you mean?' I asked him, though I knew damn well what he meant. I wanted to smash his face in.

"'What did the doctors find? Are you clean?'

"'What are you, my Jewish mother, asking me if I'm finished with my period? Tell me, Alan, would you ask me that if I were a man?' He had the decency then at least to be embarrassed. He turned bright red and said, 'I only meant, did they get all the cancer, are you okay?'"

I think about poor Alan and his choice of words. Why "poor" Alan. He's probably a barracuda, aren't they all? But I'm sure the question was innocent, without the biblical connotations the word "clean" has for Blanche. Semantics.

"Anyhow, they renewed the contract. I asked for part time, but it's a little too part time to suit me. I feel better when I'm busy, I guess everyone does. What do I do there now? I'm a consultant. When they're considering a property, they have a meeting to review it. I sit in on the meetings and make recommendations. If I don't think it will work, I tell them why. I'm the one there with theater experience. They're gigantic, but mostly in movies and records and periodicals. Theater is the smallest part of their operation. What I do, for example, they want to make a musical of Patagonia Lost, it doesn't sound like a bad idea, right? The book was on the best seller list for eighteen months. I love the book. Caswell writes like a dream. Marty Silver wants to write the music ... you know, he did the music for Mendel's Theory. But it would never make it in the theater, even as a musical. It's all scenery ...well, I don't have to go into why, it would take too long, you don't have the background. You have to have the background. That's why they pay me, because I have the background, the experience. And they pay me very well."

At our second meeting, I'd told her that it was hard for

me to talk about money.

"I've noticed that."

"You'll have to do it."

But she hasn't done it and it's begun to make me angry. Am I being used? I have to be careful when it comes to money. It's emotionally charged. Money was always the most important thing to my father, the only real value, and how I hated that! And the way it was used! It was the currency not only for material things, for necessities, for ease and comfort, but for love, approval, anger and disapproval, displays of superiority, of achievement, worth, power. It was given or withheld, mostly the latter, according to the whim of my father who made it all and had it all. I know all this, and how unnatural and demeaning it was. It came out in my analysis, along with its affect on my bowels (colitis), and much improved though I am, I still have to guard against the residual detritus of that early conditioning.

Blanche telephoned a couple of weeks ago. She had just read my book and she said she loved it. The book had been out about a month and I was pleased that she'd read it because I hardly knew her. She wanted to talk to me about it. I knew she worked for The Arista Group. When I asked our mutual friend Carla what she did for them, Carla said she wasn't sure but she thought Blanche acquired properties. Properties. Since my books have never made much money, a wild and wonderful hope instantly surged. Property is money; maybe I was about to make some. How much? Enough to become an owner instead of a renter? We made a date for dinner. Twice, she had to break our date while, almost unbearably, the suspense mounted. When at last we met at a restaurant of her choice in her neighborhood, about as far from mine as it's possible to get and still be in the same borough, we nattered on about one thing or another until I began to think that we would never get to the point of this meeting.

"How's your book doing?" she finally asked when I was on my third bloody mary and nearly insensible.

"Not well enough to suit Marble House," I said. "You know how it is with big publishing houses. They publish books like scattershot, hoping one will kill. They give up on a book a week before publication date if it's not already on the best seller list."

"Have they run any ads?"

"One tiny one in the Sunday Times Book Review."

She broke off a piece of bread from what remained of the pre-scored baguette in the basket. We hadn't yet ordered dinner, but thank God for the bread.

"How's it supposed to sell if nobody knows about it?" she asked, but I could see she wasn't really interested. She was trying to show that she was on my side and I felt grateful for that.

"Beats me. They must know something about the book business that the rest of us don't."

"It's a shame. It's a wonderful book. I read it twice. The first time I read it just to read it, and the second time I read it because I thought there might be a television series in it."

"A television series? You mean, like a situation comedy?" I couldn't imagine what she was talking about.

"But there isn't."

"Well, that's a relief. A movie maybe, but never a series."

"I don't see a movie in it, either. But you know what I did see in it, Rachel? A lot of my own life. You and I are very much alike."

I was so busy being surprised to hear this that I neglected to ask her how, in what ways she thought we were alike. As I say, I didn't know her very well, but I had known her, also not well, years ago when we were just beginning. We were neighbors then, during a six or seven year period, when we lived in the same super-complex of drab brick rectangles, she in a slightly lower-income section. Their rooms were smaller than ours and their rents were lower and they weren't permitted to have air-conditioning, but otherwise we had the same depressing standard off-buff paint on the walls, the unboxed pipes that carried heat to the radiators, the same bathroom and kitchen tiles and fixtures, the same windows. We had both been war brides, but so had all the women I knew then. It was right after Jed was born. We each had two children but that, too, was true of almost everyone I knew. Her husband, Morty, was my children's pediatrician. She and her children were a couple of years older than me and my children. She had a biting sense of humor. She said very funny things and rarely cracked a smile. She was homely but she behaved as if she were gorgeous, so it didn't matter. She was said to be bright, clever, sharp, and she scared me a little because I didn't yet know what I was.

"And God how I envy your talent," she said. "One thing I've learned after writing three hundred pages of my life is that I can't write."

I began to feel my heart sink. We were getting to the point. My book wasn't the property she wanted; her book was, and she wanted me to write it.

"What do you think?" she said, when it was all on the table along with the coffee and the crumbs of dinner. "Do you think you'd want to do it?"

"I don't know," I said. "I'd like to read some of those three hundred pages. And I'd have to hear what you have in mind."

"No,'" she said. "I've destroyed those pages. I'd want to tell it to you. You could tape it."

"I'll have to think about it," I said. "And of course you'd have to make me an offer I couldn't refuse."

So here we are a couple of weeks later, and I am still thinking it over. I need to know what she really has in mind, what she really wants. Although she denies it, I think she thinks she's dying and who knows, maybe she is, and wants to leave something behind, some record, but does she want it to be an honest one, how honest can she be, how deep does she want to go and can she, or does she just want one of those `as-told-to's' that any hack can do and that I don't want to waste time on. I don't even know if I could do it if I did want to. No, she wants me to bring my sensibilities, those she admired so much in my book, which was, of course, about me, to bear on her life. I'll have to hear her life before I can decide (have I room in my life for her life?), and learn her sensibilities. Damned if I'll lend her mine if she doesn't deserve them.

"Anyhow," she says, "what difference does it make why I want to do it? Do I have to have a motive?"

"Noooo," I reluctantly grant. But everyone has a motive, a reason. It's usually an ego thing, but what's the difference?

"I think I've had an interesting life. I don't care how you do it. Make it a novel, if that's what you want to write."

People are always telling me what a great book they could write if they only had the time, but since they're so busy how would I like to write it? And then they begin to bare their lives to me. Once they begin, there's no stopping them. It's as if I have nothing to write about and they are making me this gift of their adultery, their child born out of wedlock, the extreme poverty of their childhood, the coldness of their mother, how their husband left them for a younger woman and they found God. As if I've been sitting around dying for someone to give me a plot. Little do they know how little I care about plot, how much I can make out of nothing, how much I would prefer to make something out of nothing, rather than nothing much out of something.

Tergiversation, caprice.

At least Blanche has admitted that she can't write, even given the time.

***

A new recurrent dream. Recurrent, but with variations. Packing. I am packing to leave. There always seems to be too much stuff to fit into my luggage. And not enough time. There are always closets, chests of drawers, another room I've forgotten about, crammed with my stuff. I don't like this dream. It isn't frightening, but it's unpleasant and frustrating. Packing. Packing it in? To leave? Death? Am I preparing to die? Then why does it seem necessary to take all these clothes, papers, everything, not to leave anything behind in the rooms I'm leaving? To die clean? Maybe it isn't death. Maybe it's just change (she said wistfully). Moving into old age. It's very hard to do because of all these old clothes. I'm always wishing I had more closet space because I find it so hard to throw anything out. Hard to give up things that once fit me, things that I once liked. Youth and beauty. Love and life. My earnest, curious, engaged self.

CHAPTER SIX

"I painted this for you," Harold said. "Where would you like me to hang it?"

He had not even asked if she liked it. Arrogance. Though the artist's arrogance is somehow acceptable, more like stubborn self-confidence without which, she supposed, it would be so hard to proceed. Timidity, apology: the death of art.

She did like it. It was smaller than most of his canvases, three feet by two. The colors were marvelous. It was abstract, like all his paintings, but as she studied it, she seemed to enter it, to find herself in some dream-like landscape, an island in a darkening sea, a restful quiet place, what she from that moment hoped dying might be.

"Does it have a name?" she asked.

"No. I don't name my paintings. I number them." He looked at the back of the canvas. "This is number 397."

"My God, you're fecund for an old man!" She narrowed her eyes at the painting. "I would name it 'A Peaceful Death,'" she said.

He smiled. "That's why I don't name them," he said. "They might all have the same name."

"It's really quite beautiful." She looked around her walls for a proper place. Did she want it facing her bed? If she died in bed, it would be the last thing she would see. It would be the last thing she would see every night and the first every morning. Did she want that?

"Leave it on the table," she said. "Yes, propped up like that. Let me live with it a while before we decide where to hang it."

Harold slowly folded himself into the chair next to hers. He gestured at the pile of notebooks between them.

"Are you writing a novel?" he asked.

"No. My life."

"What are you up to?"

"Age fifteen."

"All these? What a rich childhood you must have had."

"Rich? No, it was only rich in detail, like all childhoods."

"And what a memory you must have."

"Only for the distant past. The middle past will probably go into two books."

"Why are you doing it?"

It was a question she had never squarely addressed to herself. Why was she doing it? She looked at Harold with increased interest. He was waiting. He really wanted to know. She could almost see the man he had so recently been, virile and strong and, no doubt, a charmer. He was still something of a charmer, and his eyes were clear, unclouded deep-set dark brown eyes, the whites still white, like the straight white hair that fell in a thatch across his brow.

"Why am I doing it," she murmured. "I can tell you more easily why I'm not doing it. Not for posterity, certainly. I can't imagine that anyone would be interested, and there are very few people left who would volunteer to go through the detritus I leave behind. In fact, when I came here, I pared myself down to the barest necessities."

"Yes," he said. "You threw away the drawer full of road maps, and the one with the half-burnt candles."

She laughed. "Oh, much more than that. All the accumulation of travel stuff, the outdated drugs and vitamins..."

"The bottles of designer vinegar and mustard dinner guests brought you that you never got around to using..."

"All the foodstuff. I gave it to the super."

"Books..."

"That was easy. I'd already gotten rid of the books I

knew I would never read again, and needn't have read in the first place. The rest are here in the library." You would have thought that they had lost their identity among all the other books, but no. When she went into the library, her own books practically jumped off the shelves at her, so familiar had they grown over the years. "Clothes, though. There were things I'd held onto for decades: scarves, gloves, mufflers, kerchiefs handkerchiefs, shoes, boots, costume jewelry, oh, so many things I hadn't worn in years, had even forgotten were there, things in perfectly good condition. It was so hard to part with them when I needed the space, so easy when I decided to come here, and such a relief to be finally rid of it all."

"You still haven't answered my question. Why the memoir? I imagine it's another paring down, getting rid of, putting things in order."

She thought for a moment. It wasn't just that. "I may be doing it," she said, "because I haven't anything else to do."

***

Why do you write? For whom do you write? Who is the audience you have in mind when you write? How much of what you write is autobiographical? Boring questions. I wonder how many writers answer them truthfully, especially when they are interviewed and feel a need to be original. Me, I write for three reasons: to amuse myself, to torture myself, and because I don't know what else to do with myself.

That's too glib, of course, and while I do sometimes amuse myself and more often torture myself, not knowing what else to do with myself is the truest of the three reasons. My identity is all bound up with writing ever since I wrote my first composition in second grade and it was such a hit that my teacher sent me to half a dozen other

classrooms to read it aloud. For that brief morning I was a
star. Something I had done made me feel important. It was
a first, a new feeling, and needless to say I liked it. I had
found in myself, in a precocious use of words and humor,
a power I didn't know I had that separated me for a moment
from my usual mediocrity. When I was a child, even adults
sometimes listened to me, paid attention if I used the right
words. Learning to talk was the best thing that had ever
happened to me. Words were magical. I couldn't wait to
learn more and more of them. I was never a liar; I was a
truth-teller. But to tell the real truth you need a vocabulary.
And you need a sense of the shape of things, which means
that artful alterations are sometimes necessary to get at the
real truth. These are not lies. They are fictions. Fiction is
not lies.

Blanche would never have said, "I want this book
written because I haven't anything else to do." Most people, as they get older, pretend to be busy, if not busier than
ever. How many people, when you ask them on the phone,
"Did I wake you?" ever admit that you did? There's something shameful about admitting that while others are up and
calling, you are still asleep. Idleness and sloth are never
earned, at any age.

I do sometimes wonder what I would do if I stopped
writing which, for a number of reasons would make sense.
There is less and less publishing happening, particularly of
the sort of things I write. And, as I told the therapist that
day when I was so down, I am afraid that there may soon
be less and less going on in my mind. So what would I do?
I could go with Becky to see what's happening in all the
museums. I could learn to bake. I could spend two years
clearing out my closets and drawers. More than two years.

CHAPTER SEVEN

Jilian was gone and Julian missed her achingly. He felt like a wall through whose center a four-foot hole has been punched by a bulldozer. The empty part defined him and the rest of him, the still-standing wall, was flat and dead, there only to delineate the absence. He didn't understand how this could be. He had always considered himself a complete and self-sufficient man, and Jilian had been in his life such a brief time. This, he supposed, was what it was to be passionately in love, a condition that he was only now aware had hitherto eluded him, at least at any serious age.

But with what was he in love? He hardly knew her, really. He knew her with all his senses, but not much with his intelligence. Was she considerate, thoughtful, compassionate, did she lose her temper, did she brood, did she love movies as he did and did she cry at them, as he sometimes did? He hadn't a clue.

Idly, during a solitary dinner in his kitchen, he began to make a list of these things, knowing that none of them mattered, not yet. They would be revealed gradually in the course of their time together. They would delight and please and, perhaps, occasionally dismay each other, and whatever the bonds that were forged and strengthened between them, learning each other would be part of the excitement of love.

When he phoned her the first night of her absence, she sounded distracted.

"Do you miss me?" he asked. "Do you love me?"

She was silent for a moment, a silence that sent terror to his heart. "From this distance," she said, "you don't seem real."

He tried to understand what she meant by this, tried not to feel too upset. She had been plunged back into her separate reality, one in which he had never existed, among people to whom he was not even a name. She, on the other hand, had happened in his reality, his world, trailing the scent of her perfume through his house, her voice sounding in his rooms, her body beside him in his bed. She was absent from him in a way that he was not absent from her.

"I'd better come there this weekend," he said.

"No, not yet. There's too much I have to do first."

Perry? He must try not to be too invasive. He didn't know how to behave with a woman with whom he was so much in love. How hard it was to have boundaries suddenly thrust upon you where, for the days before, there had been none.

"I won't be able to come the following weekend," he said, "and I don't know if I can stand so much time apart."

"Trust me, darling, it will be all right. I do love you."

"I don't like that 'do'. It sounds conditional. It seems to be trying feebly to cast out doubt."

She laughed.

"Do you cry at movies?" he asked.

"Never," she said. "Whenever I feel I might, I tell myself it's only a shadow on a screen."

***

"How were the apartments?" I ask my mother, who has finally, without mishap, made it over the doorsill to the interior of a place called Giverney (pronounced Give-er-knee. Hard G). When I correct her, she tells me she's sorry but that's how they pronounce it.

"Beautiful," she says, with enthusiasm. "I'd have room for almost everything. And the grounds are beautiful, too. No ocean, but lots of flowers and a stream with a sort of Japanese bridge over it, a green one. The apartment they offered me overlooks it."

"Are there water lilies?"

"I didn't notice."

"Is there a terrace?"

"Two. One off the bedroom."

"Sounds perfect."

"Flora can't afford it. She'd have to share."

"With you?"

"God, no. I couldn't live with Flora. She's a slob."

I am sure Flora is not a slob. She is always very neatly, smartly dressed and coiffed. "How?" I ask. "In what way is Flora a slob?"

"There are crumbs all over her kitchen. She doesn't see them. Anyhow, I couldn't live with anyone. They have an apartment for Flora with another woman who needs to share. We met her."

"Did Flora like her?"

"She seemed depressed. It's hard to tell."

Who wouldn't be depressed? I can't imagine two unacquainted women in their upper eighties trying out of a new necessity to make a home together, sharing a living room and kitchen, sharing the television set, waiting to die. I try to imagine the conversation between Flora and the other woman, how they went about feeling each other out.

"I just can't make up my mind," my mother says. She sighs. "You walk in and all you see is white hair." My mother, and most of her friends, dye their hair. "It's all old people."

CHAPTER EIGHT

Ida Tomashevsky had alwayss considered herself a strong, brave, happy woman. How had she come to this?

Bound by a recent stroke to a wheelchair, she could maneuver herself in a limited way with her unaffected right hand. Her damaged left hand held a small, ridiculous rubber doll, a cartoon character whose ears and eyes bulged when she squeezed it hard enough. It seemed to take an inordinate amount of strength to accomplish this, but when she did, it always made her laugh. There were few powers left to her, but one of them was making this creature's orifices pop. The satisfaction was entirely private.

It was late afternoon, and the sun was nearly gone from the west window of the room she shared with five other women. Soon the attendants would be clattering about with their dinner trays. The attendants' shift was over at five, so dinner had to be early, making the night intolerably long. There was television, and some of them watched for the hours after dinner until bedtime, nodding and snoring in their chairs, even though the sound was turned up deafeningly loud for the many among them who were hard of hearing.

Little old Rosie wandered into the room, as she did all day, her shaking hands spread open before her, her eyes behind the thin tousle of uncombed yellowing white hair empty of all but her terrible need. "Ice cream," she begged. "Give me ice cream. I want ice cream." It was all she ever said, all she asked for, but she asked constantly. Ida knew that what she was saying was, "I need, I need, I need." When there was ice cream, she was silent only for the time it took her to eat it.

"Ice cream," she beseeched Ida. The woman was mad, of course. Most of them were at least half mad.

"What flavor, Rosie?" Ida asked, as she always did, a cruel question that had no meaning for Rosie. Ida wondered what Rosie was really asking for, and was sure that it was probably everything. She wondered, too, how old Rosie was in what self-image remained to her, five? seven? What was the age of ice cream, the age when going out for ice cream was a special treat, an occasion, a reward?

The truth was, even Ida, still rational, was not as old as she chronologically was. Were any of them?

Yet the place reeked of age. Urine, disinfectant, baked potatoes, occasionally the smell of dying lilacs or roses. Illness, decay, despair. She had been consigned to this place by Molly, her only child, a weak woman married to an overbearing man, Herschel, very successful. They lived in a fourteen room house in Chappaqua where there was certainly enough room for her. There was more than enough money for a caretaker, too. Ida had always been careful and cheerful with Herschel and gotten on well with him, but she knew that now her age and her disability frightened and possibly disgusted him. He did not want to be reminded of what lay ahead. Paying her bills at the home relieved Herschel of both guilt and any further responsibility. And, while Ida knew that she loved her, Molly had long since made the compromises and adjustments needed for her marriage to function. She never argued with Herschel. Peace was all.

Ida understood. She even sympathized, though she herself would never have put up with Herschel. She would have fought him tooth and claw. He would have had to kill her, or else make a few compromises of his own. But Molly had never had Ida's stamina, her determination. She was smart, she was popular, but she was weak, a little lazy, and morally neuter.

So Ida had been, as she felt, warehoused, or set adrift on an ice floe like a useless old Eskimo woman, put away to endure among others of her kind the time until death. How she wished she had been born into a culture that honored the old, a culture of extended families. It was something she had never wished until she was old, people of all ages, bound by blood or marriage, in crowded, cluttered rooms. But oh how she wished it now. There were things she could still do. She felt sure that, even with one hand, she could cook, even bake. She could, in a limited way, mind babies. She could give advice. But here there was little for her to do but think about her own body, feed it, take it to the toilet, brush its teeth and dentures, comb what was left of its hair. And wait.

Thank God she could still see well enough to read. She read whatever books Molly brought her, and the newspapers. The world was still going on out there, and it still had the power to amaze, anger, and amuse her.

"Jonestown. Waco," she said to Daisy Kornish, who lay bedridden in the slot adjoining hers. "And now Heaven's Gate. What kind of religion could make a whole group of people commit suicide? The children, too. Death by Kool-Aid, by fire, by plastic bags."

"Masada," Daisy said. "We Jews are always getting ourselves pogrommed and slaughtered."

"That's what we were chosen for."

Daisy groaned. "I'd kill myself if I could."

"Individual suicide is different," Ida said. "You wouldn't take us all with you if you were the leader."

"This bunch?" Daisy said. "Don't be too sure."

Ida laughed. "How would you do it?"

"Give me a minute."

If it weren't for Daisy, Ida would have been completely desolate, but Daisy, though her body was failing in so many ways, was still someone to reckon with, to talk to.

"A clever combination of tapioca pudding and arsenic," Daisy said. "No, that wouldn't work. Nobody likes tapioca pudding. It would have to be ice cream. Mocha fudge."

"Daisy, how old are you?" Ida asked. "I don't mean actually. I mean really. Inside."

"Thirty-five," she said, without having to think about it. "What about you?"

"A little older," Ida said. "Fortyish."

They were silent for a moment. Ida wondered why you chose a particular age to stop at, whether that was when you had felt at the height of your powers.

"You go along," Daisy said in her small, feeble voice, "thinking that you always have the option of suicide, but by the time you really need to do it, you're too old. Imagine being too old to kill yourself! What a crowning indignity! I can't even manage to save up the pills."

"If I had my choice," Ida said, "I'd arrange myself comfortably in the back seat of a Cadillac with the garage sealed and the motor running. And I'd bring a good book to read in the meantime." Though maybe a good book was a mistake. If it were really good, she'd turn off the motor so she could finish it.

"Who has Cadillacs? Who has garages?"

Hattie, a big woman with skin that good cafe-au-not-too-much-lait color, strode into the room.

"How you girls doing?" she asked. She advanced to the side of Daisy's bed and sniffed. "Time to change your diapers," she said. Ida discreetly turned her wheelchair away while Hattie set to work.

"How I hate it that you have to do this," Daisy said. "I feel so ashamed."

"Don't feel ashamed," Hattie said. "You can't help it."

"All the same, I hate that you have to do it."

"I don't mind. It's part of my job," Hattie said. "You'd do the same for me."

"The hell I would," Daisy said.

"Hold still. I got to wash you. There. A little talcum

powder. That's better, isn't it?"

"For the time being."

"Let me take your pulse. Mmmm. See that you eat all your dinner. You need feeding. Mrs. Tomashevsky, will you see that she eats? Help her if she needs it. Her pulse is a little weak."

"I'll try," Ida said. "It's not such a pleasure to eat the food in this place."

"I know," Hattie said.

"There must be a special school for rotten institutional cooks,." Ida said. "Who would go to it?"

"Rotten people. Sadists," Daisy muttered. "The course names are: Cooking terrible, 101. Cooking worse, 102. Then, when you get really bad at it, Cooking for hospitals 103."

The three women laughed.

"Where there's life there's not always humor," Hattie said appreciatively; she was given to coining apothegms. "But where there's humor, there's usually life."

Nonetheless, some time during the night Daisy died. Ida awoke at dawn, when they came to wheel Daisy's body out, and she had a last brief look at her friend. She looked more than peaceful; she looked almost happy. Ida cried all that day and the next and the next. Daisy's death was harder for Ida than the death of her second husband. She hadn't known Daisy long, but she would miss her more than she had missed Isaac. She needed Daisy more than she had needed Isaac in those last years. She couldn't look at the new old woman who almost immediately replaced her. She wept for Daisy as she had wept for a cat she had once had for seventeen years. Her heart was broken.

***

"Do you think writing distances you from your experience, puts a sort of scrim between you and it?" a young
painter asked last night at a dinner party.

Au contraire, I think, or perhaps I tell her. What she
may mean is that when we write, we move the event, the
experience, the feelings, via the bridge of words, from
memory and gut to intellect.

The two kinds of glass through which writers see: the
window, the mirror. We all use both, but some more one
than the other. We look out at the world and see it objectively; we look into the mirror and see what we have made
of what has happened to us, what we have seen, what we
have felt. We experience our more meaningful experiences
not just once, but over and over, we worry them like a dog
a bone. We are self-conscious and self-involved. If,
finally, writing it puts the chaos of our lives into some more
manageable form, which may be a distancing, it isn't until
after the wrenching struggle with it that most people avoid,
or are able to put behind them.

"It's different for painters," the painter says. "Our
medium is more abstract. And at the same time more direct." Does she mean that because painting doesn't use
words, it isn't so closely felt? I wonder what kind of painter
she is.

It's probably true that visual thought must have preceded and is therefore more primitive than verbal thought.
Animals must think visually, in pictures, and man must
have, too, until he became sufficiently complex to begin the
marvelous business of naming, and of sharing the naming.
Making words to stand for more and more complicated
things. You can't have complicated ideas without a vocabulary. Painters began, simply, by describing with line and
color what was there: the horse, the bison, the hunter, the
fish, the fisher, the stick, the stone, the bow, the arrow.
Only later were there depth, shading, perspective, back-

ground and foreground. Language, too. But more and more words are constantly needed so that we can know what we are thinking and so that we can think about what we know and say it.

Language, writing, experience. Why have I chosen to write this book that I'm writing? Because it's outside my experience, window-writing, and therefore painless? Is it painless? Is it outside my experience? Am I enjoying writing it? No, I often hate it. Of course, when it's going well it's as good as sex. It takes you out of yourself by going so much deeper into yourself.

How peaceful it is. The Schola Cantorum singing madrigals on WGBH, the tree limbs outside my window waving in a breeze that may soon bring rain, the cat curled up on my desk, her head on the computer, almost but not quite in the way. This cat. Her legs are too short, her belly too low to the ground, and she walks like Mae West, her hips swaying, but she has an alert, beautiful face, and she strikes funny poses and runs away and hides from most people. Otherwise, she's developing into quite a decent sort of cat. Deirdre, whose hair I changed in my last book from scarlet to ebony, used to say that a writer needs a cat. How right she was. I don't think I could write without a cat. A cat soothes and calms you and sits comfortably on your pages. It doesn't intrude, yet it's company, a living, breathing, presence.

My latest fortune cookie says: EMPHASIZE ON YOUR CREATIVITY.

***

"You're not the only one who's getting old," Rebecca says.

Rebecca is a year older than I. She is probably getting old at the same rate as I am. She looks okay, though, her features a little sharper, more aquiline, a few brown spots she would never dream of having erased, her hair, what she lets grow of it, completely silver.

"You're so self-involved," she again accuses me.

"Writers are," I say, sick of hearing this from her. What makes me think I can speak for all writers? "Ultimately, our selves are our grist."

"Aren't you finished writing about yourself? What can be left? Why don't you write some fiction for a change?" She sounds like my mother.

"I'm writing a novel," I say. "I think it's about old age. I think the characters in it are fictional."

This, of course, isn't entirely true; it never is. Ida Tomashevsky is my grandmother, the loved one, made more articulate. Jilian is a tiny bit Alison, made beautiful. Etcetera.

"I don't know what I'm going to do," Rebecca says, a little later. "I can't stand anything any more. I think I have to stop going out of the house or letting newspapers come into it."

Age has not mellowed her. It has only increased her disapproval, her outrage, her indignation. She is a window person and nothing out there is done properly, decently, ethically, intelligently, or correctly. Mostly, she's right but, as I now ask her, why must she care so much? "Isn't there any way after all these years to expect less, accept more?"

"Only on my deathbed," she says.

"I admire your spirit," I tell her, but I'm not sure I do. It's such a waste of time and energy. It changes nothing. It only makes her miserable. Anyhow, who promised her a rose garden? Speaking of rose gardens, if she liked nature more and cities less, she might find some peace. Nature, except in extremis, does most things right, and if it doesn't, you can't quarrel with it.

But, paradoxically, it's manmade things she admires,

interiors, exteriors, architectural details. She will go to the ends of the earth for an interesting building, even a piece of one. Since she began using a camera a few years back, most of her pictures are of doors and portals.

I try to imagine what it would be like to outlive Rebecca, and I can't. She may sometimes get on my nerves, as I know I do on hers, but I can't imagine a world without her. I can well imagine, as I have, what Ida Thomashevsky is feeling.

CHAPTER NINE

It was Friday. Jilian would be there that night, just for the weekend. Again, Julian felt embarrassingly like an adolescent, anticipation elbowing aside almost everything else. It was difficult to concentrate on what Ida Tomashevsky was saying. Her wheelchair was surrounded by the fallen newspapers she was finished with.

"It's harder and harder to understand the world," she said. "The Serbs, the Croats, Bosnia. Muslims and Christians. Muslims and Jews. What's the good of history if nobody learns from it?" Uncharacteristically, she began to cry.

Julian, who had not thought about the world for at least the past two weeks, was moved. He handed Ida his clean handkerchief. She thrust it back at him and reached in a pocket for a Kleenex.

"I have nobody to talk to, nobody to discuss with."

There were 740 people in the home. Surely she could find someone. He began to suggest this, but then caught himself.

"You miss Daisy," he said.

She groped for another tissue and blew her nose.

"Everything is subtraction," she said, dismally. Rosie wandered past, calling for ice cream, then a small, bent man hobbled up and, leaning on his cane, stood staring at them, sucking on his gums, making little clicking noises.

"Go away, Bench," Ida said. "This is a private conversation." Bench stood there, not moving, not smiling, not speaking.

"It's an insane asylum," Ida said. "Bedlam. Soon I'll be as loony as the rest. I haven't laughed once since Daisy died."

He could feel his hand moving along the curve of

Jilian's waist, the rise of her hip, her fresh warm breath in his mouth.

"How are you feeling physically?" he asked, hating himself. "Are you getting any strength back in that left hand?"

She had the doll in her hand. She squeezed it and showed him how the doll's ears and eyes popped out, laughing at it in spite of herself.

"But what's the good?" she asked. "What will I do with this hand? Nobody wants it."

Julian sighed. She had never complained before, never shown self-pity. He knew it was the beginning of the end, that soon she would give up and die. There was nothing he could tell her. He was there only to observe her.

"*I* want your hand," the old man said.

"Get out of here, Bench," she screamed. "I can't stand the sight of you. You have no business butting in when I have visitors." The old man took a step back, but stayed.

"Would you like to start a discussion group?" Julian asked her. "There must be other people here interested in what's happening in the world. You could chair it. I could talk to Mr. Principale."

"*I'm* interested in what's happening in the world," Bench mumbled.

She could just imagine it. A few would come. They would sit there hawking, spitting, dozing off, talking about nothing that was relevant today. They would use all the old words and phrases like pinkos and commies, union busters, capitalists riding on the backs of the poor.

"No thanks," she said. "If you really want to do something for me, get me Dr. Kervorkian and tell him to bring his equipment."

"I'm sorry," he said, smiling. "They don't supply suicide doctors here."

"Nothing useful or practical," she said. "Just lousy

food. You should have seen lunch today. Smart as you are, even you wouldn't have been able to figure out what it was."

Surely, he thought angrily, it must be possible to provide decent food for 740 people. Jilian would be there in time for dinner. She had said she would bring Wellfleet oysters. He had bought two lobsters that were living sluggishly in the bottom of the refrigerator while a bottle of Moet Chandon cooled above them. Earlier that morning, he had called Cora.

"I don't want you to take this personally," he had told her, "but I think we should get a divorce."

She laughed. "Oh, you've met someone," she said. "You want to marry her?"

"Yes."

After a moment's silence, Cora said, "Who can blame you? All right. I'll talk to Jonas."

Jonas was their lawyer. That simple, he thought. Cora was such a civilized woman. He would always love her.

"When does your daughter come to visit?" he asked Ida.

"Molly will be here tomorrow. She'll bring me a container of matzoh ball soup and a turkey sandwich on rye with cole slaw and russian dressing. The soup will already be tepid, but I'll eat it for lunch, the sandwich for supper. An international sandwich." She laughed. "Turkey. Russia. On French bread if I could chew it. With a Greek salad."

"How often does Molly come?"

"She tries to come once a week, but sometimes she has to miss. She's bringing me a lawyer tomorrow. I want to write a living will. I don't want any extraordinary measures. I don't want any measures."

"Ida, Ida. How do you know you won't meet someone like Daisy again? She may even be here already. What about the new woman in your room?"

Ida sighed. "Not an unintelligent woman," she said.

"But so depressed that every time she begins to talk, she cries. I try to cheer her up, but it's no use, who am I? Her husband put her here, imagine. Eighteen years younger than her, but he says he's too sick to take care of her anymore."

Julian looked at his watch. He had been with her for an hour. He had to move on; there were others he had to visit.

"Molly will insist on a funeral," Ida said, "though I can't see the point of it. I don't mind if it's just music, though, no talking. What do you think, doctor? A Beethoven late quartet or a Strauss last song?"

"In one of his novels, I read it as a boy and it seemed the height of sophistication to me," Julian said, "Aldous Huxley had someone committing suicide to a Beethoven quartet, I think it was Opus 132...,"

"It was. The A-Minor."

"I'd have to hear the Strauss. I don't know the last songs." He got to his feet, reluctant to leave her.

"They're gorgeous," she said. "Get the Jessye Norman."

"Ida," he said, "why don't you give some thought to the discussion group? I think it might help a few people here. I think you'd be good for them."

"Take that man Bench with you, please," she said. "Otherwise he'll be standing there clicking like a parking meter all day."

CHAPTER TEN

He held her naked body firmly against his, wanting to feel the entire length of her. They had been making love for at least two hours. The oysters were chilling and the lobsters still lived, though barely, in the refrigerator. It was nearing midnight.

"Oh God how I missed you," he said into her hair. "Talking to Ida, poor thing, and most of my mind in bed with you."

"Who's Ida?"

"She's one of the people in the control group at the Home. Recovering from a stroke, but I can see that she's failing."

"You should be used to that, shouldn't you? Working with old people?"

"I like her. She's funny and smart. And, the thing is, well, I could probably save her."

"How?"

"By transfering her to Gerutopia. It would make all the difference."

"Then do it."

"How can I? She's one of the group that doesn't get the real medicine."

"One of the people who has to die to prove the effectiveness of the new drug? I always wonder about the ethics of that."

"I want to take you to see Harold's paintings tomorrow afternoon. If you think, as I do, that he's good, I'd like to contact some gallery people. See if anyone's interested in representing him. Maybe he could have a show."

"You're really interested in your people. They must love you," she said. "If he's good, I'll contact Spectrovsky for him. My gallery. They're one of the best."

"An architect is coming in the morning to see about the studio. You can tell him exactly how you want it."

"Oh Julian. Not yet."

"Why not?"

"We hardly know each other."

"That never seemed to matter before. Is your ardor cooling?" It had felt far from that until they had begun talking.

"You're a married man."

"I asked Cora for a divorce this morning."

"You did? What did she say?"

"She guessed why and then she said of course."

"No regrets?"

"I don't think so. We've been living apart for almost two years."

"It all sounds too amicable to me."

"There are no problems about custody or money. Why shouldn't it be amicable?"

"Jealousy. Passion. Possessiveness. Nostalgia."

"Cora isn't like that."

"You're crushing me."

"I can't help it. Is that better?"

"Only a little."

"Did you get rid of Perry?"

"Almost."

"What does that mean?"

"He's not as reasonable as Cora."

"He's a psychoanalyst, isn't he?"

"That doesn't mean he isn't crazy."

"Is he?"

"Yes."

"Will he try to kill me?"

"Maybe. He doesn't know about you yet."

"Then you didn't get very far with him. Did you sleep with him?"

She was silent. He shuddered and pushed her away. "How could you!" he said.

"I had to. He threatened to kill himself. I didn't enjoy a minute of it," she said, trying to console him. "In fact, I felt terrible."

"Did you really believe he'd kill himself?"

"Yes. No. It was a dreadful scene. I couldn't just let it go on and on, could I?"

"That's your way of ending scenes?" He sat up and swung his feet over the side of the bed, his back to her. "Fucking as punctuation? Period, end of scene."

"I know. It sounds shameful. But Perry and I have been ... what we've been ... for a long time. Fourteen years. Fucking him doesn't really feel like fucking."

"What does it feel like? Having a cup of tea? And what about love?" he shouted.

"Don't shout at me!"

"I must shout at you."

She got out of bed and wrapped herself in her robe. "I'll go home," she said.

"No you won't. You'll stay right here until this is resolved. And we will not resolve it sexually."

"This is our first quarrel."

"I'm furious."

"I'm starving."

"All right. We'll boil those bloody lobsters."

"Bloodless," she said, if only to have the last word.

CHAPTER ELEVEN

Emily, brooding on bodies, on her own body, surprised herself by beginning a poem. In high school and college she had written poetry, had even published some poems in a small quarterly connected to her college, but once out in the world where the serious business of her livelihood loomed, the muse had spread her wings and flown away.

She had been remembering how she had taught herself to roller skate, how impossible it had seemed at first, her feet flying out uncontrollably, her skinned and bloodied knees, and how gradually her body had mastered it and become free and graceful and completely in charge. The miracle of that transition. She could remember flying down the traffic-empty streets of her quiet neighborhood, sailing like a ballet dancer over manhole covers, whirling, twirling, finally to a stop. Her mind, her body. It had been the same with learning to ride a bicycle and, later, a horse. How her body had adapted and become one with skates, bike, horse, and moved with perfect thoughtless ease and synchronicity.

And though she remembered exactly the feeling of it, what it was like to do it, even how to do it, in memory that was more cellular, instinctual, than mental, she knew she could no more do any of these things now than she could fly to the moon. Was it loss of balance, reflexes, coordination, physical strength? It was probably all of these things, but chiefly it was that her bones were afraid. What her body had so generously given her, it had taken back

Sex, too. What a miracle it had been when it was right, the powerful, delicious, crescendo-ing eroticism, the eddying uncontrollable whirlpools of orgasm. She had not had sex, or even thought about it much in the past dozen years, but she could remember its physicality with total clarity. It did not excite her to remember, her body did not respond in any way to the memories; it was like looking at a sharply detailed photograph in an album, something that had once been so much a part of her but had separated from her, moving from subject to object.

My Body, she wrote.
My body
takes orders from me,
goes down stairs, comes up again,
gathers The Times outside the door
opens cat food and spoons it out
runs, swims, dances, does it all,
does it well, my faithful dog.

No good, a dog and cat in the same stanza. Her last cat, Gray, had died a couple of years before she had come here. She had missed him terribly but never thought to replace him, certain that a new cat would outlive her.

My body: (she continued)
Brings the news, the clear sharp day
The smell of spring, of crème brulee
Velvet of rose petals, colors of fall,
The crack of the bat meeting the ball,
Faces and voices I sometimes love.
The bell-like toll of the mourning dove.

The poem had begun to rhyme. She would have to make up her mind if it was going to be that kind of poem.

My body:
Makes demands: thirsts and lusts
hungering for sleep.
it needs fuel, I give it dim sum

it wants sex, I want love
our happy compromise: loving sex.

Food again, but dim sum? It was almost the only food she sometimes still craved, but the words on the page were jarring, alien and unexpected. It sounded silly. She used to love going to Chinatown for dim sum. But she need only mention it in this place and it would miraculously be granted, God knew how, a Sunday treat. She would try it. Speech, the magic wand.

This is my body:
changes my skin from smooth to sere,
creases me and thins my hair.
shrinks my bones and makes me less
a turncoat ghost completely in charge
old age makes it look like hell,
bringing discomfort, pain, and fear,
soon it will stop and bring me death.

She put it aside. She would tear it up later. An unpoetic poem. Even so, there was something satisfying about having written it. It had taken her barely an hour, and there it was. Instant gratification.

She looked across the room to where Harold's painting hung, and found that she was smiling.

***

What Blanche wants is for me to write the book, or a stunning proposal for the book, that will get us a contract with a publisher, and then we will split the proceeds fifty-fifty. I am, it seems, to bear the responsibility for selling it, and to give it my time on a purely speculative basis. She will contribute her life. There is no "I'll give you

X number of dollars up front, and a like amount when the book goes to contract. After that, you'll get X percent of the royalties." Blanche risks nothing. She may have had an interesting life, but Blanche is not a household name. In fact, she is known only to her friends and the people with whom she has worked. There is nothing in her name that would attract a publisher or an audience. As for her life, if I really wanted it, I could, with a few clever adjustments, steal it. I steal lives all the time.

I sigh. All that admiration for my books! It's clear that I'm not one who will ever get rich from writing.

"What do you think?" Blanche asks.

Why don't I tell her what I think? Bluntly. I don't. "I don't think I want to take the time from my own work right now," I say. It's not a lie, but I wonder how I'd have felt if she hadn't made an offer that was so easy to refuse, if I'd had to grapple a little with my soul. "If you haven't made other arrangements, we can talk about it when I finish this book I'm working on."

I may be imagining it, but she looks miffed. Does she feel that I have been wasting her time?

When I get back to my computer, I think of all the things in my life that have gone nowhere. I sink into a slough of despond. Is everyone's life so anti-climactic, or is there something wrong with me? The pattern in the rich weave of the fabric of my life is one of starts and stops, of knots and abruptly chewed off ends. It's not just Blanche who has brought on these depressing thoughts, it's Blanche, it's Alison and other false starts, it's all those who were once in my life and are no more, it's the two unfinished novels I gave so many years to, lost through death or attrition or carelessness.

But life isn't a novel, I remind myself, it's full of false starts, broken promises, dropped stitches, fumbles. One could play it safe, but what's the point of being safe?

I ended my last book with a counting of blessings, and I see now that this is a repetitive act, increasingly necessary with the passing of years. Because it sometimes helps, I count my blessings. I'm still alive. I never expected this many years. My kids are okay. I love them. I think they love me. A few friends are left. I can walk. I can see. With a little help, I can hear. I have no dentures, not a single false tooth. I still enjoy food, drink, sleep. I'd probably still enjoy sex if it were around. At this moment, my books remain in print. I still have a mother (!) who cares about me, whoever she thinks I am, and a brother who is my friend. I rarely have to worry about money; there seems, after all these years, to be enough to bring me the modest income I require. How many blessings is that?

I sit up a little straighter and turn on my computer. I love my computer, my quick, amazing computer into whose capacious memory I have put so much of what I couldn't possibly keep in my own.   The years may be making things more difficult for me, but technology has jumped into at least part of the breach; I now have this extra head. I push a switch and it lights up, bursts into color, hums softly (I *think* it hums softly) asks me what I want, where do I want to go? It takes me there. If I don't like something I thought yesterday, I can throw it out or fix it with the touch of a key. If I've had further thoughts in my attached head, I can add them seamlessly to yesterday's thoughts. If I'm stuck or depressed, I can say the hell with it, choose a deck of cards from a colorful assortment and play solitaire all afternoon, dragging the cards around with my mouse.

CHAPTER TWELVE

Julian had persuaded her to let the architect come; they needn't go ahead with anything until she was ready. It wouldn't be easy, but he would try not to push her in any way. He had almost, out of necessity, forgiven her for Perry.

"But let me remind you," he said, "that you were the one who brought up marriage in the first place. You proposed to me."

"I got carried away. It was all a dream. Also, I was drunk."

But dreams are in the mind, or just beneath it, and what had passed between them had been pure lust, more powerful than any she had felt before. She knew that lust was unreliable, but she had been immediately attracted to Julian in more than a purely physical way, and that had to be trusted, that chemistry, or whatever it was. Now she must spend some time finding out the why of that instant attraction, and whether it rested on anything that might last and grow.

Although the physical attraction was still all-pervasive, she told herself to proceed with caution, to evaluate Julian as objectively as she could under the circumstances, to wait until she could see him more clearly. She was too sophisticated to be swept off her feet. Would he continue to interest her, or might he come to bore her? He was so terribly *nice*. Did he have those qualities of mind and heart and character that she valued? Perry, whom she had never wanted to marry, had fallen far short, but he had amused her and been made to do. She had been in love before, but there had never been anyone she could imagine actually living with, at least not since her college years.

Physical love, she believed, in the arrogance born of her

beauty, one could always find. She needed a certain amount of intellectual companionship, but she didn't need it terribly.

She had always been serious about her work. She spent long hours in her studio painting, good music playing on the radio, the cats wandering in and out, rubbing affectionately against her ankles, and a day could easily pass in what sometimes seemed like minutes. If she stepped outside, there was the clean salt smell of the sea, and there was always a commotion of birdsong. Except in summer, the community she lived in was small and she knew most of its members, many of whom were artistic and interesting. She was perfectly happy with her life. What she felt for Julian, the intense desire to be with him, to be touched by him, to touch him, to know him, was exciting, but, at the same time, an imposition, an intrusion into her satisfactory, well-ordered life.

She had, nonetheless, allowed herself to be caught up in the architect's plans for "her" studio. Luckily, it could go on the north side of the house, there was not too much garden it would destroy. A couple of good trees would have to come down. Inside, there was a natural passage that would lead to the studio from the kitchen. It was convenient for the studio to be next to the kitchen since it would be easy to plumb it for water; she would want a sink there. They agreed on the height of the ceiling, the proportion of walls that would be glassed, the fluorescent lighting, the storage area, even the movable panels. Julian happily contributed suggestions, as excited as if this were as much for him as for her, as it was. There was no talk of money. For her, cost would certainly be an important consideration. She had no idea about Julian. They had never discussed money. That, presumably, lay in the future.

Now, driving up the winding road to Gerutopia, her hand on his knee and his free hand covering hers, she studied his profile. It was too perfect for her ever to be tempted to paint it, not that she was ever tempted to do portraits. It was morning and he was freshly shaved and showered and combed, and he smelled clean and fresh. Although he wasn't actively smiling, he was smiling. He was happy, proud to be showing her this place.

He drove slowly so that she would miss nothing. The grounds were immaculate and park-like, planted with flowering shrubs and towering trees of all kinds, oak, pine, tulip, copper beech, clusters of birch. The lilacs were just finishing, but their scent still hung in the air, and the rhododendrons and dogwood were in full bloom. There was a turn in the drive, and there, on the crest of the hill, sat Gerutopia, a Norman castle looking like something out of a fairy tale.

"Oh," she exclaimed, "it's beautiful! How did you ever find it?"

"It belonged, believe it or not, to a childless couple who, according to the servants, never had a guest, never entertained. He was a cottonseed oil baron, and when he died, she immediately put the house on the market. It happened to be exactly the right moment for us."

"Imagine being a baron of cottonseed oil. What happened to her, do you know?"

"She moved into Trump Towers and, according to the newspapers, goes everywhere and gives frequent, lavish parties."

"Marriages can be so silly," Jilian said.

Julian turned the car into a small parking area. He took Jilian's hand as they walked towards the building's entrance.

"There's Harold now," Julian said. Harold was expecting them. Julian waved, and Harold strode toward them. He wore a paint-smeared khaki work shirt and baggy pants, but he walked vigorously, his posture erect, the silver

thatch of hair falling across his brow. Jilian found it hard
to think of him as someone only a handful of years from his
ninth decade.

"I'm pleased to meet you," she said, shaking his hand.
"Julian has spoken so often of you, and so fondly."

"Julian speaks fondly of everyone," Harold said, smiling at Jilian. "He's the kindest man I know."

Kindness. If you had to name the three most desirable
qualities in a mate, Jilian thought, would kindness be one
of them? No, it would never occur to her. Intelligence,
humor, and that physical thing, looks, not necessarily beauty, but whatever it is that makes you smile and want to
touch someone. You would assume kindness if the intelligence was the right sort, but you wouldn't really think of it
unless it was noticeably lacking, or was so aggressive that
it constantly leapt to the forefront, calling attention to itself.
She wasn't particularly aware of it in Julian, but she knew
it was there.

He was holding her hand again as they entered the
building. Near the entry, a handsome woman sitting behind
a desk smiled at them. She looked at Jilian with interest.
Julian greeted her and introduced them.

"Portia is what would be called a manager in other
places," he said. "Here she's a hostess/mother/head
housekeeper/friend. She's been with us from the beginning."

"Everyone has," Portia said. "Nobody ever wants to
leave."

Julian was eager to show Jilian the spacious downstairs
rooms before they went up to see Harold's paintings.
Living room (not called the lounge, as it is in so many
institutions), with its comfortable sofas and armchairs, and
a card table at which four women were so ferociously
playing bridge that they never looked up. An elegant
dining room with a huge gothic stone fireplace, cupids

carved in it just below the mantle. A smaller television room and a library. All the rooms had fireplaces, Julian told her, that were in frequent use during the winter months.

"It's a marvelous place," Jilian said. "You're right. I can't see why anyone lucky enough to be here would ever die."

A small glass and brass elevator conveyed them to the third floor where most of Harold's paintings hung. She saw them the instant she stepped off the elevator, and her heart nearly stopped.

They were *her* paintings.

"B-but how did you get them?" she asked. "Is this some kind of joke?"

But no, they couldn't possibly have gotten them. She had just left them, yesterday, in Wellfleet, and the few paintings her gallery kept would never have been released except to a buyer.

They were staring at her. "What do you mean?" Julian asked. Seeing her pallor, he grasped her hand again. She was trembling.

"B-but," she stammered, her eyes darting wildly. "But."

Mystified, Julian and Harold were silent for several minutes. Then Harold, puzzled and a little frightened, said, "No one has ever been this affected by my paintings. Should I be flattered?"

She moved closer to the first painting and studied it, then the next and the next. They were nearly identical to paintings of her own, the brushwork, the colors, the concepts, everything. Now, up close, she could see differences, but these were so negligible as to be virtually nonexistent. And it was Harold's name painted modestly in the lower right-hand corners. She signed her own paintings, even more modestly, on the backs of her canvases.

"What is it, Jilian?" Julian asked.

She was unable to tell him, unable to tell Harold. It was

too frightening, too crazy. How could it be? What mysterious connection could there be between her and this
Harold? She stared at him.

"You don't like them, then," Harold said.

"Of course I like them!" she said sharply. "They're very
good."

"But?"

"Yes, Jilian," Julian said. "But? You look as if you'd
seen a ghost."

"I have seen a ghost. Harold, have you ever heard of
me? Before Julian, I mean."

"I don't think so," he said.

"Have you ever been to the Spectrovsky Gallery on
Spring Street?"

"No," he said. "I'm not much of a gallery-goer. I try to
limit my picture viewing to the museums. I'm one of those
people who can't look at more than a dozen paintings in a
day. I look at them slowly and if I try to look at too many I
get a headache."

"Julian," she said, "take me home. I don't feel well.
Please excuse us, Harold."

He tried to question her in the car, but her mouth was
firmly shut. She could not talk about it. Not yet. She was
still reeling from the shock, the ghostly horror of it. She
needed to think; what could it mean? She thought about
coincidence and the laws of chance. She thought about
those chimps sealed in the room in front of typewriters
who, in the course of time, if there was enough of it, would
write the complete works of Shakespeare. She didn't believe that, never had. The chimps would type the same
gibberish over and over and would never, by chance, by
accident, type out King Lear, not even a sentence of it. She
did believe in coincidence, however. But that she and an
old man in a retirement home, unknown to her, should have
the same intellectual approach to painting, the same ideas,

the same technique, the same impulses, all of which she had arrived at so gradually and painstakingly, was somehow too terrifying to attribute to mere coincidence.

"Well, just tell me," Julian said, "did you think his paintings were professional? Good?"

"Yes," she mumbled.

"Would you recommend him to your gallery?"

"No."

"Can you tell me why?"

"No. Please, Julian, not now. I think I'm going to vomit."

***

Last night I dreamed that Peter said he was going to shave off his moustache, but first he had to find a sweater. In the dream I found this hilarious. Dream humor. The workings of the human mind are so peculiar. Why would something be funny in a dream that isn't at all funny in waking life? Is it funny at some hidden level of the mind that has nothing to do with reason, that invents its own reasons? My subconscious mind often feels like a complete stranger to me, not someone I know or would choose to know, even though I can interpret much of the symbolism and metaphor it serves up. It has its own life, one that tends to vanish like smoke, and yet I know it is always there, lurking, waiting.

Dreams integrate my whole life. In them, I am ageless, neither young nor old, in some ways a much more solid entity, both subject and object, and yesterdays are like todays. I don't take medication or listen to my heartbeat. I don't think I've ever been lonely in my dreams. Or perhaps I'm always lonely in them.

And, except in sleep, less and less has been happening in my life. This was an event: on the bus, yesterday, I sat next to a smallish, middle-aged woman with neatly combed hair, wearing a print dress, red unchipped polish on her carefully rounded fingernails. She was writing in a notebook. What I saw before I forced myself not to go on looking said, "Thank you God that I did not throw up this morning. I am so grateful for the smallest improvements."

This morning, during breakfast, I found myself reading the wedding announcements in The Times. It's not because I wish I were married although sometimes I do, though never back in the old marriage. I like to study the pictures of the happy couples. The smiles on the older couples' faces, usually second marriages, are not as broad as those on the younger first-timers. Experience seems to have made them emotionally dimmer. Often, too, couples look alike. Opposites are supposed to attract, but the wedding pairs in The Times, and they may be a special breed, seem to have been attracted to each other narcissistically. If one is patrician, so, usually, is the other. If one looks studious, the other wears glasses. Rarely do you see a lean man with a stout woman. I am delighted to see an old couple this morning. They must be in their eighties and their smiles are small and wise, but there's no doubt that they're happy. I read about them. They are both credited with children and grandchildren and past careers, not particularly noteworthy. I am pleased for them, and pleased that they had a picture taken for the newspaper.

CHAPTER THIRTEEN

"Now that you're walking again..."

"If you call this walking."

"Back on your feet, then, ..."

"With more than a little support."

"Upright..."

"Well, almost."

"I'm forgetting what I wanted to say."

"Then it probably wasn't important."

"That's not necessarily true. Forgetting is an option of old age that has nothing to do with the quality or value of what is not remembered. I wish you didn't mind smoking."

"Everyone does now."

"I just had a very unsettling experience. Why don't you sit down and I'll tell you about it."

"Yes, sitting down sounds like a terrific idea." She glanced at her watch. "I've been standing for almost ten minutes. There, that's much better."

"Would you like your lap robe?"

"Please."

He brought it to her and draped it across her lap, then sat back down in the armchair facing her.

"Julian brought his new woman friend, who is a painter, to see my work," he began.

"The one he's fallen in love with. What's she like?"

"How do you know he's fallen in love? Did he tell you that?"

"No, but haven't you seen how changed he is? Go on."

"I think he thought she could tell him whether I'm worth finding a gallery to represent me."

"That was generous of him. What did she say?"

"Well, she ... she went completely to pieces."

"What do you mean?"

"She turned pale. She began to tremble. She couldn't speak. She was terribly agitated."

"How odd. What was she like?"

"How could I tell? Until she saw my pictures she seemed sane enough, and very attractive."

"Your paintings reminded her of something? Touched some kind of nerve?"

"Obviously. But what? Do you see anything startling in my work?"

"Not startling, no. Provocative, maybe, but nothing so extreme."

"They left abruptly. I suppose I'll hear more about it from Julian, though he was as much in the dark as I."

She watched his hand stray to the shirt pocket where his cigarettes were, then reluctantly fall away.

"Ah," he said, "now I remember what it was."

"What what was?"

"That I started to say and forgot. Emily, I think you and I should get married."

"Married! Did you say married?"

"Yes."

"Whatever for?"

"So that we can live together."

"We do live together."

"I know. But no more together than anyone else here."

"I don't know you well enough to live any more together than we already do. Do you mean share a room and a bed and a bathroom?"

"Yes."

"Why? What for? Sex?"

"I don't know. Possibly."

"Could you?"

"I don't know. Possibly."

"Well, I couldn't!" She considered for a moment. If sex was about anything, it was about bodies. With distaste, she thought again about her body. It was a while since it had been a body meant for sex. You can't have sex when you dislike your body. The longer she lived, she found, the less she demanded of her body, even as it increasingly imposed itself onto her consciousness. To perform some simple tasks and not to cause her too much discomfort was about all she could ask of it, especially since her fall. The time when she unthinkingly took her body for granted was long past; it was constantly reminding her by its limitations and demands, by its little and sometimes not so little aches and pains, by its almost daily theft of the tattered remnants of her physical beauty, by the length of time it took her to get out of bed in the morning, by the number of pills that had to be swallowed to keep this thing down and that thing up and those things at bay, by all of these and more, she was reminded that her body was a growing monster that would soon devour her spirit and mind and will and, finally, her life. Her friend, her ally, had become her enemy in a war she couldn't win.

"I wouldn't want it." she said, wondering how Harold felt about his own body. "It's been a while since I've even thought about it."

"Well, think about it."

"I just thought about it. It's not very interesting. Anyhow, sex is no reason to get married."

"No, it's more than that. I think it's because I'm possessive. I like to think that what I love belongs to me."

"Belongs!" she snorted, ignoring the "love." "What an old-fashioned notion. I'm surprised at you, Harold. Anyhow, nobody is going to snatch me away."

"You never know."

She laughed.

"And it's not sex, really; it's intimacy. And physical affection."

What was the intimacy of a couple close to death, a

couple who have not shared their lives and habits of being, she wondered, especially in a place like this where they didn't need each other to accompany them to the doctor, to help with anything, really, or to give support. They had all that. What was left? Waking in the morning to hear him clear the accumulated phlegm from his throat? Listening to each other's snores? Finding him dead on the bathroom floor? Or worse, holding his hand when he lay, groaning, dying? Or vice versa? She didn't give a hoot about vice versa.

"Having someone to talk to in the middle of the night when I can't sleep," he said, as if she had been talking aloud. "Having someone to really talk to."

"When we know each other a little longer, we'll be able to really talk to each other as we are."

"Being touched. I miss being touched."

"There's a very good masseuse here. As you know."

"And I want to have our picture taken together to go with the announcement of our wedding in The Times."

"I don't believe this!" she said, shaking her head. "You're pulling my leg."

"No. I'm serious."

She could see that he was serious.

***

"I hate it," my mother says. We have just moved her into Giverney, the retirement village.

"What's to hate?" I ask. "It's lovely. I don't think I like that gold armchair there. It's too big."

"It can go in the bedroom."

"No. Get rid of it. You don't need it."

"They shouldn't be allowed to uproot people at our age. It's cruel. Whoever thought I'd end up in a place called Giverney?" She pronounces it their way. It sounds terrible.

Once again I correct her, hoping that the French pronunciation will make the place more acceptable to her.

"It's a ghetto for old ladies. Fourteen men in the whole place."

"I didn't know you were looking for a man."

"Are you crazy? Did you see them? Did you see those faces at lunch, not just the men but all of them?"

"Lunch was pretty good," I say. "Better than you'd make for yourself."

"Yes, but did you see those faces?"

"Of course I saw them," I say. They looked no different to me than the faces in the lobby of the building she just left. "What was wrong with them?"

"They're the faces of . . . strangers," she says. "All of them old. It smelled like an institution."

"It did not!" I say. "You just don't know anyone here yet.

"I know Selma Schwartz. I can't stand her."

"Well, Flora will be here next week, and you'll make new friends. You've already been asked to a Wednesday bridge game. And you can take up painting again."

Years ago, my mother "took up" painting for a year or two. She had a teacher who put items on a table, fruit, candlesticks, jugs, and she made paintings of them. Still lifes. Lives? She was pretty good at it, in a primitive way, and would have gone on to be better if she had stuck with it, but it took too much time away from cards. At least I think that was why she gave it up. She never said.

"Maybe I'll get used to it," she sighed. "I guess I have to give it a little time."

"And you still have Majesta every morning so you aren't dependent on the Giverney van."

She is looking out the window at Monet's green bridge. There are, indeed, water lilies. The gardener knew what he was doing.

"It is pretty," she concedes. "I don't think I'll miss the ocean too much. This view is cosier, more suitable for old people."

"And you'll feel safer here," I say. "With all these people paying attention to you. And I'll feel better knowing you're here."

"I'm glad someone will feel better," she says.

CHAPTER FOURTEEN

"This is my daughter Molly," Ida said.

Julian reached to shake her hand. "I'm glad you're here," he said, pulling up a chair so that they formed a close triangle, their knees nearly touching. "There's something I want to discuss with both of you. If Ida is agreeable, I'd like your permission to transfer her to another home."

"Another home? Where?"

"It's in Westchester, about half an hour from here."

"But why?" Molly asked. "Has she been making trouble here?"

Julian laughed. "No, of course not," he said. "I think she'll be happier in the other place."

"I'd be happier any other place than here," Ida said. "Even in a coffin."

"Don't talk like that, Mama!"

"I have the papers with me. If you'll both sign them..."

Molly reached for the papers and examined them. "Gerutopia?" she said. "I never heard of it. What is it?"

"It's a private institution. Small. Very comfortable. And the food is good." He smiled at Ida. "You can tell what you're eating."

"Is it expensive?" Molly asked. "We'd have to consult my husband."

"It's not expensive. It's free."

"Free? Why? Why is it free?"

"It's funded by several government agencies and by a private foundation."

"For what purpose? Do you experiment on the inmates?"

"In a way, yes." We kill them with kindness, he almost said. "We try to keep them happy."

"That's an experiment?" Ida asked. "Happiness?"

He did not say that she was already part of the experiment. What was he doing? They had had a death, their first. The empty room cried out to be filled. But could he get away with putting Ida in it, Emily's unfortunate counterpart? Was he damaging the whole program? Obviously, he was never meant to be a scientist.

"I'm opposed," Mollie said. "I wouldn't be able to get there easily."

"Amtrak," Julian said. "A short ride."

"And I don't trust the sound of it."

"Sounds super duper to me," Ida said.

"We could go and have a look at it," Julian suggested, "and then you can decide."

"Furthermore, she seems fine here."

"I'm not fine here. What do you know?" She squeezed her rubber doll in Molly's face as hard as she could, causing its eyes to bug and its tongue to pop out. "As long as I'm out of the way, that's all you care about."

"Mama that's not true," Molly said.

"So why then am I here in this warehouse, God's waiting room?"

"Oh, Mama," Molly said, tears filling her eyes. "We've been over this so many times."

"Never to my satisfaction," Ida said sternly. She knew Molly's tears were caused not by sorrow but by guilt. She was pitiless.

"Why does she have to sign?" she asked Julian. "Can't I sign myself? I'm still in my right mind, am I not?"

"Of course. Yes, you can sign yourself. And I can sign you. I just thought, since she's your next of kin, that Molly should approve."

"All right," Molly sighed. "We'll go have a look at it. We'll talk to some of the people there. We'll see."

"Never mind looking and talking and seeing." Ida said. "Call the nurse, pack my bag, let's go."

***

Back in Florida. It's my third time down this winter. I feel like a yo-yo in the hands of a hyperactive child. She is in Hollywood Memorial hospital on Johnson Avenue, she told me on the phone late yesterday, having blacked out and fallen twice. She had been having dizzy spells since the move.

Although it's the height of the season, I manage to get an emergency flight and to rent a car at the airport, and when I walk through the open doorway into my mother's room, her face lights up. She is always so incandescently glad to see me. Ten minutes later she will disapprove of something about me, my hair, what I'm wearing, something to do with my appearance. She has always done this, yet she is always so nakedly happy at my being there. It's a mystery to me who I really am in her eyes. If she stopped to think about it, it would be a mystery to her, too.

At this point in my life, I don't think I mean as much to anyone else as I do to her. I'll miss this when she dies. I wonder if I'll mourn more for myself, for the end of myself-in-her, than I will mourn for her. I suppose that's always part of the grief at the loss of someone close. We're no longer who we were to that particular person. That part of us also dies.

"It's my darling daughter," she says, beaming, spreading her arms to embrace me. I lean to kiss her and, weakly, she hugs me.

"You look okay," I tell her, standing back. She does. Even without the usual make-up, her color is good and her hair is combed.

"They gave me a pacemaker," she says, showing me the bandage just beneath her left shoulder.

"My God, when?"

"In the middle of the night. It was an emergency, My pulse was down to thirty." She sounds immensely cheerful. "Thank God Majesta was there. Dr. Yakhandler says we caught it just in time. He saved my life, or so I hope."

"Dr.who?"

"Yakhandler. That's his actual name." She laughs. "Sounds like a veterinarian, doesn't he?" A nurse comes in to take her pulse, her blood pressure. "They do this every ten minutes," my mother says.

"Every hour," the nurse says, smiling at me.

"This is my daughter," my mother says. "Rachel, why don't you freshen up, comb your hair? You look as though you've been up all night."

My mother is indestructible. After two days, satisfied that the pacemaker is working properly, they release her and I drive her home. She seems a little more feeble than when I was down the last time, but determined. Florida is a good place to be old, I decide. They send a registered nurse every day to check her vital signs. They send a nurse's aide to bathe her and to do whatever she can't do for herself, though Majesta is there. They send a social worker to talk to her, to tell her they have a shopping service if she needs it, and a van that will take her to the doctor, or anywhere else she needs to go, and she gives my mother telephone numbers for all their services. Then she asks her if she has enough money and my mother assures her that she does. The Giverney nurse pops in and out to see how she's doing. A young man appears to tell her that if she is deaf or blind, the state will supply her with a special telephone that has Braille keys and volume and clarity control. Free. She signs the proper forms for it, though she is clearly neither deaf nor blind. "For you," she tells me when the man is gone, and when, after a few days, anxious to get home to see what my folks, Emily and Harold and the rest of the gang are up to, and assured that my mother is being more than well taken care of, I, who love gadgets, depart with her telephone.

CHAPTER FIFTEEN

"Do you mind me watching you work?" Jilian asked, sitting on a straight-backed wooden chair, the only one in the studio except for the stool near his easel.

"No," Harold said, though he did.

"Will it interfere with your concentration if I ask you some more questions?"

"No." Of course it would. What did she want of him? Well, he supposed he would find out soon enough. He was mixing a difficult shade of yellow on his palette. Not exactly yellow, golden brownish, a nasty color. Why nasty? The color of a newborn's earliest stool, the purest shit imaginable made only of mother's milk. Soft, curd-like stool, by-product of breasts he loved with sexual reverence. What sort of wastes could there be in mother's milk, he used to wonder, when he sometimes changed the twins' diapers. Dorothea and Beatrice they had named them, romantically, but of course the minute they started school they became Dot and Bea. It was only to be expected. Like their mother, they had died young, in their forties, ironically, cruelly, of breast cancer. Was it passed to them in that mother's milk? Was that why he was looking for that particular shade? Was this painting going to be about breasts? The death of his daughters? The passivity of his own genes and his inability to save them? His helplessness and fury? They had been dead long enough so that he no longer thought of them daily. Julian Keller had twin daughters, too, but Harold had never mentioned his own in their conversations.

There, that looked exactly right. How did he remember the color so well after sixty-something years?

"Yes," Jilian said, watching his brush on the canvas. "That's the right color."

Earlier, he thought he'd heard her say, "I would have done, no, I did precisely that." It was eerie. She was behaving so peculiarly. She had been following him around all day, staring at him, asking questions. What could she be looking for? He was not unaccustomed to having women fall in love with him, but surely he was beyond that now. And Jilian was supposed to be in love with Julian, wasn't she?

"Where did your forebears come from?" he heard her ask, her voice raised so that he knew she was repeating a question she had already asked, perhaps more than once. His back was to her since his easel was up against a wall. He had been discovering that more and more he needed to be facing the person who was speaking to him. The throaty timbre of Emily's voice was very congenial to his newly evolving hearing deficiency. This woman's voice, however, was a little breathy. He turned the easel around so that the back of the canvas was toward her, killing two birds at once: she would now not be able to comment on every stroke of his brush, which she seemed to be awaiting intently and, if she did, he would be able to hear her.

"Sorry," he said. "I misunderstood. I was about to tell you that I don't keep bears, certainly not four of them."

Jilian groaned. She did not appreciate puns, especially obvious ones. "Denmark," he said. Danes, he thought. Great Danes is what we kept. Why was he being so silly? He was nervous, having her stare at him, though it was better than having her watch every daub of his brush, as she had been doing. She was an extremely attractive woman, her eyes so bright and luminous, undimmed by encroaching cataracts and the other optical insults of age.

"Both sides?"

"I think there may have been a little bit of Sweden in there somewhere."

"No one from Great Britain? Wales?"

"Not that I know of," he said, shaking his head. "Is that where your origins were?"

"Yes."

"Are you trying to find out if we're related?" he asked. "What is it, Jilian?"

"I'm trying to find some common thread. There must be one."

"We both paint," he said.

"It's more than that. It has to be."

"Why, Jilian?" He peered around the canvas to look at her face. She had been pale. Now her face reddened.

"I suppose I'll have to tell you this sooner or later."

"Tell me what, Jilian?" he asked after a long silence.

She took a deep breath. "You've been painting my pictures," she said. "Somehow I've gotten into your head."

"What do you mean?" he asked, his hand pausing en route to the canvas.

"Just that. When you see my paintings you'll be as shaken as I am. The one you're doing now? I painted it last January."

He put the brush down and stared at her. "But that's preposterous," he said. She was crazy, possibly paranoid. "I've never seen your paintings. And my painting is almost entirely intuitive. It's very subjective and personal. I don't even know yet what this painting is going to be."

"I do," she said faintly. "Since I've already painted it."

He walked the few steps to where she sat and took one of her hands in his. It was ice cold.

"Are you sure you're not imagining this, Jilian?" he asked in his gentlest voice. Still, he sounded like a lawyer. Or a doctor. Without asking her if she minded, he lit one of his cigarillos.

"Of course I'm not imagining it," she said. "Why would I want to imagine anything so... so... daunting?"

For a moment, he almost believed her. But it was too

crazy, too irrational. He was a rational man. For most of his life he had practiced law. Although it sometimes seemed otherwise, there were no fantasies in law.

"Well, how do you account for it?" he asked, not knowing what to say next.

"I can't account for it," she said impatiently. "That's why I'm following you around so stupidly, asking you all these ridiculous, unavailing questions." She began to cry.

"There, there," he said, patting her hand, wishing Julian would appear and take her away.

"I'm sorry," she said after a minute or two. She blew her nose. "This is too idiotic."

"There is obviously," he said, "no connection at all between us except that we both paint and that your meeting Julian has brought you to this place where old age has deposited me."

"I wish I had never met him," she wailed. "I wish I had never known anything at all about you."

How did she imagine he felt?

"Would you like to come with me to my gallery? To see my... your... our paintings there?"

No, he would rather not. But suppose it were true and not a wild figment of her insane imagination?

"Yes," he said. "We'd better do that."

Through the open doorway, a strange woman in a wheelchair appeared, Julian behind, pushing the chair.

"Jilian!" he said. "What are you doing here?"

"I... I came to see Harold," she said. "To... to watch him paint." It was nice of her to be interested in Harold's work, but Julian was perplexed. She had been behaving so oddly since yesterday's meeting with Harold. He felt a stab of fear.

"This is Ida Tarkovsky," he said, collecting himself. "Our newest member. I've been showing her around the place. Ida, this is my friend Jilian, who's visiting. And this is Harold Johanson."

She beamed at them, and Harold came and shook her hand. "Welcome," he said. "I think you'll be very happy here."

"Never mind will be. I'm already very happy here," she said. "And I haven't even eaten yet."

Both men laughed, but Jilian was chewing her lip, Julian saw, looking distracted, interrupted.

"The food," Harold said, "is outstanding. I can't imagine that they could possibly pay the cook as much as she's worth."

"We're very lucky," Julian said.

"All these paintings on the walls," Ida said. "You painted them?"

"Yes," Harold said. "I... think so."

"They're beautiful."

"They're not meant to be beautiful," he said, not unkindly.

"Then you fell on beauty in spite of yourself," Ida said. "And they're mysterious, also. Maybe some day you'll let me choose one for my room."

"Happily. Thank you."

"Well, we must be moving on," Julian said. "I want to help Ida settle in." He turned the wheelchair towards the door.

"Oh, Julian," Jilian said. "Is it all right if I take Harold off for the afternoon?"

"You don't have to ask me," he said testily. "Harold is free to come and go at any time as long as he signs out."

"I'll have him back in time for dinner," she said.

There were only three of her paintings at the gallery, but they were, as she'd predicted, enough to cause his heart to start pounding. He was forced to sit down, to take deep, measured breaths.

One of the pictures he had not yet painted, and now

never would, but the two others he had done not six months ago. It was uncanny.

He knew immediately that she had ruined his life, what remained of it, that he wanted to kill her. It was clear that one of them had to go. But if she were dead, could he go on painting her unpainted pictures, or would he dry up and die also? Possibly the latter. She had been painting first; the muse, the afflatus must be hers, somehow, God knew how, passed to him at second hand, and from a distance. No matter how unconsciously, he was nothing but a reproducer, a sort of ethereal copy machine. She was the transmitter and he a receiver, something in his brain tuned just so to her channel, a vessel like a radio or television set through which her messages could pass.

He didn't believe in this rot. He had never been drawn to science fiction or movies, killer cucumbers and all that. But how account for this? Could it be coincidence? That seemed as unlikely as any other explanation, though there was even a word that he couldn't remember for the not uncommon phenomenon of two scientists or inventors, completely independent and unaware of each other, making the same discovery at the same time. What was that word? He hated losing words, as he more and more did. Two or three days from now it would pop into his head as if he had a search function going in the computer that was his unconscious brain.

But there was more than coincidence to that kind of phenomenon. There was a logic. There was a problem that needed solving and there were steps within that particular discipline to which both scientists, and many others, had been led. There was a flow, a common river they were traveling. It was bound to happen. This was different. This would have to be a much blinder coincidence.

"I may not be the only one," he said. "There may be others. Have you thought of that?"

"I think you must be the only one," she said.

He shivered and lit a cigarillo, drawing deeply at it. Smoke issued from his nose, as from a dragon's, in two streams. He could not know how angry he looked.

The young woman in charge of the gallery appeared and said, "I'm sorry. We don't permit smoking." She handed him an ashtray. Fiercely, he stabbed out the cigarillo. Was there no place an old man could go with his lifetime habits? Did they really expect him to give up smoking at his age? And not for his health, but for theirs? How selfish they were. He almost felt like crying. He did feel like crying. His only honorable recourse was to destroy his paintings. And then what? What was he going to do with his passion, this passion he was so thankful to have been allowed to let bloom at a time when his life would otherwise have been so empty.

"So you see," Jilian said softly, "you've either got to give up painting or find a way to break free of me."

His anger subsided. How was he to do that? He had only just learned that he was her thing, her pawn, this stranger he'd never seen before in his long life. And it was only a few hours since she had learned that she had one, a pawn, a robot, a clone. Each had frightened the other nearly to death.

"Oh, God," he groaned. His desolation felt bottomless.
"Yes, I know."

"I would have to intellectualize what I do," he said slowly. "It would no longer be spontaneous, free. It would lose its mystery. I would lose the suspense of it. What I love about painting is its unconsciousness, the way it seems to flow out of this deep, wonderful place in me that I never knew was there."

And now, who knew, might not be.

"Yes," she said, though she was schooled and much more aware of what she was doing.

"All of them?" he asked. She had seen more than thirty of his paintings. "Are they all yours?"

"Yes. No, the one in that woman's room. Emily? It's in the style, but I don't remember that one."

He had thought of Emily almost the whole time he'd painted it. He had known he was going to give it to her. He felt a little more hopeful.

Still, he looked pitiful. For the first time, she felt sorry for him. She had robbed him of what was most important to him. She put her hand on his.

"Since this has all happened," she said, "when we were miles apart and totally unaware of each other, maybe the answer would be for us to live together for a while, to really get to know each other as intimately as possible."

He stared at her. Live with her? Intimately? What did she mean by intimately? He had just proposed to Emily. He loved Emily. But he knew, now, that he was bound to this young woman, this Jilian, as if by invisible, unbreakable chains. Maybe she was right. Maybe familiarity would breed a little distance, if not contempt.

"What about Julian?" he asked.

She hadn't thought of Julian. "I'll have to explain it to him. He'll understand. He's very good at understanding."

"I just don't know," Harold moaned. "I need time to think. This is all so sudden."

***

Where does all this come from? What in my life? This business of creativity, of making things out of thin air. But is it thin air? We know the air is charged with electricity, with air waves, with other voices, the voices of multitudes. We know our minds are multi-layered, that they contain in deep or shallow levels, not only clear and present thoughts and memories, but scraps of so many things read, seen, heard and then consigned to some long, subterranean tunnel, forgotten or, we think, irretrievable. Are we ever really making something new?

CHAPTER SIXTEEN

"I knew from the minute I laid eyes on you," Ida told Emily, "that we would be simpatico." Ida was beaming, her eyes sparkling. At Ida's request, Molly had brought her some new clothing, and she was wearing a skirt and an apricot-colored silk blouse.

"Not those old lady things, those cotton prints with the little lace collars," Ida had commanded. "Stylish. Like you would buy for yourself."

"What do you need them for? "Molly asked. Ida had more than enough clothes. She had seen to that, at least.

"I'm too shabby."

"Shabby! You never thought so before."

"I never thought about it before."

Ida had been at Gerutopia less than a week, but she and Emily were already like old friends, completely at ease with one another. Emily had admired Ida's outfit and told her that she looked ten years younger.

"It's this place," Ida said. "I don't think I've ever been so happy, even in the days when I was happy. It doesn't seem fair when so many people are so miserable."

"You'll get used to it," Emily said.

"To happiness? You mean it will begin to seem ordinary and then I won't be happy? God forbid!"

"You'll stop being so aware of it," Emily said. "You'll have other things to think about."

"I already have other things to think about. Iran, Afghanistan, Darfur. The death of children." She had the New York Times every morning with her breakfast, and the Gerutopia library subscribed to Time, Newsweek, The Nation, Harper, The New Yorker, even some literary quarterlies. Plus all the good books in the library. Where did she find the time to sit here talking to Emily about happiness?

"But for myself I'm still happy. It's separate compartments," she said. "If you had come from where I was. It's like you were in hell and an angel came and said, sorry, we made a mistake, and took you to heaven. Talk about from one extreme to another!"

"It was so bad?"

"It was from another century, medieval maybe. They worked hard, the staff, but even so, the smell alone. But the saddest part, it was the people there who made it so terrible. They had no lives. So much misery concentrated in one place. I think that was the smell."

Emily loved the way she talked. The lingering trace of a Yiddish accent, the lack of education, the sensitivity and humor and intelligence.

"When I first felt it, I didn't know what it was, this strange new feeling. And then a light went on. It's happiness, I said. I'm happy." Emily laughed. "It's like I was on some kind of new drug. Prozac, maybe. Tell me, what are all those school notebooks? Are you taking a course?"

"I'm writing my memoirs."

"You're such a good writer! I used to read you religiously. I missed you when you stopped. I always liked to cook but you know how it becomes second nature, you stop thinking about it? But not after reading you."

"Thank you."

"Making dinner became ... interesting. "

There was a light knock on the open door, then Julian strode in.

"Ah, here's my angel," Ida said. "My deliverer."

"Good morning, ladies. How are you? What a pretty blouse, Ida." Both women were seated, Ida in her wheelchair but with her new walker beside her, Emily with her cane across her lap. "How's the walking coming? Are you making progress? Let me see."

The two women obediently struggled to their feet. It was a little easier for Emily, who was making real progress, but Ida leaned heavily on her walker. Since the stroke, she had not been encouraged to walk until she came to Gerutopia. Nor had she seen much reason to try. It was painfully difficult, but now, just being in an almost upright position made the world and her relationship to it different. She was no longer a prisoner. She felt confidence seeping back.

The women shuffled across the room, Emily ahead, Ida pushing the walker, a few steps behind, dragging her bad leg.

"Twinkletoes we're not," Ida said.

"It's wonderful seeing you both on your feet," Julian said.

When they were seated again, Julian pulled up a chair and said, "I'm glad you and Emily are friends. I'm going to tell you something in strictest confidence."

"I wouldn't breathe a word," Ida said.

"As in all controlled experiments," Julian began, "each of you here in Gerutopia has, or had, some of them have died, a counterpart in another, ordinary old age home."

"Ah!" Ida said, "Like the Tremont Home for the Golden Oldies."

"Yes, like Tremont," Julian said.

"Don't tell me," Ida shouted, "that I was Emily's, what did you call it, counterpoint? I knew it! I knew we had something unusual in common."

Julian smiled at her, his bright pupil. "Yes," he said.

"So you ruined the experiment," Emily said.

"Just this one part of it," Julian admitted. "I've chosen someone else there to replace Ida."

"Why, Dr. Keller? Why did you do it?"

"I thought it would be an even more interesting experiment," he lied, or half-lied, or rationalized, "to see how you responded to this place. I felt you would soon give up and die there."

If Ida had died there, and Emily gone on living, it would have been another indication of the viability of the project.

"How do you know you won't grow just as fond of Ida's replacement?" Emily asked. How sharp she was, Julian thought. He really did love her. She was a woman who would never have bored him. Would Jilian ever bore him? Where could she have gone off to with Harold that day?

"For one thing, there are no more empty beds here," Julian said. "I suppose it's always a risk though, isn't it, getting attached to those who are meant to be your statistics."

"Only for those who are in the business of collecting statistics," Emily said.

"You make it sound so cold," Julian said.

"It is cold."

Jealousy was new to Julian. He had never been jealous of Cora. But he had reason to mistrust Jilian. Perry. Still, with Harold it could only have to do with painting, his painting. But why had she been so upset by Harold, so unable to discuss whatever it was with Julian?

"It is cold, naturally" Emily said, "because it's so completely impersonal, though obviously not with you. I suspect you're a man whose feelings often get in the way."

"In the way of what?" Julian asked, interested.

"Reason. Though I'm very glad it got in the way and brought us Ida."

"For my part," Ida said, "I'm glad Dr. Keller is a man of feeling. The world could use a few more like him."

He had never thought one way or another about himself as a man of feeling until Jilian had so overwhelmed him. As promised, she had delivered Harold back in the late afternoon, but both of them had seemed unusually subdued, dejected. Harold still did. Jilian would be arriving early this evening, after only a few days' absence. He had missed her from the moment she left, but he had found himself feeling more guarded with her, less free. There was so much in her life he didn't know.

Julian left the women and went next to the painting studio where Harold would normally be at this hour, but it was empty. Julian glanced at the unfinished painting on the easel. There wasn't much on the canvas and what was there looked forlorn, abandoned. He found Harold in his room smoking.

"Can I talk to you, Harold," Julian asked, "or would you rather I go away?"

"No, no, come in."

"I thought I'd find you painting..."

"No, I've stopped," he said, gloomily. "I've reached a ... an impasse."

"You'll overcome it, I'm sure."

"I... I guess I'm just burned out."

"Harold, are you feeling all right? Do you think you should see the doctor?"

"No. I'm all right.

"But..."

"Why don't you sit down, Julian? You're hovering. There, that's better. I have something to tell you."

"Yes?"

"I'm going to have to leave."

"Leave Gerutopia?" Julian said, appalled. Harold nodded. "But you can't, Harold. Well, of course, you can, but you shouldn't."

"I know I signed an agreement, and I'm sorry. It may be only temporary, a month or two. Maybe even less. Couldn't we call it a leave of absence? Could you keep my room for me?"

"Would you care to tell me why you're leaving, where you'll be going?"

Harold stabbed out his cigarillo and sighed. "I'll be going to Wellfleet," he said. "Jilian has asked me to stay there with her, to work with her. I want to go there to try to paint, to see if I can get over whatever this is in a different setting. I'm sorry, Julian."

Julian, stunned, was speechless.

"It's not what you think, Julian," Harold said. "At least I don't think it's what you think, since I don't know what you're thinking."

"What am I to think?"

"I'm an old man, Julian." These were words he had never uttered before. He had never really thought of himself as an old man until now. Odd to feel that way when he was going off to live with a beautiful, intelligent, gifted young woman.

"But why do you think that you'll be better able to paint there? Is Jilian going to tutor you?"

"Yes, in a way. Oh, it's such a complicated thing, Julian. Perhaps Jilian will explain it better." Slowly, he got to his feet. "I've got to go see Emily now. Will you excuse me?"

Emily's door was ajar. She was writing in one of her copybooks.

"Am I interrupting you?" Harold nonetheless asked. She looked up at him, slowly re-focusing from the far place she had been. She had gone back to her eleventh year. She had just learned that her father was not dead, as she had believed, but was living in the south of France with a man. Oh, a man, she had thought at the time, then that's all right.

It was amazing to her that she could recall in such detail events and feelings from so long ago, almost seventy years, when most of last week was a virtual blank, when words she had used all her life often eluded her for hours at a time. The mysterious brain.

Reluctantly, she closed the copybook over the pen she

was using, marking her place.

"Come in, Harold."

"I'm sorry to disturb you," he said, "but it's important. I'm leaving, you see."

"Leaving?" she asked, dismayed.

"Yes, leaving Gerutopia. On Monday. This is so embarrassing," he said. His eyes filled with tears. "Since I just asked you to marry me. And meant it. And still do mean it. I love you, Emily..."

"Why don't you tell me about it. Has someone from your previous life come to claim you?"

"No, no, it's to do with my painting... It's Jilian. I'm going back to Wellfleet with her for a little while."

"Oh, has she taken an interest in your painting? Does she feel you need lessons from her?"

"On the contrary. Listen, Emily, I want to tell you about it but you must promise not to laugh at me. It's too seriously true."

"I'll try not even to smile."

"If Jilian and I were to have a joint show, her paintings, say, on one wall and mine opposite, you would think one wall was simply a mirror. Except that the canvasses wouldn't be transposed, as in a mirror."

"What do you mean?"

"I mean that without ever having seen Jilian before, or even heard of her, or seen any of her paintings, every one of my paintings is an almost exact replica of one of hers. Except for this one, the one I painted for you. I don't know what it means, but I've been painting her pictures and this is unbearably disturbing to both of us."

Emily was struck dumb.

"Exactly!" Harold said.

"I can't believe you could have imagined this, or made it up. You're a sensible man."

"Thank you, Emily. It's easily proven. All one has to

do is see her work. And mine."

"So that's why she reacted the way she did when she saw your paintings. How do you know she hasn't been painting your paintings?"

"Oh, hers predate mine, sometimes by years."

"So you've been ... bewitched."

"Do you think Jilian is a witch?"

"I don't believe in witches, do you?"

"No, but I don't believe in this, either."

"Besides, in all the stories, witches act with intent."

"Yes. What's happened between us has been entirely unconscious on both sides."

"Still, you have been bewitched."

"Jilian believes, or hopes, that if we get to know each other, and paint side by side in the same studio, we may be able to exorcize the... I don't know what to call it."

"Spell? Bond?"

"The connection, whatever it is. She's as appalled by this as I am. Except it's worse for me, feeling this flow of inspiration and energy that doesn't come from me. What have I been doing these past few years? And, even more important, why?" He looked at his gnarled hands, spreading them out before him. "Whose hands are these?" His eyes filled with tears again. Moved, she leaned forward and covered one of his hands with hers.

"Poor Harold," she said. "I think Jilian is right. You must go with her. Yes, you must certainly go."

***

When Jilian came through the door, she dropped her suitcase, threw her arms around him and murmured "Darling," then raced to the bathroom. It was her usual arrival, and usually it was followed by their going straight to bed.

"Why did you come?" he asked, when she emerged from the bathroom. His voice, which he had hoped would sound normal, was bitter.

"What do you mean? Weren't you expecting me?"

"You came only to fetch Harold, didn't you?"

"No," she said. She took his hand and led him out of the vestibule into the living room. "It's been a long drive. Can't we sit down and have a drink?"

He fetched the pitcher of martinis from the refrigerator.

"Now," she said, when they and their drinks were seated. "It's true that I'll be taking Harold back with me on Monday. Did he also tell you why?"

"No."

"But that's not the only reason I'm here. I came to see you, Julian, to be with you, to talk, to make love. I won't be seeing you for a while after this weekend. I don't know how long it will be, but I want you to know that I think I really do love you."

His heart sank. It was the kiss of death, wasn't it? Think? Really do? That "really." And especially that "do" again, as though she had been debating it, as though there were a lurking "don't." How could anything so direct, so instantaneous, so pure, so intense, so mutual as what they felt for each other have come to this? Could she have fallen in love with Harold through his paintings? He waited for her to tell him. She began to tell him and when she had told him he didn't know what to think. It was so unexpected, so strange, so unbelievable.

"Exactly the same?" he said.

"Virtually. You would have to be me to see any differences."

"And you think that getting to know each other might sever the... whatever it is?"

"I hope so. Since it was all absolutely unconscious... I don't know if unconscious is even the right word. Preconscious. No, it had nothing to do with consciousness. I'd call it coincidence but it's too elaborate to have been that."

"What a shock it must have been for you," Julian said, shaking his head. "My poor Jilian."

***

Once again I'm back in Florida although three months have passed since my last visit. My mother, it appears, is not going to adjust to Giverney. "I've never felt so old in my life," she complains. "This place is for old people." She is probably the oldest one there. "And it's too far away." It's twenty minutes from where she'd been living, but I know what she means. I've come down to see if we can extricate her from Giverney without too much loss.

She has signed a long lease but they'll let her go for $2600. Then there are the moving expenses again. She has her eye on an apartment a few doors down from the old one, a building where Flora is already installed, having been talked out of Giverney by my mother.

"I guess it's fair, $2600, considering everything. It's only money, right?"

This is an uncharacteristic thing for her to say, this woman who thinks twice about taking taxis when she is in New York, even though she will no longer consider public transportation. A long time ago in high school she was trained to be, among other things, a bookkeeper, and she's still quick at business arithmetic, but she really has no idea about money. She can never remember what anything cost, but if there is a 30 cent charge on her phone bill for a call to an unfamiliar number, she will call the phone company to question it.

"What the hell," she says, "right?"

I am always thinking of my book, as I do now, of Emma, Harold, Ida. I miss them. They have taken on a life

206

beyond me, almost beyond my control. I don't know what is going to happen next, but I trust them to tell me. I wonder if death must be part of this book since they are all so close to it, since death is a part of life and certainly of old age? Must I have one of them die? Which one? Why? Why must I?

CHAPTER SEVENTEEN

"I think we should take off our clothes," Jilian said, peeling off her sweater and stepping out of her jeans. It was late afternoon. Although they had arrived only an hour ago, they were already in her studio, a barn-like space with a north-facing windowed wall. The place was full of cats.

"You mean ... paint naked?" Harold asked, trying to keep calm.

"Yes." She reached around to unhook her bra.

He forced himself to look away. The glass wall. Beyond it lay a sparsely wooded area leading to a pond.

"Oh, no one ever comes," Jilian assured him. "They know I'm working. They wouldn't dream of interrupting." Her breasts slipped free of the bra. She bent to peel off her panties.

"I've thought it through, Harold," she assured him. "There must be nothing hidden between us. We must become entirely familiar to each other. Take off your clothes. If it's not warm enough for you, I'll turn up the heat."

She was already at her easel, studying the unfinished painting on the canvas, readying herself for work as though this were a normal day like any other. One of the cats twined itself around her ankles. Another peered out from behind one of her finished paintings, which were stacked against the walls. Of the paintings that he could see, four were ones he had done. The rest he had not yet gotten to and now never would. She had been painting for many more years than he, but he had ascertained that he painted faster. He could finish a painting in less than half the time it took her. It made sense, since inspiration, thanks to her, must come to him full-blown, while she would have to struggle for it.

Slowly, he began to unbutton his shirt, not looking at her. The last thing in the world he wanted was to bare his body to this woman, a virtual stranger, not as lovers but in this peculiar context. But he was the trespasser, the poacher, she both victim and constable, and he was entirely in her hands. He was not used to being passive but clearly, in this case, it was her ground he had been infringing upon. Still, there was a lingering doubt, the possibility that she was the invader and he the victim. She had told him that it was futile to think in such terms, to try to assign blame, or even cause and effect. He must stop thinking like a lawyer.

He picked his discarded clothes up off the floor, snatching his underpants from a gray tabby, and, trying for insouciance, he carried them to a chair where he placed them, neatly folded. Back at his easel, he stared at the blank canvas. Jilian had supplied both canvas and easel; he had brought only his brushes and some paints. He looked across the room at Jilian. She was working away, completely focused on what she was doing. She had a perfect body. As a younger man, he could never have stood here like this.

"Why do you have so many cats?" he asked her. "Don't you have them neutered?"

"Yes. They're all fixed. Still, they accumulate. You're not allergic, are you?"

"No," he said. "You have a beautiful body, Jilian," he said. She looked up and smiled, a distracted smile.

"Thank you, Harold," she said, "So have you."

Surprised, he looked down at himself. As it had always been, his body was lean, but he saw all the places where his failed hormones had surrendered the field to gravity, saw the sparse white hair on his chest, saw his penis languishing uselessly, though at the moment, pleased with the compliment his body had been paid, it seemed to have responded by ever so slightly hardening. Poor thing, he thought, it was a long time since he had given it anything to harden at. Unlike the cats, it was time that had neutered him. On the other hand, it had been years since his genitals had demanded anything of him. It wasn't that he missed sex; he missed missing it. When he thought about it, he hated the serenity of old age. He had always been a passionate man, passionate in everything he did except the practice of law.

He was here to paint, not to think about his body. An empty canvas had never frightened him before, but the longer he looked at this one, the more menacing it grew. He stood, naked and paralyzed, staring at it for half an hour. The white of it could blind you, he thought, like snow.

"I'm a little cold," he said at last. "Would it be all right if I put on a sweater?"

She put down her brush and went to turn up the thermostat. "It warms up very quickly," she said and, back at her easel, abandoned him to the arid wasteland of his canvas that seemed to be crying out to him for the relief of something, anything, an image, a blotch. What on earth could he possibly put on it? He must paint entirely differently, and he had no idea how. He was terrified to begin; it was impossible!

Then it occurred to him that the one thing Jilian would not be painting was a portrait of herself naked in her studio, painting. He smiled. But he had never done figurative painting and had no idea if he could. He would not be too literal. His slightly blurred vision should help, and by half-shutting his eyes, he could unfocus her a little more. The important thing was the color of her flesh, her hair. The colors of the studio. The cats. The light. The brightness of the colors on her palette. He moved his easel slightly for the angle he wanted, and began, hungrily, as though he were preparing a delicious meal, to squeeze paints onto his palette, and to mix them.

Doing the only thing it knows how to do, time passed. It might have been minutes, it might have been hours, but the day had slipped away, the light was nearly gone. Jilian put away her brushes and stretched her arms over her head, raising her lovely breasts. She was entirely unselfconscious.

"Time to quit," she said. "Unless you want me to turn on the lights."

"No," he said. He was feeling tired. "No, don't look at it. Not until it's finished."

"All right." She turned to the glass wall. Someone was there, tapping softly.

"Oh damn!" she said, going to open the studio door to the outside. The figure at the window disappeared, then emerged through the door and stamped his feet as though he had come in out of the snow. There was no snow; it was June. He was a short, stocky man with a bushy red beard and a look of puzzlement on his face.

"I thought your father was dead," he said.

"This is not my father. Harold, this is Perry. Perry, this is Harold." Harold, scrambling into his trousers, had no hand to offer. He nodded.

"Well who is Harold?" Perry demanded. "And why are you both painting... ah, in the buff?"

"Harold is a friend, Perry, and would you please go away."

"Absolutely not! Put some clothes on so we can talk."

"We are talking," she said. Nonetheless, she began to dress. "No, Harold, don't go. I want you here."

Dressed now, Harold sat in the chair where his clothes had been and put on his socks and shoes. He was a tall man, but he felt very small and quite old. He wondered how much of Jilian he was going to be able to take.

"Is this the man you've been threatening to leave me for?" Perry asked.

"I have left you, Perry, in a manner of speaking. Why don't you go home and make your wife happy?"

"Madeleine is gone."

"Gone?"

"She left me. She and Dennis ran off together. Taking the children."

Jilian began to laugh. "I know it isn't funny," she choked. "But it's funny. After all those suicide threats."

Messy, Harold thought. Jilian's life is messy. What was he doing in the middle of all this? He wondered how much of this Julian was aware of. Poor Julian. Such a decent young man.

"I'm sorry, Perry. There's nothing I can do. I'm committed. Happily."

Perry looked at Harold with disbelief.

"He paints?" he asked Jilian.

"Yes."

"Well, Jilian dear," he said pompously, "I count myself as more than a student of human nature, and I can assure you that you're making a tremendous mistake. To have found a father figure who also does what you love best is unhealthy, at the very least."

Harold waited for Jilian to disabuse Perry, to deny that they were lovers.

"When it comes to pitting myself against your scientific detachment," she said, "I'm at a disadvantage. I'm not going to argue with you. Now go away."

"Don't you have any feeling for me?" Perry asked, his voice breaking. "I've been faithful to you for more than a dozen years."

She laughed. "Faithful!" she said. "Of course I have feelings for you, Perry, but not very complicated ones. You must find someone else to be faithful to."

Later, when Perry had been persuaded to leave and they were having a light supper in the kitchen, Harold asked

Jilian why she hadn't told Perry that they were not lovers.

"It's really none of his business, is it?"

"But what about my business?" he asked.

"Did you really mind?"

He thought about it and, in all honesty, he could not say that he minded what Perry thought. Who was Perry?

"It's been a long day for me," he said. "I know it's early, but I'd like to go to bed."

"Of course, Harold." She put the last of the few dishes in the dishwasher and sponged the crumbs off the table. He assumed she had a guest room, and she did, but it was not for him. She led him to what was obviously her bedroom.

"You mean for me to sleep here?" he asked.

"Yes. I'll be up in a little while."

"I don't think it's a good idea," he said. "For a lot of reasons. Also, I snore."

"I'm a very sound sleeper. Don't worry about it."

The smallest of the cats, a white one with black bangs, sat at the foot of the bed, watching him as he drifted off. He was asleep when Jilian slid into bed beside him. He was dreaming.

In the dream he was lying in bed, as he was in reality. A figure hovered over him, about five feet above the bed, not a sexual figure, no. He knew it was a woman, but it was not Jilian. The woman trailed yards of gauzy stuff and her face was also veiled.

"Who are you?" he asked.

"I'm your muse," the figure said, the notes of her voice round like bells. "I've come to apologize."

He waited for what she would say next. His anger towards her was extreme.

"Sheer laziness," she said. "I'm so sorry."

"Laziness?" he bellowed.

"Yes. It was inexcusable. I thought I could get away with it. I thought you'd never know."

"You're supposed to be MY muse," he shouted. "MY muse is not supposed to be lazy and dishonest, since I am not. Are you all like this?"

"I can't speak for my sisters, but in my line, with painters, you know, it's so easy. They're always stealing from each other anyway, or else working so hard at not copying, at breaking new ground, as if there were any, distorting themselves, and ignoring my input, that they begin to lose any trace of their true selves, if they ever had them. It's hard to have much respect for most of them Once in a while, oh so rarely, there's a real one, like Jilian, with whom all that's needed is the occasional nudge."

"Are you saying that I have no true self?" he asked, subdued.

"That remains to be seen, doesn't it?" She yawned. "I'll try not to be lazy with you again."

"I'd appreciate that," he said, but she was gone. While he had her ear, and he knew this was an unusual reversal, he had wanted to ask her why the muses were all female. He knew they were Zeus's daughters, and in Zeus's time he was sure all the bemused were men. Ah, women! The roles they were required to play.

He awoke to the body snuggled up against him. He had no idea how long he had been sleeping. His mouth no longer tasted of toothpaste. Worried that his breath might have gone sour, he nonetheless told her his dream. They both laughed.

"I bet it's begun to work already," she said. "I can't wait to see what you're painting. Harold, put your arms around me."

"Jilian, I think I must tell you this," he said, desperately. "I'm engaged."

"What do you mean?"

"Engaged to be married."

"How nice," she said. "So am I. I think."

He was pleased at her easy acceptance of his announcement, as though it were perfectly natural for him, at his age,
to be engaged to be married. "I mean, she hasn't exactly
said yes, but neither has she said no."

"Who is she?"

"Emily."

"Oh, yes, at Gerutopia. She's lovely. Harold, put your
arms around me. Hold me. It would be good if you could
enter me."

He was shocked. Was she wicked? Or was she sincere
in her notion that complete intimacy might break her hold
on him, or at least alter it. But "enter me?" What a cold,
mechanical way to put it, as if she were a room with an
open door, out of Alice in Wonderland. But how should she
have said it? Make love? No, love wasn't part of the
equation. Have intercourse? Copulate? Fuck me? Yes,
that would be best.

"What are you thinking?" she asked. "You must tell
me. You mustn't hold anything back. Are you shocked?"

"Yes," he admitted.

She was beautiful, she was young. Any man would
consider himself lucky to be lying in her bed, holding her
in his arms, feeling her body against his, let alone a man of
his age. He felt a faint stirring. It grew a little stronger. He
thought of Emily. He thought of Julian.

"I don't think I can," he said.

He wanted to kiss her. He ran his tongue around his
mouth, around the space where four of his teeth were
missing. The partial bridge with his four adopted teeth was
in a small green plastic box on the night table beside the
bed. No, he would disgust her. It would be awful for him
to sense her revulsion.

"Sex as creative therapy," he said. "How can you want
it?"

"Oh, you're romantic," she said. "An old-fashioned

man."

"Never mind the fashioned, I'm an old man."

"I don't think of you as old." She put her hand under his pajama shirt and ran it over his chest.

"The feel of my skin," he mumbled.

"It's you with your years on you. But it's still you."

It was a strange thing for her to say. "But you don't even know me, and certainly not the earlier me. You don't know that 'you.'"

"Of course I do," she said.

He sighed. "How lucky I should feel."

"You're afraid."

"Yes."

"Then we won't rush it." She yawned. A minute later she was asleep. He listened to her soft, gentle breathing and thought with what he realized was pleasure about the picture he was painting. As he often did, he tried to stay alert to the mysterious transition from being awake to sleep, that incredible hopelessly elusive moment of yielding. But when sleep, delayed by this effort, finally overtook him, he was as always unaware.

CHAPTER EIGHTEEN

"Mommy says you asked her for a divorce," Gwen said. The twins were wrapped in towels, their lips blue after an hour of frolicking in the surf. The ocean was still too cold for comfort but the twins were so active they hardly noticed. Besides, they never caught cold.

Julian had brought them to a remote part of Fire Island for the day. Cora had insisted on providing the picnic lunch which Julian was now spreading before them. It was a typical Cora lunch, lots of raw vegetables and grainy bread and three bananas but nothing, really, to eat. The girls were used to it, however, and made no verbal judgment, though he had no way of knowing what they were thinking. Dutifully, noisily, they munched on celery, carrot sticks, cucumbers, radishes, watercress, and chewed endlessly on the chewy bread. If it had been left to him, they would have been feasting on thermoses of hot chowder and thick rare roast beef sandwiches, potato salad and crisp garlic pickles. Cora's interest in food was almost non-existent and her attitude to it responsible and virtuous, never sensual or joyous. She had learned what was good for you and then never thought about it again. Once in a while, the girls expressed sad yearnings for peanut butter and jelly sandwiches, nostalgic and lustful as though it were caviar they were missing, protesting that all the kids in school ate them and seemed none the worse. "Some of them are even taller than us," they said, "and just as strong." Once in a while, Cora would succumb, a special treat, though she drew the line at grape jelly, which was what they specified.

Food had been another of Cora and Julian's incompatibilities, though hardly a serious one. Still, how he had appreciated Jilian's greediness. He loved to watch her eat and marveled at the flatness of her stomach.

"Did you hear what I said?" Gwen asked.

"About the divorce? Yes." Cora told the girls every-thing, treating them like the adults they were not, while still liking it that they called her Mommy. They called him Julian. "Nothing will change."

"Yes it will. You won't be married to Mommy."

"Well, we're not really married now. Not living togeth-er..."

"Legally."

"What has legally got to do with it?"

"Julian, don't you want some of these radishes? We're gobbling them all up."

"No thanks."

"Legally means you can't marry anyone else. Do you want to marry anyone else?"

"Is that why you want to divorce Mommy?"

A gull had been hanging around nearby, watching their picnic from its single profiled eye. The other eye, presum-ably, was engaged elsewhere. Julian tossed a chunk of the bread high in the air and, while it was still on the rise, the gull flew up and caught it. "I might," he said, aware that a couple of days earlier his answer would have been an unequivocal, resounding yes. "I was hoping you'd meet her this weekend but she couldn't come."

The twins exchanged a despairing glance. Overhead, more gulls gathered, swooping down to join the first.

"What's her name?" Polly asked politely, though it was clear that she didn't care.

"Jilian."

The girls snorted in unison. "You made that up," Gwen said.

"No. Listen, it could have been Julia, or Juliet. The world is full of coincidence. Look at you two."

"Are we a coincidence?"

"In a sense."

Polly, who was more intellectual than Gwen, thought for a moment, nibbling her lower lip. "I don't think so," she said. "We were caused by the same thing."

They looked at each other again and giggled.

"Whereas," Polly continued, "your name and your ... your new friend's name were not."

He smiled. He was proud of her. They were both precocious, but Polly was more verbal.

"So who is she?" Gwen asked impatiently.

"Someone I met at the Millers. She's an artist. I think you'll like her."

"How many times has she been married?"

"Zero"

"How old is she?"

Julian told them.

"Oh, a spinster!" Polly said.

Julian laughed. "There are no spinsters any more," he said.

"Is she ugly?"

"No."

"Is she a virgin?"

"Really, Gwen!"

Even Polly was embarrassed by Gwen's question. Polly was a reader, therefore, worldly.

"What kind of artist?" she asked Julian, quickly changing the subject.

"A painter."

Gwen began with sniffles to cry and was soon sobbing. Julian gathered her into his arms.

"Why are you crying?" he asked. "Nothing will change."

"Of course it will," she blubbered. "You and Mommy won't ever live together again."

"We wouldn't anyway."

"Well, that's a shame because it's what Mommy wants,"

Gwen said.

"Who told you that?" Polly asked sharply.

"Nobody. I just know it."

"You want that," Polly said. "Not Mommy."

"Don't you?" Gwen asked her.

"It doesn't matter what we want. You can't always get what you want. Not in this life."

Julian sighed. "Well, anyhow," he said, "it's not happening yet."

CHAPTER NINETEEN

Sunlight shining brightly through the windows, Harold awoke with a feeling of excited expectancy, something he hadn't felt in so many years that at first he wasn't sure what it was. He felt rejuvenated, like an adolescent, all the sap running. It was the new painting; he couldn't wait to see it.

Oscar Wilde said that the tragedy of old age is not that one is old but that one is young.

Then he remembered Jilian. Her side of the bed was vacant, a note pinned to her pillow. He groped for his glasses. "Off doing tiresome errands," the note said in a strong hand, "back by noon. Coffee on stove. Help your-self to anything else you can find."

The wonder of it! He had slept all night beside a beautiful woman, her body curled against his, had slept sweetly, deeply, peacefully. He had even forgotten to take the mild sedative he took every night that enabled him to fall back to sleep should he wake during the night which, for a wonder, he had not.

He got out of bed, restraining himself from going straight down to the studio to see the painting, going in-stead to the bathroom to tend to his bladder and take his shower. It was not a very good shower; the pressure was weak and the water temperature shifted erratically. How spoiled he was by Gerutopia, where the water pressure was as perfect as everything else. He thought of Emily. He felt more than a day and a few hundred miles away from her, although he had not yet begun to miss her. But he thought of her with quiet longing, almost nostalgia. She was a woman of such calm intelligence and perception.

He did, then, something he never did: studied himself in the full-length mirror on the back of the door, trying to see himself as others, Jilian, saw him. Not too bad for an old man, yet an old man, his body hair gray and sparse, skin that had once been tight loose over muscles that lacked tone and confidence. As a young man, he had rarely thought about his body, had never had to think about his weight, which had remained fairly constant since his thirties. He had never been vain. Still alive when so many who had been in his life were not, still in reasonably good health, with all his faculties, he felt blessed. And he had his painting.

Or did he?

He shaved and dressed, then poured himself a mug of coffee in the kitchen and took it to the studio. The painting was there, waiting for him to go on with it. He was pleased with it. He had never tried anything that was not abstract, that was not about the purity of space and color and form, the purity of art alone without conscious reference to his outer eye and the world it beheld. This was a painting that combined the two, the inner and outer, mirror and window. He had intentionally exaggerated the colors beyond truth, into what seemed to him a truer truth, and the light, though it needed work, was good, mysterious. The figure of Jilian naked at her easel, still rough and far from finished, none-theless already reflected her grace and a hint of her beauty. It wasn't a large painting; he could finish it in a few days. Jilian, he was sure, would not have been able to resist looking at it. He wondered what she had thought. And then, of course, he needed to see what she was doing. Nervously, he crossed the room, increasingly terrified at what he would see.

The painting was not covered. He could see at once that, like his own painting, it was a portrait. It was a portrait of a naked man standing at an easel in this studio. His heart thumped painfully. Her colors matched exactly his own distorted, exaggerated colors; the light in the studio differed slightly, but only, he felt sure, because of the angle of her vision.

He felt as if he had fallen into a swamp of cold despair. He fetched his own painting and easel and stood them side by side with hers. It was uncanny. They were indisputably paintings by the same hand. He was her mirror image, or she his.

His heart still racketing, he sat heavily down in the studio's only chair. She would have thought, as he had, that this was one thing he would not be painting. He knew that if he died, when he died, she would go on painting as she had always done, her paintings, for which she had begun to be known. But if she died? Would he be unable to paint? Would inspiration die with her? He could not imagine that if she ceased to exist he would not go on painting as he did. But the likelihood of his ever knowing was infinitesimal.

Unless he killed her.

But could he? He tried to imagine a way to do it that would not come directly from his hands. Not that they weren't strong enough; it was his will that would not be up to it. He could not imagine literally holding someone's life in his hands. Poison was the only way, but he knew nothing about poison. And it was too slow, too passionless.

He went again to study her canvas, interested now in how she saw him, as only a moment ago he had tried, in the bathroom mirror, to see himself through her eyes. He could have saved himself the trouble of that earlier perusal, for here their views diverged. She had painted him as an aged man, but virile, powerful, Picassoesque, though she had not given him Picasso's compact, taurine physique. He was himself, but she undoubtedly saw him as still a sexual man. He couldn't recall if he had ever considered himself a sexual man. On her canvas he was himself, but seen through the eyes of a sexual woman, translated by her. How interesting. There was nothing sexual about his painting of her, though her beauty already shone through.

There were, he saw, nuances in figurative painting that had no equivalent in abstract art. Here, then, their individuality declared itself, here they weren't entirely one, no matter how subtle the differences.

A ray of hope?

Almost without thought, he picked up her palette, chose a brush, and began to repaint himself on her canvas. If she stayed away long enough, he could finish her painting. Let her finish his, if she liked.

"But you've taken all the life out of him," she said from the doorway. He jumped; he was unaware of time having passed and hadn't heard her come in. "The shoulders, the knees. Is that how you see yourself?"

"You're not angry?"

"No. I think it's an interesting idea, painting each other's paintings on the same canvas instead of on two. But why did you sap him of all his quality?"

"Only his sexuality," Harold said, going on painting.

"No," she said. "His vigor, his passion. Passion isn't necessarily sexual. When you paint, Harold, you're passionate."

You. He. He was her you, his own I. Who could say which of them was right. He saw himself through the eyes of all his former selves. Self-consciously. With mourning for the losses, but with acceptance, without self-pity. She knew him only as he was and what of his past her imagination might trouble to reconstruct. Honesty had nothing to do with it.

"No," she said. "Don't think. Speak. Think aloud. Remember why we're here."

"Neither of us is really objective," he said. "True objectivity happens only in the first moments and is soon overlaid. People change as you absorb their words, their thinking, their gestures, their personalities. People become beautiful before your eyes, or ugly, or boring."

It was difficult saying your private thoughts aloud; he sounded pedantic, perhaps because it was necessary to shape his thoughts into neat, grammatical sentences, thereby, no matter how slightly, altering those thoughts.

"Yes," she agreed. "First impressions are rarely reliable. Transformation comes with familiarity, with one's own judgments and prejudices." She sighed. Briefly, she thought of Julian. "Oh, how can two people ever really touch!" she moaned.

"But in some impossible and disturbing way," he said, putting down his brush and turning to her, "they do. You and I touch. More than touch. Connect."

He sat down on the hard, wooden chair and lit a cigarillo.

"More than connect," she said.

"More than connect," he agreed. "Overlap."

"Finish the painting," she said. "I'll finish yours. And then we'll start on a joint painting."

"How?" he asked. "The logistics, I mean. Will you do the right side and I the left, like piano duets? Or will we take turns? You first, then me?"

"No. You first. We'll see. Oh, this is so exciting, so incredible!"

***

Days have gone by and I haven't added a page to the novel. Instead, my mouse and I play a new game, Bookworm, on my computer, game after game, obsessed, adicted, in a hypnotic trance.

Despondent. No, drugged, out of it. An idiot killing the days, these lovely summer days, feeling the whole summer slip away, lost and irretrievable. When did it get to be summer? It was just winter, wasn't it?

Ergo, I've consented to be on this ship with my mother.

It's what I consider a stupid cruise. It stops at ports along the coast of New England, where I have spent about a third of my adult life, then on up to Canada and Nova Scotia, where I've also been several times. Two weeks, much of the time spent in places one could drive to in a day or two and see in much more depth. My mother doesn't care about the stops; it's the ship that matters to her, the shipboard life: duplicate bridge in the card room, lavish meals (not that she is a lavish eater), dressing for dinner, blackjack in the casino, the frenetic shows at night. She would just as soon the ship never stop, since this is definitely not a stop-and-shop cruise.

"Did you buy any clothes for the trip?" she asked me on the telephone a week before we sailed. I told her no, I had enough stuff left over from past cruises.

"What about you?" I asked.

"No. Oh, just a couple of shorts sets."

"You're going to wear shorts?"

"Why not? There's nothing wrong with my legs."

I had resisted her invitations to join her on this cruise. She didn't need me; two of her friends were booked, one with her caretaker, Sally. I, so concerned with my own aging, am going to spend two weeks with three wealthy women in or near their nineties! Women who love to dress up and spend hours doing it. Plus the early sitting!

"It costs so little more for a second person in the room," my mother kept saying. She would be paying for me and she wanted me to know, for some reason, that she wasn't being extravagant, as though she was afraid I'd think she was robbing me of my inheritance.

"How much more?" I asked once, idly curious.

"Oh, I'm not sure, a couple of hundred dollars."

Hundred. Thousand. She doesn't really know the difference, rarely knows what anything costs, what she can afford. It always drove my father insane. If his violence had been as physical as it was verbal, he would have killed her before my brother or I had a chance to be born.

My mother, who has filled three walk-in closets at home with her clothes, closets for any one of which I'd trade my soul (the closets, I mean, not their contents}, has brought most of those clothes into our tiny stateroom. I help her unpack and hang things up because I am now the young, tall, strong person. (If I outlive her, her death will finally release me into my proper age). We have a four-section closet, each section about 12 inches wide, and I give her three of these, making each hanger do double and triple duty, but there's still far more than we can manage.

"I don't know when you think you're going to wear all these duds," I tell her. "This isn't a world cruise."

"You said it!" she agrees. She sighs. She is telling me that she is incorrigible and she is.

"How will you ever make all those decisions?" I ask. She is terrible at decisions, like me.

"What decisions?"

"Whether you want to be powder blue today, or pink, or scarlet?"

"It will depend on the weather."

"...and then there are the evenings when you'll have to decide whether to be silver or gold or black or..." I hold up a chiffony thing ... "flamingo?."

"Shut up," she says.

I hang things on hooks on the wall facing the closets, and then line up the empty suitcases along the wall, and fold slacks over the suitcases. We will have to go in and out of the cabin sideways since the corridor is now stuffed with her gaily-colored pants and shorts sets.

So goes day one of the cruise.

As for the ship, it has sailed out of New York harbor, swung left past Brooklyn and under the Verrazano bridge, and is now steaming up the Atlantic toward its first stop:

Newport, Rhode Island. And almost immediately, it's time for the first seating for dinner. It's a long walk to the dining room and my mother is not the walker she once was. She is again a toddler. Or a totterer. I am tottering slowly along behind her, trying not to trip over her heels.

"Must we do the early-bird?" I whine. "You're not going to save any money." In Florida, when they go out to dinner, they often avail themselves of the early-bird special, which is cheaper, dining at five-thirty. They're all so wealthy that I know it's not to save money; it's to allow them to get home in time for their television shows.

"That's what the girls want," my mother says. By "girls" she means her two nonogenarian buddies. They have always referred to each other as "the girls." When they still had husbands, however, these were referred to as "the men," never the boys. It said a lot about them, about the kind of women they were.

On the second day out, one of the old women, the one without a companion, Lucy, falls and breaks an arm. They can't get her off the ship fast enough. They pack her up and whisk her off to the Newport hospital before any of us even knows about it. I am, frankly, relieved, and it makes me feel unfeeling, but she was a non-stop talker. And now that we are four, we can move to a table at a window. I persuade the survivors to change not only our table but our sitting and we are all much happier, though from time to time, one of us says, "Poor Lucy."

So here I am for fourteen days, committed to this life of ease, of feeling so much younger than I have come to feel in my own world, of not having to think about those other old folks I've been living with inside my computer, of not having to think about anything, really. I've brought along some books I expect to enjoy. I'll stroll around the streets of Bar Harbor and look out from the top of Mt. Desert at the sea and our ship lying in it. I'll go to Peggy's Cove and stand on some rocks with a few hundred other tourists, taking pictures of a lighthouse. On one gray, rainy day, I'll board a small, noisy boat and sail off on a whale watch, and we'll actually see a whale surface and spout half a dozen times, and I will find this the highpoint of the trip.

And then, I hope, I'll come back refreshed and go on with my other life, the life on my desk, that by now is more real than this one.

CHAPTER TWENTY

"I think it's extraordinary," Jilian said, stepping back from the canvas and narrowing her eyes at the finished painting. "It's the best thing I've ever done!"

"We," Harold said.

It was their third partnership painting. That is, they had both painted it, taking turns, each one picking up where the other had left off. Stepping in with no difficulty, completely at home with what was on the canvas whether it had been painted by himself or the other. The transitions were as fluid and natural as if they were made by the same person. Each painting was better than the previous one.

"Of course, we," Jilian said. She laughed and looked lovingly at Harold, who had begun the painting. She had been the last to work on it, finishing it. It had gone very quickly. Neither of them ever felt that they had to go over anything the other had done, or to explain themselves and what they were reaching for. "I can't wait for you to start the next one."

He already had. He was almost as excited and enthusiastic as she.

"I'm still not sure this is a good idea," he said.

"Why not? It works!"

"Because it contradicts completely what we set out to do. Instead of freeing me from you, it's binding us inextricably closer."

"I know," Jilian said. "But maybe this is what we were meant to do. And with you starting the paintings, there's no question that in some way you're echoing me. We're obviously more than the sum of our parts. We're complementing each other." Her voice dropped to an awed whisper. "I think this painting may well be..." She couldn't quite bring herself to say "a masterpiece." "It's better than anything I

... we ... either of us has ever done before."

It was. It was certainly better than anything Harold had ever done. But how much of it could he take credit for? Her youth, her ebullience were clearly there. But what had his age brought to it? He studied the parts he knew he had done, though it was already nearly impossible to separate them. Did he temper her with mellowness, sagacity, caution? No. His touch was even bolder, fiercer, than hers. Still, nothing in the painting warred with anything else. They were entirely compatible. And it was true: they were more than the sum of their parts.

"We'll paint a series and then we're going to have a show," she said.

"Whose paintings will they be?"

"Both of ours, of course. 'New paintings by Harold Burton and Jilian Stern.'"

"They'll want to know which are mine and which are yours."

"Then it will be 'paintings by Burton slash Stern.' "People will know. Program notes. Publicity. The gallery will take care of all that. Oh, God, this is exciting." She turned to Harold and put her arms around him. "I'm scared," she said, beginning to tremble. It was refreshing to see her vulnerable, troubled. It made him feel protective, something it had not occurred to him he could feel towards her.

"We are so ... married," she said. "Maybe we should actually marry."

"We can't," Harold said. "I'm engaged to Emily. And you to Julian."

"I'm not engaged," she said. "Not even really promised," she mumbled. He could feel her tears on his cheek and in a moment she began to sob. He took her hand and led her away. Reluctantly, she turned from the canvas and followed him into the living room where he sat her down.

He handed her his handkerchief and she blew her nose in it, then blotted her eyes.

"We have to talk," he said, sitting beside her on the sofa. He had been standing much of the day and, even with his faulty ears, he heard his knee bones pop like Chinese firecrackers a block away.

"How can it be? It's all so insane," she said."

He lit a cigarillo and coughed. "You love Julian, don't you?" he asked. Julian had been phoning every night before dinner, and every night Jilian told him: Soon. No, not yet. Don't come.

"Yes, I think I love him," she said. "But love seems so trivial beside this ... this thing ... that's happened to us."

"Why don't we separate the work from our private lives?" he said in a reasonable, lawyerly voice. "Why don't we just meet during business hours, like partners?"

"Because we're not ... business partners. We're ... soul mates. We're more than that. We're almost the same person."

"Be realistic! I'm a tired old man and you're a beautiful, vital young woman. My whole life until we met has had its own history, and so has yours. We scarcely even know each other."

Her weeping grew stronger. "We know each other in a way that has nothing to do with history. We know each other ...so ... basically ... cellularly."

"We must go back and meet with Emily and Julian," he said softly. He stroked her back, trying to comfort her. "I'll go home to Gerutopia and you must marry Julian and build your studio. I'll come and work with you there."

"You don't understand," she sobbed, shaking her head. "I don't understand how it can be that you don't understand, you of all people!"

"You're hysterical."

"I know."

"It will pass."

"I know."

"How much longer do you think I have to live? And then what?"

"I don't care. You're alive now. Here."

Harold was moved. It was a declaration of perfect love: he was alive now; he was here. Time and place. That was enough. He cupped her chin and turned her face toward him. It was wet with her tears. He wiped them away with the palm of his hand. Then he kissed her. It was sweet to kiss her but when she responded with passion he withdrew. But of course it wasn't love; it couldn't be.

"In our lives, apart from the painting, we're still complete strangers," he said again.

"That will change," she said. "It's already changing."

****

I am wandering through the vast Barnes and Noble in Chelsea, warm with dark bookshelves and their orderly armies of books, trying to get my bearings, thinking that, like the Metropolitan Museum, they ought to supply diagrams. There is an Information counter but, since I don't know what I'm looking for, and the two young people who are womaning it seem to be inseparable from telephones, I continue to wander lonely as a cloud until I stumble on a section of paperbacks headed "Literature." What, I wonder, do they mean by "Literature?" They mean fiction, apparently, both contemporary and relatively recent. I have always believed that books considered Literature have stood the test of time and graduated. I begin to browse, trying to recall the names of books and authors Becky has recommended. They are all British writers who, Becky seems to feel, have more interesting things to tell us in more stylish language, and with more subtle humor. This

233

is often true, but not always.

As I usually do, I look for my own name and don't find it, alas. I back up a bit and see a spine with the name Jackson on it. Probably Shirley, I think, pulling it out, but it is T. L. Jackson with a title I never heard of. I'd been thinking so much about Tully, remembering our long-ago time together while writing the beginning of Julian and Jilian's affair, but mostly wondering if she really belongs in this book and debating whether to take her out of it. For months, my ambivalence has been paralyzing. Stumbling on a new book of Tully's feels like a sign, a promise, a possibility, the Chinese cookie that's about to give you the message you've been waiting for. The book's title is "Death Cave." Naturally I take it home and read it immediately.

It's not my kind of book but I recognize Tully's voice at once. The book is a sort of science fiction/mystery with a Pueblo Indian heroine named Joe, a youthful member of an archeological group digging in the Southwest. She becomes a valuable member of the team when she accidentally discovers that, under the influence of peyote, she can commune with her twelfth century forebears who, like tourist guides, explain the meaning of the cave drawings and other artifacts as they are revealed. I realize that this book was written to make money, like Tully's earlier Kit Lansburys, the ones to which she would never sign her name. The frontispiece indicates that there have been two earlier books in this genre.

When I finish the book, I write to Tully at the last address I have for her, just a note, telling her how exciting it was to discover that she's still alive and pulsing with her special energy. I tell her that I liked her book, especially the Indian lore parts, and that I will order her earlier ones.

One thing, as it tends to do, leads to another. A few nights later the phone rings. I instantly recognize Tully's voice.

"It was so good to hear from you," she says. "I've been thinking about you a lot lately." She sounds almost nostalgic.

Me, too, I tell her, not meaning that I've been thinking a lot about myself lately though God knows I have. We tell each other that we are fine and Tully asks if I'm "with" anyone.

"No, I think those days are over. What about you?"

"No," she says, "I seem to have run out of the good hormones."

"Tully, I can't imagine you without hormones, you had such an abundance of them."

"Yeah. I was just telling a friend that of all the women in my life, you're the only one I could have lived with."

For about a second, I'm speechless. "Then why didn't you?" I do not say, since she would then ramble on about that time in her life and her breakdown and etc. We chat about other things, who died, who didn't, what we look like now, our cats.

"Are you happy?" I ask.

Silence.

"What kind of question is that?" she finally asks.

"I couldn't agree more. Sorry."

She asks me why I don't come visit and I think: why don't I? and tell her yes, I will, very soon. I'll let her know.

When I hang up I run to the bathroom to look at myself in the mirror and, alas, I'm not who I just was on the phone, I continue to be this aging, heavier person with sags and wrinkles and bulges and veins, this stranger who has engulfed me. Will I never return? Will Tully be shocked and dismayed? Will she even recognize me? Will I know her? How long has it been?

Long.

On the plane, less than two weeks later, I try to examine my feelings, as though through some equation of reversed symmetry, the altitude at which I am being borne will make it easier to go down deep. I tell myself it's merely curiosity but I know it's more than that. I know there is something hopeful fluttering nearby, but I don't know what it is. Do I want to resume a long dead relationship because Tully now thinks I was the one she could have lived with, though of course she couldn't have and neither could I.

I try to imagine what it would have been like. We would never have been able to stay in New York; I would have had to leave family and friends and go wherever, for the moment, she felt comfortable. I would have missed many of the things that happened to me in those years, loves that didn't last but that I value nonetheless, people who became friends, places I've been that we couldn't have managed together. I might never have seen the pyramids, the Taj Mahal, the Great Wall, the Columbia glacier, David and Mona, or eaten wild boar. Spending a little time with Tully may be revealing, now that I know where the road taken has taken me, and perhaps I'll gain some insight into where the road abandoned, if it had not been, might have led.

It gets earlier and earlier on this westbound plane, and I don't know which is real time, mine or theirs. Two stewardesses are approaching with the beverage cart between them. The stewardesses look cheerful and relaxed, which I rarely am when I consider all the empty space there is beneath the thin skin of the belly of this plane, how far and fast one can fall through it, how big and final the bang at the end. Too early, no matter how you figure the time, I nonetheless ask for two bloody marys with extra lemon. When it's all laid out on my little shelf, the tumblers filled with ice cubes, the cunning plastic bottles of vodka trying to ape the grown-ups, the can of mix, the stirrers, napkin, lemon segments, the tiny aluminum-foil-wrapped package of salted peanuts, I feel, completely irrationally, that all this detail must mean that I am safe.

But instead of feeling cheered as I sip the first drink, I begin to think again about my life and how much time and emotion I've wasted! How much of my life has been devoted albeit often passively, to the pursuit of love. The poor suit of love, for clothing it is. Without it I feel locked naked in the closet of increasing age, deafness, apathy, unimportance. Half of my adult life! But no, conquest was never what I was after, just the intimate connection that I still seem to need to make me feel alive. Yet there is a sense of power, of triumph, and exhilaration, in the achievement of love (and sex) and a sense of defeat in its failure. No wonder so many people choose monogamy at any price.

If I had been in a stable relationship all these years, a monogamous one, I might have been so much more pro-ductive, even with Tully and all the problems we would have had to work out with each other. But would there have been enough to fill the well? Creativity grows more diffi-cult with increasing age. People cease to be endlessly fascinating, as they once were, the future less exciting and promising as it shrinks, life's miracles not really miracles at all. Only nature remains awesome, magnificent, satisfying; there is nothing like a long vista, rolling hills spread out before one like a complicated map of the world, sloping green velvet pastures, a distant barn, its silo burning in the sun, the distant line of pale blue mountains beyond. This is what I often look at as I write, later, after the facts, in Jed's rented country house, this and the more immediate, intimate foreground: the park-like setting with its lawns and tall young oaks, the perimeter of denser trees segueing into forest, the stone walls harboring squirrels and chip-munks, mourning doves fluttering to the ground like falling leaves, hawks wheeling high above on invisible currents, nuthatches describing busy zigzags on the tree trunks.

Age. I know now that I am never going to be able to

name all the birds, the trees, the wildflowers, the mush-rooms. I will never be fluent in French or Italian. My musical memory will never improve. I may never finish Proust. I may never finish writing this book.

However, back to the plot. I am on a plane traveling to the southwest to meet my first woman lover, someone who was incredibly important to me at the time, and the time was long ago. And so it is not untoward that I should be thinking like someone near the end of her life, which is how I more and more feel, and perhaps there's a faint element of say-it-ain't-so, even of hope in this voyage, hope, perhaps, of surprise, or of some sort of resolution to my life or, more important, of my book. What I really want is an epiphany. God, I'd give anything for an epiphany! I want a bomb bursting in air, a rocket's red glare; I'm sick of soft, quiet insights and sage, inconclusive little conclusions.

I tell myself that I am impelled only by curiosity, and aren't I lucky there's still curiosity.

Once again a survivor, I am rebirthed from the plane's unsteady womb through the red-carpeted vaginal passage into the world, the waiting room where I immediately spot Tully among the greeters. She is still handsome, her short hair now thick and silver. She is looking my way, not sure.

"Rachel?" she says, when I smile at her. I put down my carry-on and we embrace. I try not to think about what she may have been anticipating, and what she sees. She'll get used to it. Or not. Nothing I can do about it.

She stands back, holding me at arm's length. "How'd you get so old?"

I laugh. "I didn't get old. Old got me. But it took time. It wasn't easy."

"Me, too, I reckon."

"You look pretty good," I say. "I'd forgotten that I was taller than you. Unless you've shrunk.

"I haven't shrunk," she says indignantly, and rattles off

a list of all the food supplements she takes. In the next week, I'll be hearing a lot about these.

"We match here, however," I say, patting my belly, which I hate though not enough to do anything about.

When we get to the parking lot, I admire her car.

"It's a grown-up's car," I say. "Four doors and everything."

"Not like the little beetles I used to favor."

I remember a crippled VW she was once conned into buying, one of her many horrible New York Experiences, a particularly galling one since she prided herself on her knowledge of automobiles. Wisely, I don't mention it.

"You still talk like a southerner," I say.

"And you're still very much the New Yorker."

"I never left for very long."

In the car, Tully rattles on in her southern and faintly nasal voice about the growth of cities, about how money has ruined Santa Fe, about how she thinks of leaving it. Restless, she always wanted to leave wherever she was, as though she would not find herself waiting wherever she went. She was always a talker and I relax as I realize how little is demanded of me. I am engrossed by the scenery. The southwest is so raw, so dramatic, so fiercely, threateningly gorgeous. Nothing like the green or white landscapes of my northeast, my New England.

"Here it's as if it all just happened yesterday, those violent upheavals, and nothing's had time to settle yet," I say. "It's so much gentler in the northeast, as though it's had time to heal. Such diametrically opposite scenery."

"You call that scenery where you come from?" she scoffs. "That's not scenery, it's upholstery."

"Let's not quarrel so soon," I say. "I'm not saying one is better. Just different."

I like the warm buff color of Santa Fe, the earthy clay sameness of its buildings with their softly rounded edges.

The sky is cloudless, intensely blue. We stop in front of Tully's house, a modest adobe distinguishable from its neighbors only in minor details.

"It's what I hate about living here, why I want to move. It's a Goddamn *neighborhood*."

She shows me the house. It only takes a minute. A comfortable house, pleasing, nothing jarring. Her two cats appear and accompany us. She gives me her bedroom. I object. She dismisses my objection; the bed in her work-room is even more comfortable than the one in her bed-room. Also, she will have to do some work and she needs to keep the study free of me.

"Why don't you stay longer?" she asks. "Five days is nothing. I thought you'd be coming for at least a month."

I laugh. "Five days will be more than you can stand."

Later, settled in the back yard, a lovely garden made by Tully, at a table under a tall, wide tree which Tully tells me is an elm, we spread cheese on crackers and sip scotch and sodas. The cats chase each other, happy to have an audience.

"I've asked some people to brunch tomorrow," she tells me. "They want to meet you."

"Why?"

"I've told them about you. One of them, Fran, read your last book."

"I'd have thought everyone in Santa Fe would have read it. Isn't everyone here gay?"

"Only everyone I know. Most of them really don't read that much. We never talk about books."

Not talk about books? Tully?

"What do you talk about?"

"Everything else. Pets. Politics. People. Gossip. Health." `

"Why did you say I was the only one you could have lived with? We fought all the time."

She looks at me in amazement.

"What do you mean? We had *fun*."

I look at her in amazement. Did we have fun? Ah, memory! Of course we had fun. Of course we fought all the time. As has happened before, I'm struck by how diverse is the experience of two people who think they have shared an intimate relationship, of how differently the moments are processed in those separate, walled brains. It's hard enough feeling so lonely in my life now without being made to feel lonely in my past.

"What happy, fun-filled moments come to mind?" I ask Tully.

"Oh, many," she says. "The friends we had, the trips we took, the love we made. Seems to me we laughed quite a lot."

We spend hours recalling friends we had then, friends we made together, Cheryl and Peg, philosophy professors who had a pet rabbit named Wittgenstein they were trying to paper-train; enormously wealthy June who lived with handsome Dorothy, her slave, who later died of rancor (almost an anagram for cancer, the official "cause of death"), but whom we visited often in June's splendid house on a rocky spit of Maine coast; Samantha, a high-powered business woman, the illegitimate daughter of a Portuguese fisherwoman, and whoever it was she was living with then.

I'd kept up with some of these women after Tully left and I could fill her in on what happened to whom. I tried to make the stories amusing but they weren't really; they were horrible. Peg, who was crippled, sat heavily on the sofa one day and crushed to death Wittgenstein who matched the upholstery almost perfectly. Dorothy had confessed to me that in addition to the cooking and hostessing and work in the office, her role was to make love to June, and that it was years since Dorothy had had anything but a self-inflicted orgasm since June never reciprocated. "I'm not like that," June explained. "I have no interest in making love to anyone, but I do need to be made love to." And then June fell in love with another woman who saw, in June, a means of climbing a few steps higher in her professional world, and who subsequently made a fool of June. Dorothy was messily, hurtfully, cruelly dumped. She hired a lawyer and made a feeble effort to be given at least what financial compensation she felt she was entitled to after the years of partnership not only in June's life but in her businesss. But June was tough; I don't believe she had a tender bone in her body. She had her own lawyers who easily outwitted Dorothy and hers. Then Dorothy got the aforementioned cancer and soon died. (Sorry, Susan S., I do believe that sometimes there is a connection). When, in due course, it came time for June to be dumped by the new woman, Pat, June cried a lot and made scenes in restaurants and other public places, but she finally had to accept that it was over. On the rocks one day, looking out at the northern blue sea with its small green islands and the lighthouse beyond, June told me about the lovemaking with Pat. "Spontaneous it wasn't," she said. "Once a week. Sunday mornings. It was a ritual. She would bring me breakfast in bed, wait for me to do my 'ablutions,' close the blinds, then get into bed with me. No conversation. God, it was like church. I once asked her if I should wear a hat."

"Nobody since for June?" Tully asks.

"Just her sister, who built an expensive house on an adjoining pile of rocks after her divorce. She and June have been inseparable, as far as I know. Travel everywhere together. I've lost touch in recent years."

"I don't know why she ever put up with you," Tully says. "She was so anti-Semitic."

"The question is, why did I ever put up with her? I didn't take her anti-Semitism very seriously."

"She was rich."

"And talented. She even designed her own doorknobs and had them made. And the kitchen and bathroom tiles. Everything reflected her taste and she was sure of herself."

"Money."

"Yes. It enabled her to have everything her way."

"But she couldn't always do it with people."

"And when she couldn't, it made her wildly angry. One drunken night she wanted me to go to bed with her and I wouldn't. I really couldn't. I tried to be tactful, told her my heart was elsewhere. She wouldn't let it go. She pleaded and then she began wrestling with me. She was a lot stronger than she looked."

"So how did you fend her off?"

"Laughter. It struck me as absurd and funny and for a while I couldn't stop, and I guess that did it."

"See? I told you we had fun."

And so the days with Tully go harmlessly by. I meet her friends who invite us to lunch or dinner, all lesbians I think, and I like most of them, though the food is mostly less than memorable. Their lives, at least at first glance, seem easier, and I envy them a little. Tully is the only writer among them. She tells me again that they never talk about books. I can't imagine Tully never talking about books. She gives me one of hers to read, one not yet published, a serious one about a former lover. The Important One, the one that hurt the most. I read it out in the yard under the elm tree while Tully is in her studio, working. It's a good book, and my opinion seems to matter to her, which surprises me, remembering my literary subservience to her in our early days. She tells me about all her lovers since me and why they failed. Like me, she has never managed to form a lasting attachment, although she doesn't appear to regret it as I do.

She seems totally uninterested in hearing about my

intervening lovers or, really, anything much about me, about anything in my life that doesn't touch on hers. When I try to talk about myself, I can see her eyes wandering, her mind behind them. The most personal things we talk about are vitamins and minerals and immune systems. Tully knows all about these, about what is necessary for what, good for what, helpful to what. It pleases her to lecture me. This is about as personal as we get. She'd have made a terrific doctor.

Still, I enjoy being with her. Even after all these years, and all those lovers, she is so familiar to me that I feel we are related, and that maybe this is a kind of love. And then, on the penultimate day, it occurs to me that this visit has had something of the quality of that correspondence between us, the polite letters that I loathed so much. What had I expected? If I can touch a raw nerve (she has so many of them) if I can make her cry.

Ten minutes later she is crying.

What I did was to remind her of the furniture she'd given to the building super when she left me and the apartment across the street (that I'd helped her to furnish) when she took off for the southwest with her messy hippie. She was in such a hurry to leave.

"Remember the dining table?" It was a mahogany table that folded but was still a bit too large for her small apartment. "For years after you left," I said, "my father asked me if I knew what had happened to it, and I played dumb." He had put it in a storage space he kept after he and my mother moved to Florida, from which I'd liberated it for Tully. They'd had no need of it there; it wasn't what they thought of as Florida furniture. "He kept telling me that it was a very expensive, valuable English piece, Sheraton or Hepplewhite, he wasn't sure which." He had bought it from wealthy friends who had preceded them to Florida by several years.

Tully looks at me as if I'm out of my mind, and then bursts into tears. Is she really crying? She goes on crying for an hour, and I am reminded of all the painful moments we had, of how raw and vulnerable she was and how hard it was for me to keep from saying something that might set her off. With no one else had I ever been considered tactless or insensitive.

"Why are you crying?" I keep asking her.

"Why did you tell me that? About the table."

`I thought it might amuse you," I lie.

"To make me feel that I was irresponsible and careless?"

Yes, but not about the table. About me. I'm ashamed. I can't believe that I still feel, even faintly, this residue of anger and hurt. I can't think of anything to do except to apologize and to agree with everything she says. She doesn't remember the table. She remembers another one, a cheap one.

"And why would I have given it to the super?" she sobs, denying that it had ever happened, implying that I had made it up. How strange, I think. Why would I have made up something like that, except in my fiction? Ah, memory!

"See?" she says, after a while, "it wasn't always me. It was you, too. You're ... cruel."

I tell her I'm sorry. "I didn't mean to make you cry, to upset you," I lie again, but she goes on crying for a long time and when she does get past it, it remains there between us.

Later, I try hard to plumb my depths for the impulse to make Tully feel bad enough to cry, remembering the pain of her departure, the bitter poems I wrote and sent her that she jauntily submitted on my behalf to an editor/friend of a poetry journal who published them (with my permission, of course). But then I give it up. Old buttons. Very old buttons. It's just not terribly important now and I find that I'm really not much interested.

And so, when I leave, and I suspect it's not a moment too soon for Tully, I've not had my epiphany, only the dismal realization that whatever we had during those years together needed the fire of sex and of intimacy to make it matter, even to make it interesting. Love and friendship. Surely all those years ago we were friends as well as lovers, but it was a friendship in which everything was colored by the emotional intensity that isn't part of an ordinary loving friendship. We went on to love others, and that we managed, however sporadically, to maintain a "letters to my aunt" relationship was a feat of will.

CHAPTER TWENTY-ONE

"I can't marry you, Julian. I'm in love with Harold."

"Nonsense!" he said. Their phone calls had prepared him for something like this. "What does Harold say?"

"'Nonsense.' He says 'nonsense' too." She was crying. She hated to cry.

Work had begun on the studio, her studio. She was both touched and angered. Touched by Julian's hopefulness, angered by the arrogance of his self-confidence. But it wasn't self-confidence; it was bravado.

"Nevertheless," she said.

"Harold is almost three times your age. It's not love. It can't be."

"But it is. What about Picasso? Chaplin? Oh, so many."

"Oh, Jilian, you're beautiful. I've missed you terribly. Haven't you missed me at all?"

"Yes, of course I have. But what Harold and I have been doing is exciting, and other-worldly."

"Exactly! Let's do something this-worldly. Let's go to bed. I'm starved for you."

Was he crazy? She had just told him that she loved Harold.

"Don't you want to make love with me?" he asked.

"Yes," she said. She did. She loved the way he made love, instinctively attuned to her, tender and sure. She loved the look of him, his eyes, at once innocent and knowing, the cleft in his chin, the hard line of his jaw, his strong arms and wonderful hands, the grace with which he moved. There wasn't an inch of his body that she didn't find attractive. How else would she have been instantly drawn to him at their first meeting? "Of course I want to make love."

"You and Harold haven't been having sex?"

She shook her head, tears still spilling down her cheeks.

"He's unable?" Slowly, he was unbuttoning her blouse.

"I don't know. He may not want me that way."

"But that's important to you."

"Yes. But that's merely lust." Her blouse was off, and her bra. His warm hands cupped her breasts. A mindless thing, she thought with contempt, she could feel her body responding. She tried to resist, but an urgency had grown during their separation. She moved against him. "This is merely lust," she said. "I'm ashamed. It's that idiotic chemistry."

He laughed. "It's love," he assured her. "It's my loving you and you loving me. Think about it. But later, not now."

Naked on the sofa, the afternoon sun shining in, they made love, and then they made love again, and in between she thought about love, and tried to count the ways she loved Julian, if it was indeed love. She felt young with him, mastered, in a way that she liked. Paradoxically, because it was her work that bound her to Harold, there she was the older one. Her work was her life, not this with Julian. Still, Julian was a charming, sensitive, caring man. She loved to look at him, to touch him, and they laughed and had fun together. He was a loving man, as well as a man who gave her intense, blissful orgasms.

"I could be your mistress," she suggested into his chest.

He smiled down at her. "You are my mistress."

"But I don't want to be your wife," she said.

"We don't have to marry. But I do want you living here with me."

"Why?

"Because I love you. I feel incomplete without you. And often lonely. Don't you?"

"Never." And certainly not now with Harold. Her soul

mate.

"Still, I think we've just demonstrated that we don't live very well without each other."

She had hardly thought of him during their separation. If it hadn't been for Harold's mentioning him so often, she might not have thought of him at all. She didn't tell him this.

But Harold was new, and what was evolving between them unusual. In time, given time, who knew what their relationship would settle into. It could go well. It could go badly.

She tried to think what it would be like to live with Julian, a conventional life, painting in his beautiful made-to-her-order studio, doing something about meals together, having his yet unmet children spend weekends with them, making mutual friends, listening to the details of his day, going with him to his funerals, having lovely, frequent sex. But take away the sex?

But you don't take away the sex. Not while the hormones flow. How important is sex? Very. More than you know at the time.

So, a life with Julian? Not bad, she thought. She wanted both, but at this moment, sexually at ease, she wanted Harold more. It was true that she and Harold could work together here, but she wanted more than that. She wanted the full depth of their connectedness, of whatever that was they were trying to exorcise. She couldn't envision it, couldn't play it out in fantasy, couldn't even tell if what she wanted was nothing more than fantasy, but she wanted it.

You can't always get what you want, she told herself. No small consideration is Harold and what he wants, which is Emily and Gerutopia. He had hurt her when he told her that he missed the meals at Gerutopia. She wasn't much of a cook, in fact he was a better one than she. But to be with her, to be making their amazing paintings, and to miss Gerutopia's cooking!

"I'm a lousy cook," she told Julian.

"But such a superlative eater," he said.

***

"Emily!" he said, striding into the room. He would have liked to embrace her but she was in her chair. Instead, he reached for her hand and folded it into his.

"Harold! Home from the hills? You remember Ida."

"Yes, of course," he said, trying not to show his disappointment at not finding Emily alone. "How are you, Ida?"

"It's nice to see you, Harold." Her eyes sparkled happily. Her lap was full of newspapers. "We missed you here." She looked at her wristwatch. "Oy! I'm late for my physical therapist, if you'll excuse me. Are you back to stay?"

"Oh, yes."

"Then we'll meet again soon."

Harold closed the door behind her, then brought a chair and sat on it, his knees almost touching Emily's.

"You look well," he said. She did. "How is your hip?"

"All but mended," she said. "I would be dancing this very minute, but the orchestra went home for lunch."

This was not Emily's sort of levity; it was Ida's. They must have been spending a lot of time together.

"Did you miss me?" he asked. He held both her hands in his. They felt as frail and alive as birds.

"Y-yes," she said, tentatively. "You weren't really gone long. How long has it been?"

"A month. Almost five weeks."

"How did it go? Did you and Jilian solve your problem?"

"In a way, yes," he said, grimacing.

"How?"

"We are now painting the same paintings together."

"What do you mean?"

He tried to explain it to her. He wanted to tell her everything that had happened, how they had begun by painting naked, how he had been sleeping in her bed, how she had tried to persuade him to "enter" her, his muse dream, all of it, even that Jilian had fallen in love with him. But he told her only about each of them taking up on a painting where the other left off, and how in this way they had produced three remarkable paintings.

"When we have enough of them," he said, "Jilian wants to have a show."

"Then instead of severing your painting from hers, you're collaborating?"

"Yes."

"Then you are more bound than ever?"

"Yes, I suppose so, though it feels different. I feel less unconsciously led, now, more in control."

"Jilian likes this arrangement?"

"She's excited by it. But time may change that. She may tire of it."

"Then you won't be staying here. You'll be going back with her?"

"Never," he said firmly. "I've missed you too much. I'm hoping that Julian will persuade her to stay with him and that we can paint in the studio he plans to build for her. And that you and I will marry and live happily ever after."

She laughed. "Oh, Harold, that's silly. We're not going to marry and live happily ever after, whatever ever after is."

"Why not?" he asked. "I thought it was all settled."

"Did you? A very private fantasy."

"I've been telling everyone we're engaged."

"Who's everyone?"

"Well, Jilian."

"And what does Jilian say?"

He couldn't recall if Jilian had said anything. "Jilian likes you," he said feebly.

"Well, we're not engaged. We were never engaged. I'm quite sure I never said anything to lead you to think we were."

He let go of her hands and reached for a cigarillo, then remembered. He felt wretched.

"I don't understand you," she said. "We can have everything we could ask for from a close relationship here. I think what you want would in any case be impossible. You want the companionship old couples feel, people who have been married for most of their lives, together and sharing. People with a history."

She was probably right. How would he know? He had been unmarried for so long. He had had affairs over the years, but yes, it was a special intimacy he wanted with her.

"What I want, I think, is to know you better than anyone else knows you. I want to know you deeply, everything about you," he said. "I feel that I belong with you. I want to feel that."

"That's impossible," she said, impatiently, though she was trying to be kind. "What a romantic you are!" She looked at the stack of notebooks, the ones in which she was depositing her life. There was so much of it she herself had forgotten, no longer knew, that she had put it aside, at least temporarily, and begun to write a cookbook for the aged.

"Don't look sad," she said. "Most of what there is to know about anyone is unimportant. And not very interesting."

"Not when you love them," he said. "I don't think anything about you would ever bore me."

"What a burden," she said. "I'm too old to have to worry about never boring you. I think I've earned the luxury of being boring."

He smiled. "I don't think you have to give it a thought," he said. "Please, Emily. Let's have a wedding. Let's have our picture taken for The Times. Let's ask Julian if they have a room here suitable for a couple. Let's live our lives as though we have a future, even if it's only a short one, not as though we're just hanging around, waiting to die."

"You're very persuasive, Harold. You say you love me, but you've never inquired about my feelings for you. Don't you think that's a little arrogant?"

"Yes. And presumptuous. And confident. I know you like me. A little more familiarity will breed love."

A kitchen, she thought. "I wouldn't mind having a little kitchen," she said. "Did I tell you I'm writing a cookbook for the aged? Special comfort food, simple but delicious and tempting and nourishing. Meals for the dietarily restricted, as well. Separate sections for heart, for blood pressure, for diverticulitis. The Final Cookbook. I don't know yet what to call it. Every day I toy with a new recipe and a new title." She laughed. "Ida suggested Alta Kocker Cookery."

"What's that?"

"It's Yiddish. I think it means old shitters. Literally, that is."

He laughed. "That's what we can do, evenings by the fire. Think up titles. But nothing with Senior or Golden or Sunset in it."

"Absolutely not!"

"And if I have to give up painting, I'll help you with recipes."

"God forbid! Ida's a big help. She says almost all Jewish food is comfort food, not just chicken soup. She's right. Matzo brie, blintzes, cheese kreplach, Ukrainian borscht, kasha, mamaligger. I've been elaborating on some of them."

"Adding porcini mushrooms."

She laughed. "That, too. We try them out in the big kitchen, but we have to do it after hours."

"You and Ida have become good friends."

"Yes."

CHAPTER TWENTY-TWO

Sometimes it's spelled with a capital L sometimes not," Ida said, looking up from The Times. "Why, I wonder, the confusion."

"If it's a native of Lesbos, and it no longer ever is, it's capitalized. If it's a homosexual woman it's lower case," Emily said. "I no longer remember why, but I looked it up once."

"I see. So now if they spell it with a capital, it's because of the pride business." It was Gay and Lesbian Pride Week and Ida had been reading about it in the Times. There was a picture of a ragged, boisterous parade. Or at least a march. No, not a march, a walk. Well, a lot of mostly young people in the street, facing forward.

"Pride," Ida said. "That's the opposite of shame. So when they say pride, they are emphasizing that there is no longer shame. They are referring to shame. They shouldn't. If they were smart, they wouldn't. Imagine having a heterosexual pride week!"

"It was certainly shame when we were young. The words for it were 'sick,' 'abnormal,' 'perverted,' 'disgusting.' The kindest word was 'unnatural.'"

"I hardly even heard of it in any words. Where did they all come from? There are so many of them. There couldn't have been that many in our day. All I knew about was Gertrude and Alice. And Gertrude was a crazy genius who could have been anything she wanted and gotten away with it, so she didn't really count."

"Oh, they were there. They just didn't talk about it."

"Much less march. And insist on being proud."

"Were you ever attracted to a woman that way?"

"No, I don't think it ever crossed my mind," Ida said, her eyes twinkling. "I was crazy about men. What about you?"

Emily was silent for a moment, memory clouding her face. "Yes," she said, "I was once madly in love with a woman. I idolized her. For three years." It had been like discovering a marvelous new food, a juicy, warm, sun-filled mango; tender, grilled langoustes dripping with butter. Her name was Virginia, a brash, cocky, brilliant, arrogant poet. A good poet. She lived in Greenwich Village and her circle was what was then known as Bohemian. Offering love, a new kind of love, she had lured Emily out of her faulty marriage into that circle, and Emily came fully awake for the first time in years. The excitement of it! A wave of feeling washed over her, a memory of what was surely ecstasy, mixed though it was with shame and secrecy, at least outside that magic bohemian circle and in the world where she had other habits and her work.

She suddenly felt an urge to write about it. She glanced at the table where her notebooks were stacked. She wished she was further along, well out of her childhood. She laughed. After all, nobody was standing over her with a whip demanding that she be strictly chronological, nobody but herself. She would open a fresh copybook and write about those years.

"Are you shocked?" she asked Ida.

"I don't think so," Ida said, but she looked as though she were, a little. "You were more emancipated than I ever was. Although to tell the truth I never felt unemancipated."

"I don't know if emancipation had much to do with it. Were you happy in your marriage? Did you love your husband?"

"The second one, Isaac, I liked, I was fond of. But Max, the first one, Molly's father, " Ida said. "He was a wonderful man." She paused, her eyes growing moist. "So strong, so wise. I was crazy about him. His sense of humor, how he could make me laugh! We didn't have much money but we had a good life. He died young, not yet fifty. It broke my heart."

"All the same, you were lucky."

"Yes." But she had felt far from lucky then when he was dying. "Near the end I could pick him up in my arms and carry him to the bathroom. There was nothing left, he was so slow to die, so reluctant to leave. Such a strong man he had been. Once, nobody knows this, not even Mollie, he killed a Cossack with his bare fist, one blow, a big, tough Cossack who was terrorizing the shtetl, insulting the Jews. That's why Max came to America. He had to flee, so they sneaked him out in the dark of night. Just a boy he was, eighteen."

A strange woman wanders into the room, looking a little lost, a little surprised.

"Hey, this is nice," she says, looking around the room. "Even nicer than I imagined it."

"Hello," Emily says. "Who are you?"

"My name is Rachel. Rachel Levin."

"Are you new here?"

"No. I mean I'm not a resident."

"Then you're visiting?"

"No. Yes."

"Who?"

"You."

"Which you? Emily or me?"

"Both."

"Do we know you?"

"No. Yes. I'm your author."

"Our what?"

"Author, creator."

The two old women turn to look at each other, agreeing

in their exchanged look that this new person is meshugah.

When I write about people, I tend to leave their physical selves blurred. I don't want them too defined. I like to give the reader a little latitude, some blanks to fill in, to allow the characters to look a little as the readers imagine them. But these two women, I am surprised to see, are very definite, specific beings. Emily is thin, delicate, almost gaunt with hollowed cheeks and large, mournful deep-set gray eyes, a patrician nose. It's not that you think how beautiful she must have been. She is beautiful. Ida is rounder and, of late, twinklier. The hair she chopped off at the Home is growing again. Soon it will be long enough for her to knot into a bun, as she had always worn it during what she called her "real life."

"Are you saying," Emily asks, in such a way that it is clear that she is humoring me, "that you are using us as characters in a book? Your book?"

"Yes. That is, I'm not using you. You are characters in my book." But now I'm not so sure. "Although you seem very real to me."

"We seem real to us, too," Ida says, laughing.

"At least for the nonce," Emily says, and she, too, laughs. "What an idea! Are you planning to kill us off?" l can tell that she is still humoring me.

"It crossed my mind. One of you, anyway."

"Which one of us?"

"I hadn't decided. And it wasn't integral. It was only because I feel there probably should be a death or two in a book about old age." But now I'm not so sure. I think I won't.

"Was it you who killed off Daisy?" Ida asks bitterly.

"Yes. I'm sorry."

"Why did you do it?"

"Oh, she was so ill! And I wanted to see if I could get you into this place."

"You're really serious, aren't you? About your being our author."

"I don't know. Maybe it's the other way around." I can see that I am beginning to frighten them a little. "I mean, what *am* I doing here?"

"I was just going to ask you that."

"I got lost," I say, trying not to sound self-pitying. Trying not to say that I had nowhere else to go. "I wandered in."

"You're not old enough for this place," Ida says.

"By the time this book gets finished, I will be."

"You write slowly?"

"It's not that I write slowly. I spend a lot of time not writing at all. Tell me, Emily, do you think you'll marry Harold?"

"Don't you know?"

"No."

"Are you as indecisive in your life outside this novel?"

"Yes."

"Then that's why you're so slow?"

"Possibly."

Paralyzed by the possibility of the wrong choice. But you can always undo the wrong choice, especially with a computer. It's not as though you don't do it all the time.

"Why are you having us talk about lesbians?" Emily asks. She is no longer merely humoring this woman, their author, although she is comforted by the thought that they would never admit her here. You had to be, at least in the beginning, sane. But suppose this woman is telling the truth? The thought chills her. If she and Ida are someone else's fiction, does that mean God exists? If he does, and he pays so much attention to detail, he must have an inordinate number of assistants and this woman may be one of them. Is she an assistant to God, even unwittingly? Dare she ask?

"Are you planning an affair between Ida and me?" she

asks instead.

"Lesbianism is a particular interest of mine," I confess. Still, why should it have anything to do with these two crippled old women? One of them has just confessed that she has always been fervently heterosexual, the other, although she has had homosexual affairs, is perhaps becoming deeply involved with Harold. "Even without sex," I say, "the relationships between women interest me. Especially older women. The emotional attachments can be so powerful." I've seen it with my mother, in Florida, where the cast of characters is all widows. The attachments and rivalries, I'm convinced, are what keep them alive. And sometimes kill them. And in this morning's Times there was an interview with two elderly women who had collaborated for years on scholarly books about the seventeenth century, and had been living together for over forty years. The interviewer asked what had kept them together all these years and one of them said, "Friendship. Work." Then she left the room to fetch something, and the other woman said, "Perhaps I shouldn't be telling you this, but what has really kept us together is a deep and abiding love."

It made me cry.

"But no," I say. "Not a lesbian affair. Just a deep and loving friendship."

The two women exchange a glance. They are both smiling.

"And Harold?" I ask. "What about him? How do you feel about him?"

"Why don't you tell me?"

"Do you think you'll marry him?"

"Does it really matter?"

"It does to him."

"Well, what about a deep and loving friendship with him, too?"

"All right, we'll see," I say getting up and walking

toward the door.

"Where are you going?" Ida asks.

"I shouldn't be here. I'm leaving."

When she was gone, Ida said, "And not a minute too soon. That was very strange."

"Yes," Emily said.

But there were more important things to talk about. She picked up the notebook in her lap, the cookbook notebook. "Now," she said. "Tell me about your chopped liver."